Tuition

RICHARD POST

PAGE PUBLISHING, INC.
Conneaut Lake, PA

First originally published by Page Publishing 2020

ISBN 978-1-6624-1869-3 (pbk)
ISBN 978-1-6624-2645-2 (hc)
ISBN 978-1-6624-1870-9 (digital)

Printed in the United States of America

For:

A world as lost as the evil monsignor

Special thanks to:

My wife, my best friend and most honest critic
and to
Tommy V…a great coach, a greater man, and a true friend.

Contents

Chapter One

Blackmailed

ON A CRISP, springtime morning, before the interruption of man-made noise filled the boardwalk, one could almost forget the soiling of this once-prominent town. Before 7:00 a.m., when the high pitch of swooning gulls and crashing waves were the only sounds that permeated through the cool air, a guy could be taken back to when the town was young, when he was young. Through the streams of glare caused by a bright sun that had been waiting all night for the earth's spin to again allow its rise to glory, the old priest sat on the boardwalk bench. It was the kind that allowed a person to shift its two-board backrest to either side of the bench's seat, giving the option to sit and face either the ocean or the boardwalk. Today, this would be the monsignor's easiest decision.

Not quite willing to wait for the old-fashioned coffee maker in the president's kitchen to brew a fresh pot, the priest needed some chilled air, the kind that would soon turn to warm breezes as the morning evolved. He needed a place that would help him think. It had been another long, sleepless night but this time more urgent, scarier than the typical unease that kept his once-peaceful mind from relaxing.

My god, he thought, *I am almost seventy years old*. He remembered when he was a young priest, a time so much easier to think good thoughts and convince himself that he was worthy of the mostly positive and respectful reactions from others. He always blamed his promotion to monsignor as the beginning of a time where he lost sight of his mission, gobbled up in thrills of power and responsibility that over time served only to decay his once-noble life plan. It was hard for him to believe and accept himself as an aging, overweight, and conniving priest with memories that appeared more storybook now than actual happenings in his past. He thought back to that first night in the rectory where he crossed the line and began his obsession with both the thrill and the torture. Still, he was President Clark now, an often-practical, "do most anything for desired results" man of the cloth. As he had become so accustomed to, he needed again to wield his white collar to manipulate events and relationships and camouflage his stained past. Only now, the threat that had caught up to him was all too real, as he recalled yesterday's punch in the stomach.

He had been standing at the edge of the college's football field, leaning on a fence, and watching the football team run through their spring workouts. The team was located at the far side of the field. He could hear the sounds traveling forty to fifty yards to where he was standing. As he tended to do more and more these days, he lost himself in an empty-headed state, gazing outward with no real urgency to do anything or be anywhere. He watched Coach Sully barking instructions and occasionally blowing his whistle in short, loud tweets. He remembered thinking how the coach epitomized Pious College and its place in this ever-changing Wildwood, New Jersey, beach town. Such a shame, he had thought, that his once prominent Catholic college now struggled to keep its doors open. It was a time of decreased enrollment, a growing reputation moving more toward unsavory than reputable, limping amid a poor economy and a largely unprincipled group of archdiocese figureheads, administrators, teachers, and staff. And while the college's downturn had not fully been avoidable, it was under his leadership that it had become what it was. His only out was his age and his comforting recognition that he would soon make it someone else's problem for he had long lost the strength, morality, and decency to turn it all around.

Jerry Sully, the school's head football coach was his hire, employed without much thought or comparison to others. He could not even recall if the coach had been recommended, so typical of his lack of real care for any of the college's programs. "Sully," in just a few short years, had become known as a loud, barking, somewhat-crude mid-aged coach who would do anything to win. He had little regard for any rules. When he was not dealing with the rigors of trying to field a team, his single life often found him around the blackjack tables in close-by Atlantic City or in bars watching his latest sports bet on TV.

The priest also remembered approving the hiring of Shane Ferrigno, the assistant coach. He recalled his meeting with Shane, instantly placing him in the category of a young heartthrob of a man, and someone he fondly welcomed into the Pious fold. Shane, once the college's senior quarterback in Sully's first year, was the one for whom the new head coach had pulled strings to ensure that the boy would graduate, despite his academic deficiencies and unwillingness to go to class. The young kid's passions had not changed much since graduation. They remained football and women, not always in that order. His latest fling, another eye-raising event at the college, was with Ms. Dolly Jackson, the school's less-than-successful, African American women's head basketball coach.

It had been getting late. Day was turning to dusk, and the campus was littered with a moderate number of students moving to their next destination. Isolated cars were leaving the school's parking lot. Three female students were sitting up in the stands, and he could hear the faint sounds of laughter from the giggling trio. He saw right through them, recognizing that they were far more interested in the football boys' glances than any details that the workout revealed. He remembered thinking that they were pathetic, only now considering whether his reaction to them was the lone, truly-pathetic element of that scene.

A man, about in his early thirties, had appeared from the end of the field's entrance ramp and approached him. The stranger was dressed in jeans, a T-shirt, and sneakers. A sports jacket oddly covered his casual wear. As the man drew closer to him, he recalled that

Coach Sully's barking and sounds from the workout could still be faintly heard in the distance.

"Such high hopes during spring workouts. I remember those times well," commented the newcomer.

Taken aback by the man now clearly entering his space, he had responded, "Uhh, yes…an exciting time of year."

The man continued, "You're lookin' good, monsignor. Pious must be treating you well these days!"

"Always challenges, young man," he had answered, "always challenges. I'm sorry…my memory fades with my age. Have we met?"

"No, no, noooo! Steve Summers," the man responded as he extended his hand toward the priest. He remembered shaking the man's hand and thinking he would make quick work of the visitor's expectation for conversation.

"Just a loyal Viking supporter, are you?" he asked the man.

The man responded, "Nah, just here to share in the some of the Pious wealth."

He, now tired of the exchange, commented with an intentional rudeness, "Excuse me? There is very little wealth here, young man. And of what concern would that be to you?"

Seemingly, as if on cue, the man removed a small folded yellow Post-it from his pants pocket. His smile quickly turned to a serious glare peering directly at the monsignor's now wide-eyed expression. The man handed the Post-it to him, and he remembered taking the handoff with an exaggerated annoyance, unfolding it, and reading it. The paper revealed only two words, written neatly in a black bold marker.

JESSE KANE.

He recalled fabricating a mask of confusion, as he tried hard to hide his sudden feeling of panic. He stared up at the man, demanding, "What is this?"

The man smirked, grabbed the priest's forearm, and pulled him closer, saying, "Oh come on, monsignor. You remember Jesse, your thirteen-year-old rectory boy." The stranger continued aggressively,

"He's thirty-two now...and with me! Remember those winter nights, monsignor? Those uncontrollable urges?" The now-revealed man leaned into the priest, causing him to lean back. "You sick fuck! Ten thousand dollars! Small bills! You have exactly one week."

With his message delivered, the man began to walk away, down the ramp toward the parking lot, now with but only a few cars left on campus. The monsignor almost shouting, bellowed, "Hey, you! Don't walk away from me. You're crazy, mister. I don't... I can't..."

The man stepped back toward him. "I don't blame you for choking on your words, monsignor. You are in one shit of a situation. One week, you dirtbag, or your molesting of Jesse goes to every media outlet in Jersey, followed by a sobbing press conference by Jesse himself." With that, the man stepped toward him, removed an envelope from the inside pocket of his jacket, and tossed it on the ground at the monsignor's feet.

"Sleep well, monsignor. And oh hey, good luck with that football thing." The man walked away, as the monsignor picked up the envelope. With the intruder now out of sight, he remembered staring at the words scribbled on the front side of the envelope. It simply read, "PRESS RELEASE—COPY 1 OF 200."

From across the boardwalk a Mexican man, clearly recognizing the old priest, called out, bringing the monsignor squarely back to the present. "Are you okay, monsignor? President Clarke, are you okay?" Receiving no answer, the worker stopped pulling on the chain that lifted the iron gate to the arcade. From directly across from the monsignor's boardwalk bench, the man walked toward the stoic, seated, and shaken priest. Realizing he was being called for an answer, the monsignor conjured a small smile and raised his right arm, waving an okay, hoping to once again avoid a conversation, but to no success. The arcade worker, now a few feet away, began to apologize. "So sorry, monsignor. I saw you sitting, looking so worried. Were you praying? So sorry to disturb you."

The monsignor stood up and patted the man on the shoulder. "No, I'm fine. Just thinking, my friend... Have a good day." And with that he walked away and down the boardwalk, away from the arcade. Once a good twenty yards away, the priest turned back and saw the man completing his morning's task. Iron gates were a relatively new thing on Wildwood's boardwalk, a now-required and unfortunate necessity to keep the overnight vandals from causing destruction and havoc. The monsignor recalled a time when they were not needed but then quickly turned his thoughts back to the worker's words. He felt his eyes well up with tears. The monsignor hadn't meaningfully prayed in years.

Chapter Two

The Meeting

It was a little before 8:00 a.m. The monsignor, fighting the hangover that only comes from blackmail and a past that has long since been unchangeable, drove slowly through the Pious College campus, returning from his boardwalk skull session. It had provided no answers. After departing the boardwalk and with no pathway for action, the depressed monsignor even considered doing nothing to address yesterday's visitor. Driving through the Wildwood streets back toward campus, he wondered, almost out loud, where his fight had gone. Was it age? He convinced himself that back when he was younger, he would have come up with something. Back then, he was the aggressor, so much more willing to wield his powerful wand, slicing the heads of anyone stupid enough to question him or get in his way.

Arriving on campus, he headed toward his two-story residence, the one the college's board had approved as his, soon after naming him president some eighteen years earlier. He recalled that he once enjoyed the ride back from the boardwalk to his once-very-comfortable home in this once-very-comfortable town. On this day, however, the almost one-and-one-half-mile ride from Wildwood Beach was filled with reminders of too many things changed, evidenced by the car's path along the far side of campus. Both time and mismanagement had eroded the once-modern college grounds and facilities. Maintenance funds had been cut on numerous occasions in favor of payroll needs, and increased costs in almost all categories. The once-impressive sports fields were now as tattered as the year-after-year losing records of most of the college's sports teams. The spring grass, craving the long-since-cancelled fall fertilization, didn't perk like it used to in early April. Too many buildings needed refurbishment from old age and the constant effect of sea air from the mighty Atlantic Ocean. The hope that new student candidates and their families wouldn't notice during the recruiting tours had been replaced with sorry and fabricated tales of the college's aggressive plans to pump money into facilities, money that at present did not exist. With its once-proud endowment dwindling as fast as the town's boardwalk entrepreneurs, the college was in trouble, the financial kind of trouble.

For the monsignor, this morning's campus seemed extra eerie, as all students were packed and leaving, annual rituals at the start of the college's Easter break. With yesterday's sledgehammer of a visitor so fresh in every one of his thoughts, the monsignor needed to ready himself, for today was the April administrators' meeting, a 10:00 a.m. start. Like in each of the last several years, the April meeting would be attended and run by the college's board chairman, Mr. Tony Sacco. The agenda was brief but this year also unnerving, as it would consist solely of the financial status of the college.

Tony Sacco, chairman of the Board of Trustees of Pious College, was appointed almost five years ago. He was a well-dressed, distinguished-looking man in his early sixties. Often flaunting his wealth, he ran the school's board on the pro bono request of President Clark. Tony was a tough guy and the owner of nearby Cape May's exclusive golf club, Club Eighteen. While most in the community suspected his involvement in the mob's underworld, nobody dared ever suggest such a thing, not even behind closed doors. Like most mobsters, Mr. Sacco's life was akin to a doubled-edged sword. If you found yourself in the crosshairs of his business dealings or even if you just managed to rub him the wrong way, you could be looking up at daisies real quick like. On the other hand, if he liked you or perhaps you represented an avenue to promote his human side, he could help in many ways, often earning your much-expected loyalty. When asked to chair the school's board, Tony Sacco had decided to be a good friend to the college, a category diminishing in numbers with each passing year. The monsignor liked him from a time where power, the rub-elbows type, meant something in Wildwood. Never thinking that he would ever need his muscle, the monsignor did always count on his chairman to nudge the local bank to do the right thing by the college. It was Mr. Sacco who had convinced the town's local banker to lend far more to the college than what the school's financial statements made prudent. Nobody dared ask how he had gotten the bank guy, known for his conservative lending approach, to willingly comply with the monsignor's request for an extended and robust line of credit.

After today's meeting, also to the chagrin of the monsignor, the school had scheduled its traditional staff and faculty gathering at Milligans, a less-than-elegant restaurant and bar on Wildwood Beach's boardwalk. With his required attendance at both the meeting and the social, the monsignor would force himself to struggle through the day, resigned to abide by Robert Frost's three-word masterpiece, *life goes on.*

Alone, upstairs in his home, the old priest paused in prepping himself for the meeting. Sitting on the edge of his bed, his mind drifted, recalling times long ago when his urges pushed him to act in ways that would stain him forever. He remembered how he went through a period where during overnight dreams, he would get caught committing his despicable indiscretions, waking suddenly out breath, sweating and fearful. He remembered the thankful and overwhelming feeling of relief when he realized that it had only been a nightmare, unreal, with his soiled secrets still hidden from all that could hurt him. All these years later, he thought he was free, having escaped any possibility that his crimes would surface. And while never truly forgetting, the feelings of fear and paranoia that he would be caught had long left him. With yesterday's visitor, all that had returned, along with a stifling inability to keep that fear from dominating his every waking moment. He now clearly remembered, in fact, he was reliving the torture.

Today's meeting would include the usual cast of characters from Pious College. Along with Mr. Sacco and the monsignor, the group would include Darlene Davidson, the school's CFO. Darlene had a long history on Wall Street's accounting stage. She was a petite, middle-aged woman of strength and charisma. As seemingly with most at the school, the Pious CFO was divorced and underpaid. A recent hire, she had ventured to supplement her less-than-accommodating college income as a foster mother of two minority teenagers (Ash, a sixteen-year-old African American from the ghetto in Philadelphia and Verona, a pretty fifteen-year-old Puerto Rican girl). Ms. Davidson took great pride in letting everyone know that she was both unattached at the moment and liberal in things more than simply her politics.

Adrian Kenny, known mostly as AK, would be there. He was the school's academic dean and once proud magna cum laude graduate of Pious College. Now in his forties, AK was known as an often-nasty, unapproachable dude with an insatiable appetite for power and notoriety. The man was also a heavy drinker, a trait that often impacted both his performance and his attitude. Long abandoning his once-greedy plan to rise to the top in both position and salary at a top-rated university, AK gave off a scent that the world had somehow cheated him, and with that robbed him of his ability to contribute positively in ways that few others could. To the dean, life was unfair, depriving him of those things that were inherently due to him.

Patty Simon would attend. Patty was the performing arts director, a beautiful, blond-haired late-twenties young lady, an ex-dancer, who served as the director of the school's try-hard, not-very-good arts program with her trustworthy gay assistant, Ms. Britta Holland. Young for her position at the college, Patty had taken advantage of the less-than-serious, informal hiring practices at Pious. To achieve her status as the director of a college performing arts program at such a young age, one might have assumed that she knew somebody with the juice to pull strings, perhaps a legacy child from a big donor or famous graduate. But there was none of that, just a young lady who happened to be in the right place at the right time, literally satisfying a desire of the monsignor to get the open requisition off his desk. For the president, anything lacking in Patty's experience was more than made up for in her looks and below-the-norm salary.

And then there was Gary Lee, the athletic director. Gary was a former track star at Notre Dame University. He was young, Asian, unproven, and wealthy. He lived in one of Wildwood's most prominent homes, owned by his millionaire father who now resided in Florida. The father, Kip Lee, who inherited his fortune from his shipbuilding family, was Gary's track coach at Notre Dame, having retired only after securing Gary his position at Pious College. Gary also served as the school's current track-and-field coach. His actions were normally well intended, if not consistently thought out.

The meeting would not be the same without the presence of Sister Mary Dija, a pretty Spanish nun in charge of raising money and promoting the school. Sister was often flirty and atypical of someone who had chosen a habit-wearing life. While not completely versed in American ways, she understood well the plight of the school and was willing to cross most lines to raise money and keep the school open. She lived in the town's wealthy convent on the beach, knowing full well that only her job secured her place in this upscale lifestyle. Losing her job would no doubt result in her order sending her back to an impoverished parish in Ecuador. Sister had committed to her vocation very early in life, before she could fully comprehend the difficulty of leading a life of celibacy. For that, inwardly she fought a constant battle with loneliness and struggled with oversexed hormones that far too often found her locking her bedroom door and masturbating the night away.

There was Father Jon Cusick, the career-development director and Provost Kevin McMatty. Father Jon was a young priest in his early thirties, who did his best to provide career opportunities to the college's students. He, more than most, represented the school's voice of genuine morality and common sense. Kevin McMatty, on the other hand, had the reputation of a narcissist, often involving himself in the pursuit of good-looking women. His skirt-chasing, self-promoting ways often placed him at the center of the school's watercooler gossip. He was fifty-something, strong, good-looking, and well spoken. As Provost, Kevin was self-trained in the art of providing administration a superficial expertise in the various campus programs and activities. Monsignor Clark had, early on, seen right through the Provost's shallow effort and his phoniness to relay an effort level far above than what was truly put forth. For Kevin, like so many others at Pious, he learned to take advantage of an environment that lacked accountability and rewarded those who didn't make waves. Although never spoken about, Provost McMatty was married to an institutionalized woman with severe physiological disabilities. Their son, Dylan McMatty, a chip off the old block, was currently a student at Pious and one of two student council presidents.

Finally, there was the monsignor's secretary, Jenny Flopalis, also attending to keep the meeting's minutes. Ms. Flopalis was an aging secretary, increasingly incompetent and often forgetful. Many believed she had the beginnings of dementia. As her errors increased, she often used the excuse of lack of recollection as her explanation. Some thirty years back, she had lived in the same parish as the Shawn Clark, a simple priest prior to his promotion to monsignor. An overly sexed Greek woman with a young and voluptuous body, Jenny was said to have had a love affair with the priest and thus she now remained untouchable at the school despite her declining looks and subpar performance. At Pious, she was the classic example of incompetence left alone, bringing a buffoonery to the administrative offices that could make her, well, a main character in a book about a failing and poorly run institution of higher learning.

The Club Eighteen conference room was an elegant large space on the clubhouse's second floor, with floor-to-ceiling windows on the far side of the room displaying impressive views of the golf course's first tee. The ability to watch golfers tee off had become an attractive, unspoken sidebar to the meetings. Pious administrators who were bored and largely uninterested with these college-planning sessions had learned to arrive early, attempting to secure the side of the table that provided the required angle to view the first tee without conspicuously turning one's head.

The near sidewall of the conference room displayed a long, thin blackwood table, in which an assortment of morning delicacies had been placed, along with stainless steel containers of coffee, water, and juices. The actual conference table was a long oak stained wood structure with six high-back leather chairs on each side, matched by identical chairs on each end of the sleek surface. The end chair on the far side of the table was customarily not used to allow full view of a screen displaying presentations from available laptop stations at each of the table's settings. The projector was mounted facing the screen from the ceiling directly over the center of the conference table. There was a single flat speakerphone that sat wireless on the center of the table. Funny only to those paying attention, since Tony Sacco began holding the college's meetings here some five years ago, neither the projector nor the speakerphone had ever been used. Technology or even the thought of attending a session from a remote location were availabilities reserved for groups a bit more sophisticated than Pious's management team.

It was bright and sunny in the Wildwood and Cape May areas and forecasts were for a beautiful spring day. All those in attendance were formally dressed in suits and dresses, with the exception of course of the monsignor who was wearing his customary black shoes, black socks, black pants, black belt, and black shirt with white clergy collar.

Each Pious bigwig entered the meeting room and took their royal seat, with each individual's table setting containing a notebook and pen, along with cups, glassware, eating utensils, a white cloth napkin, and small plates of selected food. Some participants had bought their Pious-labeled folder containing the meeting's agenda and other relevant documentation. Laptops or technical devises hadn't hit the scene yet at Pious as the school liked to think of itself as "old school," a 2010 term used for people and institutions typically too dumb, cheap, or lazy to jet set into the twenty-first century.

As all were now comfortably seated, the meeting was ready to commence.

Tony Sacco started. "Good morning, all. It is my pleasure on this wonderful spring day to call the meeting to order. As is our first priority, I ask the monsignor to start with a prayer."

For years now, the monsignor had become more and more tired of the ritual that all things start with prayer. Once meaningful and truly genuine to the monsignor, starting things with prayer—be it meetings, dinners, speeches, ballgame, whatever—had become nothing more than a mandate of his trade, something that reserved for him his demand and right to respect, little else. Fact was, the monsignor had long-ago abandoned and forgotten the unpretentious nature of his faith. This is not to say that he was atheist-like but rather while still believing in God, he just couldn't muster much time for the Almighty one. It became somewhat irrelevant that despite his insincerity in such matters, he was still quite good at coming up with on-the-fly prayers. Hiding that he thought this a fairly useless exercise, the priest responded, "Thank you, Mr. Chairman. I ask that we all bow our heads in the name of our Lord. In the name of the Father, Son, and Holy Spirit. Father, we come before you today as your servants in faith. Please grant us the wisdom and courage to lead our school in service to you and the many fine young students who have entrusted us with their education, care, and morality, such that they will leave us strong and capable of serving you and their chosen communities. As with all things, we ask you this in the name of Jesus Christ. Amen."

As all repeated the sign of the cross, Tony Sacco spoke up, "Thank you, monsignor. I move for the approval of January's 2010 minutes. All in favor say aye." A number around the table chimed aye. "Second?" Several in attendance responded second. "Opposed?"

Adrian Kenny, displaying his somewhat off-centered and foul attitude, blurted out, "OPPOSED!"

Mr. Sacco, a bit taken aback by both the opposition and the manner in which it was delivered, responded, "AK, your reason for opposition to last meeting's minutes?"

Adrian replied immediately, "Mr. Chairman, Tony, you will recall that at the January meeting, I gave a rather long and detailed presentation on the school's academic progress, plans for new programs including enhancing the school's overseas relationships to expand our Study Abroad Program...an extensive effort I might add, put forth by my department. You will also recall that it was under your advice that we schedule that presentation last at the January meeting *and* that the ensuing discussion on my report resulted in extending the meeting for over an hour past its normal length. The point is, Tony, that I do not see this item in January's minutes, and I am rather curious as to the reason for, in my view, this gross omission."

Tony Sacco raised his eyes at Adriane's choice of words but continued professionally, "Ahh yes, I do recall, Adrian. Quite a good report I might add." Adrian Kenny nodded an approving gesture as Mr. Sacco continued, "I don't know that I would label the omission gross, however, but point taken... monsignor, any comment?"

The monsignor turned and stared at his assistant, Ms. Flopalis, expecting comment, as she was the keeper of the minutes. Jenny Flopalis, as typical, appeared flustered and confused. "I'm so sorry. In doing the minutes a few days after the meeting, I wasn't clear on whether the group wanted Mr. Kenny's report in the minutes. So sorry."

Adrian Kenny shook his head and let out a sigh for all to hear.

The monsignor addressed the now almost-shaking assistant, "Jenny, while we all appreciate your willingness to keep minutes, not always an enviable task, we ask that all agenda matters be minuted, with any exceptions clearly and only at the request of this group."

Ms. Flopalis responded, "Yes, monsignor, yes... Actually yes, yes, I do now recall, yeees, yes. I remember I was having trouble with my pen as it was intermittently working, running out of ink, monsignor... So, so sorry, I do apologize and commit to better care."

The group struggled to conceal their expressions of embarrassment over the assistant's pathetic explanation.

Father Jon Cusick spoke up. "Excuse me, while on the subject of protocol, may I recommend that this group's meeting package be distributed earlier? Fact is, I only received this package late yesterday. And with my schedule, frankly I have not had time to even look at it. A more appropriate time period for review, *prior* to the meeting, would be more productive."

Tony Sacco agreed. "Agreed wholeheartedly, Father Jon. In fact, I have not yet received my package, usually arriving by mail a day or two before the meeting."

The monsignor angrily glared at Jenny Flopalis.

Tony Sacco continued, "Okay, all agreed, let's move on."

Adrian Kenny sarcastically chimed in, "Before we do, Mr. Chairman, may I suggest that it be minuted today that in all future meetings, Ms. Flopalis arrive with a spare pen, to be used in cases where her primary pen fails."

The group all laughed, with the exception of the clearly annoyed monsignor who again stared with red-faced anger at his assistant. Ms. Flopalis blushed as her body sank lower in her chair.

Tony Sacco moved on, "Again, Mr. Kenny, point taken. Next up…"

Mr. Sacco, not having a meeting packet, leaned far to his right to read the agenda sheet in front of the monsignor, causing the priest to again stare down his assistant. Mr. Sacco called out, "Ms. Davidson and her financial report."

Hearing her name, Darlene Davidson perked up in her chair and began talking. "Thank you Tony. I ask that the group follow along on the packet's enclosed spreadsheet labeled *2010 Fiscal Year Status.*"

Not having a packet, Mr. Sacco stood and rolled his chair around the table's corner to be literally arm against arm with the monsignor, so as to share the view of Ms. Davidson's spreadsheet. The glare from the monsignor toward his assistant was now fully recognized by all in the room.

Darlene Davidson continued, "While it is my department's responsibility to manage the college's funds, providing solutions to fund the school's various programs and operations, it is also my dutiful obligation to report the very real financial challenges which face our institution." Ms. Davidson paused and peered up at her audience. If not evident day-to-day, it was at these times that the new CFO clearly demonstrated her comfort in addressing a governance group. Her posture made clear that this was not her first board meeting. Visibly, the good-looking accountant was versed in both speaking to a financial figure as well as showing off her own.

"For the third year running, the school will operate at a loss in 2010. You will note that expenses are projected to be 11.6 million in the current year with revenue projections totaling just under 11 million. This will result in a projected net loss to the school of approximately 700,000 dollars."

Ms. Davidson paused, again scanning the room as if to accentuate her bad news, and continued, "We will again draw on our dwindling endowment to make up for this loss. Unfortunately, unless our fundraising or enrollment increases fast"—again pausing, this time to nod in the direction of Sister Dija—"this will be the final year that such a solution will be available. Another annual loss of this magnitude will force the school to either extend its already large loan debt—if we could get another loan—or I'm sorry to say…close the doors to the college." Ms. Davidson stopped talking, waiting for the group's reaction to her rather-daunting statement. Tony Sacco looked at the monsignor quizzically. Ms. Flopalis, on the job, quickly turned from Ms. Davidson to Mr. Sacco. Seeing he silently was calling for the monsignor's reaction, she shifted her stare to the monsignor and exaggerated the readiness of her pen, waiting for him to speak. The monsignor glanced a quick look of disgust at his assistant and began to rub and scratch his forehead, forcing those in attendance to wonder if his reaction was a result of Ms. Davidson's report or the sheer buffoonery of his Jenny girl.

Sensing the tension from the monsignor's expression, Darlene Davidson spoke up. "Perhaps I should first finish my report, as I am just about at the end?"

"Okay, okay, good idea. Please do, Darlene," responded Mr. Sacco.

"So," Ms. Davidson said, this time head down focusing on the paper sheet directly in front of her, "with the projection of using 700,000 of our reserve, our endowment at the end of 2010 will be reduced to approximately 240,000 dollars, eliminating the option to next year again draw on that reserve to cover a similar shortfall. In addition, the school has had to abandon its plan to accelerate repayment of its loans from Wildwood's Savings and Loan. While we have had the ability to keep up with loan payments, I would remind this group of its plans to prepay such obligations, freeing up funds for other important and much-needed improvements in the college's facilities and programs. Unfortunately, I must recommend that we curtail those plans and, for the time being, hold on tight to the remaining funds in our endowment account."

Mr. Sacco, well on board in the discussion, asked, "Ms. Davidson, what is the current outstanding owed to Savings and Loan?"

Darlene Davidson responded, "Approximately $670,000 dollars."

Mr. Sacco addressed the monsignor, "And, monsignor, what are the projections for next year's enrollment?"

The monsignor took a deep breath, then a gulp of much-needed ice water and carefully placed the glass in front of him. Finally, as if remembering where he was, he responded, "Unfortunately, we project an enrollment number almost identical to this year's graduating class, thus no projected increase in revenue from tuition. As you know, Tony, without the ability to market improvements in our offerings, recruitment is becoming increasingly difficult. The good news is that Sister Dija has some very aggressive plans for fundraising in efforts to rebuild our endowment. Additionally, I continue to work with the Wildwood Township to establish a grant program that will offer funding for scholarships. If approved, this program should increase our enrollment a bit in the future as well as provide monies for program improvement."

Father Jon Cusick spoke, "Monsignor, this has been an ongoing project for some time now. Can you comment on its current status?"

The priest responded, "Most of the local politicians are on board. However, the delay relates to a few of the more prominent voices within the township, specifically opposed to funding an institution of a specific religious denomination."

Kevin McMatty, typically quiet at these gatherings, chimed in, "Not the greatest of times to donate to the Catholic cause, I'm afraid."

Mr. McMatty's comment drew an aggressive smirk from the monsignor.

Tony Sacco continued the conversation. "Well, one does not have to be a Warren Buffet to conclude that, in the short term, at least until the school can make strides in increasing its enrollment, great focus needs to be applied to fundraising to rebuild this institution's reserves and endowment. Can you comment on your plans for fundraising, Sister?"

Sister Mary Dija perked up from the end of the table, drawing an overfriendly expression from Kevin McMatty. "Oh, I very excited. Me have many appointments coming up with alumni, local businesses, and friends of Pious to raise money. I working very hard. I sure we raise lots of money. Me not want to go back to Ecuador."

The group all laughed.

Gary Lee, typically somewhat out of place and also usually quiet and reserved at these meetings, added an unexpected comment, "If I may, Mr. Chairman, while not a bottomless pool, I am certain if the school can show progress in its enrollment and improvement in programs and facilities, my father will help to address the school's current financial condition…for a limited period of course."

Tony Sacco, gratefully responded, "Thank you, Gary. Your family has always been a good friend to Pious."

With that, and no longer seeing any need to put the monsignor on the spot to comment on the all-to-clear status of the college, Tony Sacco looked to wrap up the conversation, first glancing at his watch and then saying, "Well, I want to thank all members of the group for their efforts. As usual, Ms. Davidson, your report, while not the best of news, was clear and comprehensive. I strongly believe that Pious is an institution worth saving. I would ask that the following occur over the next few months. Sister, please be prepared at our next meeting early this summer to present a report on the status of your fundraising efforts."

Sister Dija nervously nodded yes and almost frantically began scribbling in her notebook.

"And, Ms. Davidson, with the counsel of the monsignor, please come back to the next meeting with proposals which would reduce expenses, including employee headcount, whereby without any further options, the school could make up a portion of projected losses for next year. While not the preferable option, it may be one in which the school is forced to take. Are there any questions before I adjourn the meeting?"

Before anyone could answer, the meeting was interrupted by Tony Sacco's secretary as she knocked once, then quickly but quietly entered the conference room and handed Mr. Sacco a Pious folder containing today's meeting packet. "Just arrived in the mail," she whispered to Mr. Sacco.

The whole group, again with the exception of the monsignor, laughed out loud, drawing a red-faced Irish anger from the aging priest. Oblivious to the embarrassing folder handoff, the priest's assistant was preoccupied taking frenzied, multiple bites from her plate's uneaten oversized bagel, as if her craving during note-taking had finally overpowered her. Breathless from an overloaded mouth, the feeble-minded secretary began forcing body shimmies in her chair in a mindless effort to create some room between seat and table, so as to find the needed space to stand and ready herself for exit. Mr. Sacco briefly looked her way left, faintly gave the expression of beginning to offer a kind comment, but then apparently thought better of it and quickly turned his focus right, showing the monsignor slightly raised eyebrows and a sheepish but understanding smile.

Mr. Sacco addressed the group one last time. "One last thing. As always, the contents of this meeting are confidential. This is not information that anyone can afford to become public throughout the school or the community."

The statement drew a laser-like stare from Adrian Kenny directly at Ms. Flopalis, clearly showing concern about the assistant's ability to abide by the chairman's confidentiality mandate.

Mr. Sacco concluded, "I hope to see you all later. Meeting adjourned."

Pious employees began to rise from their chairs, gather their materials, and casually begin to leave the conference room. As was customary at the conclusion of these meetings, Mr. Sacco and the monsignor lagged behind to share a few words. They strolled toward the room's large window and began to gaze at the course's first tee as the golfers below readied themselves to start their round. The view of the course's manicured green grass, which carpeted the first hole's rolling hill, was magnificent. The golfers, each branding colorful shirts, smart slacks, and an assortment of colorful golf bags, showed off the best of wealth here in Cape May.

The monsignor caught himself from entering his safe, empty-headed zone, and forced himself back to the present. "Such a beautiful sight. Thank you again, Tony, for your willingness to volunteer so much of your time to our school. We all recognize that you have many important things on your plate."

"Nonsense, monsignor," responded Tony Sacco. "I am pleased to help, and you must realize, I rather enjoy it."

The monsignor grinned. "Well, I hope you can stop by this afternoon. Your presence means so much to our staff."

Tony Sacco confirmed, "Not at all a problem. I will be there, for a short time anyway."

The monsignor and the chairman shook hands and turned back to gaze down through the second-floor window onto the plush green of the golf course. Almost in unison, they noticed a man standing to the side of the refurbished coral-type fence, opposite the waiting foursome, up next at the tee box. Looking up at the large second-story window, the man was waving at the now statue-like duo of priest and chairman. The monsignor, not recognizing the man, deferred to his chairman to initiate a wave back, softly saying, "Such a happy member. You must be doing something right here at the club."

Tony Sacco chuckled, responding, "Yes, another happy new member. Always smiling. I believe his name is Kane, Jesse Kane." The monsignor's expression instantly turned pale and cold.

Feeling his almost seventy-year-old knees beginning to buckle, the priest turned away and moved toward the room's large oak table. With a consciousness to hide his now quivering hands, he gathered his materials and with an abruptness somewhat inappropriate for the moment, glanced at Mr. Sacco and said, "Thanks, Tony, got to get on with the day… See you later."

Quickly exiting the room, the monsignor headed for the elevator, not willing to risk his trembling body on the one-story staircase.

Chapter Three

Beach Kids

THE MONSIGNOR APPROACHED the path to his residence that had been his home for the last eighteen years. He pulled into the parking spot, just up the road from his front door. His gaze was straight ahead, noticing for the first time that the spot's wooden sign, once bright and bold with the words PRESIDENT, was faded and worn, ostensibly aligned to how he was now thinking of himself. He was beaten. The events and resulting stress of the last twenty-four hours and its impact on both his mind and body sapped any strength he had left for today's facade of leadership. With still a few hours before his presence was expected at the staff gathering, he decided just to turn off the car and sit back. The leather seats in his aging 2004 Honda Accord were at least as inviting as his house's white-walled interior, adorned with crucifixes, pictures, and paintings whose meaning had long since left him. He knew he would have to get on with it, but not this hour. Not right now. He would just sit and empty his head, his only remedy these days to anything that resembled comfort.

The day was a glorious one. The beach, rid of the overnight vacuum trucks, was a fine layer of sand, broken only by the prints of a handful of local Wildwood residents drawn to an 11:00 a.m. sea. Like most Jersey-shore towns, the locals' time to enjoy the beauty of their community had dwindled to portions of spring and those few weeks at summer's end when school opened and chilled air and changing leaves were on the horizon. In between, Wildwood was filled with visitors, many who lacked the respect that one used to have for another's hometown. Most intruders were just looking for good times and memories to get them through the long winters back home. In recent Wildwood summers, the bars would mostly be filled with those lacking the usually inherited ability to get drunk with a touch of class. The boardwalk was now a haven for drugs, even some prostitution for those looking real hard. Each early a.m. summer, the Wildwood streets resembled the morning after the annual St. Patty's Day parade in towns across the country. Litter, mostly in the form of empty beer cans and liquor bottles, were strewn within an assortment of empty fast-food bags and cigarette butts, taxing the attitude of the once-hardworking local sanitation crews. Long gone was the pristine aura of the crests and parks in Asbury, Seaside, and Wildwood. Fresh and unspoiled shore towns had been preserved for the high-end real estate communities in places like Deal, Avalon, and Stone Harbor. Even Atlantic City was now filled with a lower class of people. Gone were the days where wealth was defined by big cars and bigger tippers. No, for the older gents and ladies who were around during the days when thick cash rolls bulged from pockets of so many, it was easy to notice the growing number of vacancies and bankrupted casinos. Still, for Wildwood, summer meant an influx of cash, even if its pockets arrived more from busloads than fine cars.

This morning, a spring morning, the beach seemed to forget the comparisons to years gone by. It was not a day to replay the past or even fast-forward. Today, the weather insisted that all things be positive and in the present. No one had yet taken to being in the water, but some walked its edge, while others played with dogs or ran their morning mile. Even lifeguards were out this morning, not yet to impart a watchful eye on swimmers, but busy doing preseason readying. Some were organizing equipment where the sand was still firm from early morning's high tide. Others were grouped near a few upside-down lifeboats, sanding, wiping, and painting. A few of the male guards had broken away from the morning's work to play a volleyball game up at the net, much closer to the bicycles and baby strollers now busying various parts of the boardwalk. One of them was Cory Penstar, the head lifeguard. Cory was a good-looking mid-twenties young adult, known for lifeguarding by day and partying by night. Too often, the local chatter was centered on his latest *young pretty*, thinking that she had won his love, only to become another member of Cory's broken hearts' club. Always a fine line between love and hate, many had taken to saying that the number of young ladies who hated Cory was gaining on those who felt the opposite. For Cory, though, summer meant taking a break from the local lasses, those unfortunate souls stuck to Wildwood's four seasons. At this time of year, Cory's antennae often pointed toward newcomers, those temporary bikini showcases looking to fill their suitcases with unforgettable stories and Kodak memorabilia to take back home.

Up on the boardwalk, people were walking in all directions. Seated on one of its benches, holding hands, talking and laughing were Britta Holland, the college's theater teacher and her new girlfriend. With her other hand, the one not causing a spark that only a new relationship can provide, Britta was holding her mini collie on a leash. With this afternoon's staff party reserved only for the college's employees, Britta has arranged for her new partner to take her dog while she fulfilled her college obligation with a quick face-show before excusing herself in an early exit. The Lassie handoff was her way of ensuring a meetup later when night would begin to settle in and daytime inhibitions headed for the hills.

Sitting by the water were three teenagers, Ash and Verona, foster children of the college's CFO Darlene Davidson, and another minority boy named Blo. Ash was black, sixteen, and full of mischief. When he talked comfortably and not when being introduced by his new mom, he yakked with the slang of an inner-city street kid. Verona, better know as V, was a gorgeous Spanish fifteen-year-old who looked much older. The boys were dressed in tank tops and oversized dungarees. Verona was casually dressed, maybe too casual in a see-too-much short cotton housedress. She was braless, and her maiden skin and curves could hypnotize even the most righteous males in town.

Ash, real comfortable like, turned to his friend: "Yo, Blo. Break out the bunch, boy. You got us waiting on you."

Blo responded in his equally street-like tone, "Chill, dude. Can't you see the water boys' right next to us? Those boys don't get it. They'll be hurten' our good time."

Ash responded to Blo's cautiousness, "Worry, worry, worry, man that's all we get from you. Man, you the one who needs to chill."

Verona, hearing the two boys, let out a sigh of disgust and addressed her new stepbrother "Ash, stop it! You are so one-minded. Let it go. Besides, you said we were going for a walk. Mom will be here in a little while. She said she would give us some money for lunch before she heads to her party. Let's get some exercise."

Blo interrupted, "Sure you don't want to catch the eyes of those water boys, V? We got your thing."

Verona answered Blo somewhat emphatically, "Screw you, Blo boy. The only thing you got is an empty head. Yo, Ash, did you catch Ms. Holland's new fling on the love seat over there? Looks like the real thing."

Ash, laughing, replied, "Yea I saw. Crazy shit. Maybe we should pop her bubble when we get back to her sorry class."

Verona responded, "*Noo.* Leave it alone. She ain't hurten' nobody. 'Sides, look who *you* hanging out with. Blo brains."

Veronica's comment caused all three teenagers to break out laughing.

Verona continued: "Anyway she be siccen' that little dog on you, Ash, and you be running up the beach with those fool pants fallen down."

All three howled with laughter at Verona's comment. Her comedy routine also seemed to calm Blo's worries about the lifeguards, still tending to their chores some fifty to sixty yards from where the kids were seated. Blo leaned back into the sand to better angle his hand's access into his right front jeans pocket. He took out a small pipe and removed a small piece of tinfoil, there to protect its screened-in contents. Pulling out a lighter from the opposite side of his pants, he put the pipe to his lips and lit it, taking a long, strong drag. Smiling, he handed the pipe to Ash. Ash grabbed the lighter out of Blo's hand and repeated Blo's drag, trying now to hand the pipe to Verona. Aggressively, she pushed his arm away, and said, "Get that shit away from me, boy. Damn fools, both fools!"

Addressing Verona's comment with his best tough-guy look, Ash smirked, and then repeated his inhaling on the pipe and handed it back to Blo.

From a good distance away, Blo caught a glimpse of a blue police truck heading toward them, crawling along the water's edge where sea met sand, a somewhat routine springtime exercise for the beach police patrol.

Blo barked in a panic-like tone: "Shit, here come the blue man. Be cool."

Verona, anything but cool, responded, "Oh my god! Where's the bunch? Put it away. Bury it."

Blo, now acting as if he had things under control, responded, "Chill, V. Let um go by. Don't be stupid!"

As the truck approached the three kids, it slowed then began to creep directly in front of them and stopped! The passenger's-side cop opened the door and slowly stepped out. The three teenagers, pipe and lighter now secure back in Blo's pocket, froze in their seated position, desperately trying to act cool, but clearly failing anything that resembled relaxed.

The cop who exited the car positioned himself directly in front of the seated Blo and stared down at him, "You kids ever hear of binoculars?"

The kids remained silent, too afraid to comment, as the cop continued, "Well, have you? You see, binoculars are these little glasses like the size of my hand. They let you see things from far away. All sorts of things. Sometimes we use them to search the water for sharks…you know, to keep everyone safe. And sometimes we use them to see kids doing dope on the beach…you know, again, to keep everyone safe."

Hearing this, Blo panicked, jumped up, and started running toward the boardwalk. The cop reacted quickly, chasing Blo through the sand. Seeing the action, the driver's-side cop jumped out of the truck and screamed, "Freeze!" Ash and Verona stayed frozen in their seated position. Ash turned to look at the chase, now quite a distance from them. Verona sighed and helplessly put her head between her legs, resting it on the sides of her angled-up knees.

Behind them, Blo had increased the distance between himself and the cop, who was struggling from running full uniform in the sand. Seeing a ramp at the opposite side of the volleyball court, Blo headed straight for it. Seeing this real-life episode unfold, Cory Penstar jumped into action, taking a direct angle toward the fleeing youngster and like someone experienced in tackling, the football kind, he flung himself at Blo, wrapping his arms around the fleeing boy's legs and brought him down. As Blow struggled to free himself, Cory rolled him over and placed both knees in the center of his back. The black boy was now covered in sand, unable to escape, as the chasing cop finally got within arm's reach. He bent down, grabbed the back of Blo's neck, and instructed him to place his hands behind his back, allowing the cop to quickly cuff the teenager. Quite impressive, the cop's skills made it evident that he has done this many times in the past. Not obvious to all, he nodded at Cory and began to drag Blo toward the two teenagers still seated down by the water. Cory, now completely engaged in today's action, followed them to the ocean's edge.

With the group now all together, the cop threw Blo back to the sand next to his silent friends and glanced up at Cory. Cory, unaware of the cop's intention to speak, was staring at Verona, clearly moving on from his fourth down tackle. With a thoughtful expression, the young lifeguard looked at the cop, realized that he was being watched back and nodded toward a spot a few yards away, behind the truck. Cory quickly walked behind the police vehicle, partly hidden from the rest of the group. The cop followed.

Cory, almost whispering, started the conversation, "Listen, Dave, I got a little problem here. You see, busting these kids will no doubt come back to our lifeguard unit…and to me. You know that part of my job is to control this area, and as you witnessed, I wasn't exactly doing a great job. We could also get screwed if they found out we were playing volleyball when we were supposed to be working. Can you do me a big favor? Don't take them in. Let me scare these kids, and it won't happen again on my area. Please, man, we all need our jobs this summer."

The cop, clearly annoyed, responded, "Shit, Cory, no way."

Neither Cory nor the cop immediately continued the conversation…the cop looking back at the three seated teenagers, and Cory's eyes set only on the pretty one.

Finally, the cop continued, "Damn, Cory, you're lucky that I know you forever. Okay, this one time, one fucking time only. And you're damn lucky that I'm taking my wife out tonight. I could do without all the bullshit paperwork anyway. I'm counting on you to scare the shit out of them." He began to circle back around the truck, suddenly stopping to turn back to Cory. "Listen, Cory, two things: one, that was a hell of a tackle. And two, don't ever fucken' ask me anything like this again."

Cory just grinned and nodded his head as the cop approached Blo, giving him a nasty look and then uncuffing him. Turning, he nodded to his partner who quickly caught on. Both men climbed back into the truck and slowly continued their trek down the beach.

Before the kids fully recognized that the event was over, Cory turned to the teenagers and said, "Today is your lucky day. I kinda felt bad about tackling you, kid. Not too long ago, I majored in doing stupid shit on this beach. You should know, though, I just called in a very valuable chip to get you guys off. This one time only! From now on, no more of that dope shit in my area. Got it? *Got it?*"

The two boys nodded nervously. Verona was a statue, never moving.

Cory, addressing only the two boys, yelled, "Now beat it! And you," he motioned to Verona, "you stick for a second."

As instructed, the two boys rose and began slowly walking through the sand toward the boardwalk. Blo, bent forward to aid his sand-walk, was staring at his feet and shaking his head in disbelief, while Ash repeatedly turned to check on his stepsister.

With the boys now out of earshot, Cory turned toward Verona and said, "Listen, the truth is"—pausing for an impressionable effect—"I really did this for you. Just couldn't see such a pretty lady taking the fall for two knuckleheads."

Verona responded, "Really? You did this for me? I mean, I really appreciate it. That's my stepbrother that you helped too, but you're right… They are damn knuckleheads."

"My name's Cory."

"Verona but they call me V."

Cory, acting like a guy straight out of a Frankie Avalon movie, continued, "Well, V, it's my pleasure to help such a gorgeous creature. Honestly, you kinda caught my eye from a distance before any of this shit happened."

Verona, not without skills in dealing with come-ons, replied, "Yeah right."

Incapable of stopping himself from laying it on a little too thick, Cory continued, "Serious! Can't you hear my heart throbbing? How old are you, over eighteen, right?"

Before Verona could answer, she spotted her mom waving to her from the boardwalk. Blo and Ash were nowhere to be seen, no doubt on to their next dumb thing. She turned to Cory, touched his hand, making sure that hers quickly got back to safe space, and said, "Thanks again, gotta go."

With that, she walked off toward her mom, with Cory's eyes frozen on her exit.

Chapter Four

Milligans

MILLIGANS, A LARGE restaurant on Wildwood's beach boardwalk, had seen better days. Back in the eighties, long before the century turned and with it most of the care and pride of local entrepreneurs, the establishment was known for high-end quality meats and seafood, shipped ironically down from Maine, ignoring the complaints of local Jersey fishermen. Ronnie Milligan, the owner since passed, carried a reputation as one of the area's top chefs. It was not uncommon for patrons to arrive all decked out in their finest casual wear, men in sports jackets and their dates in summer dresses, navigating their high heels carefully through the long parallel slits between the boards on a less-weathered newer boardwalk. The cocktails served back then were poured from expensive brands of liquor and fine cordials. The drinks were served to people in fine glassware and to drinkers who knew the difference. The restaurant had been sandwiched between a ladies' apparel shop and a ramp, some eight feet wide and thirty feet long, leading to a parking lot behind the restaurant. Young boys, looking to make a few bits but mostly looking to move up the list and be considered for the desired interior waiter jobs, acted as *welcome guides* to those eager customers pulling into the parking lot. This was Ronnie Milligan's idea, a real entrepreneur: good-looking, clean-shaven seventeen and eighteen-year-old boys with bleached white T-shirts, red vests, and black slacks offering a young arm to elderly diners up the rather steep ramp, or playing traffic cop for patrons pulling in and out of the crowed lot. On rainy days, the boys provided umbrella-holding for patrons walking from their car to the restaurant's front door.

On the other side of the ramp, nestled between the restaurant and where the boardwalk stores restarted, sat an always freshly painted round gazebo, complete with benches and hanging plants. The area served those wishing to enjoy an after-dinner cigar or those waiting for the rest of their party to arrive for dinner. Patrons had come to know the need for reservations, still many arriving earlier to enjoy a before-meal cocktail at the long elegant bar situated in eyeshot, not earshot, of the dining area.

Ronnie Milligan had gone before his time, some say from the endless workdays and disciplined attention he gave to every detail. With him gone after only fifty-nine years, the restaurant was taken over by his son, Ronnie Jr. Most knew that father and son shared name only, as the younger Milligan could never muster the work ethic or talents of his father. After failing miserably to maintain the same quality of food and atmosphere, most patrons ultimately went elsewhere. Ronnie Jr. sold the place before it lost all its value to a new wave of gentleman, looking more for a quick buck than a long ride. Since then, the restaurant had turned owners a few more times, now more of a burger-and-beer joint under the ownership of two Pakistani brothers. Not bad guys, just not willing to set the bar (pardon the pun) very high for either the food or service. Funny thing, though: each new owner insisted that the deal require the inclusion of the Milligan name, a joke to the old-timers and local guys who remembered what it had once been.

The restaurant had been reserved a few months back by Jenny Flopalis at the request of the monsignor; the assistant, clueless in the lack of quality that the establishment provided and the monsignor not willing to splurge the college's dwindling purse on what he had always perceived as an unappreciative staff, looking to cut corners and take advantage. Arriving early, Ms. Flopalis began strolling through the restaurant, nodding her head in approval as if measuring the tacky establishment against some other fine place of notoriety and style. Truth was, she wanted to be there when her boss arrived. She was determined to show the monsignor that she was on top of her game, despite her apparent unknowing of a lipstick smudge that ranged too far above her upper lip and a dress string that started by the backside of her left knee, drooping down to almost the top of her left heel. The string, no doubt the result of overwear, followed her like a sad puppy would follow its owner, once realizing that it was about to be left alone again.

On this sunny Friday, the most appealing aspect of the restaurant was that the weather had hit the lottery this day, and the front of the restaurant opened to the sunshine and warmth of springtime. Most of the boardwalk shops, from restaurants to retail, were built allowing their front walls to slide open, resulting in a floor-to-roof opening to the boardwalk view, air, and potential patrons.

Today, the restaurant, while lacking elegance, at least looked clean. The wood tabletops of scratch-and-spill stains were covered in blue plastic tablecloths. A row of large buffet tables, the folding kind, was arranged with various finger food offerings. For no apparent reason, the actual bar was closed, and a smaller folding table had been set up with various house liquor and cheap wine bottles, along with piles of large red plastic cups. A beer keg sat atop an upside-down gray garbage can. A Magic Marker poster sign hung on the wall directly next to a large cluttered and *not-needed-this-day* coatroom. The sign read, "Welcome to Pious College's Easter Break Staff Party," followed by a hand-drawn smiley face, no doubt the secret signature of the monsignor's assistant. The back of the coatroom allowed entrance to a scarcely functional office with a desk, phone, small-but-tattered love seat, and a few chairs.

The restaurant began to fill with the full cast of the college's characters, including Tony Sacco, chairman of the board of trustees. Just after 1:00 p.m., the monsignor asked all to quiet down, so he could address his guests.

Holding both hands in the air, open palms in a nonverbal request for quiet, the monsignor spoke up. "Welcome all, welcome all. As always, I wish to start our seven-day Easter break"—a few quick hand claps followed by some laughter temporarily forcing the priest to stop and then continue—"with a few words of thanks for everyone's hard work. As we all know, these are challenging times at Pious but never too daunting to stop, enjoy our Lord's blessings and the genuine friendships that we share in our school community. And as always, we start by bowing our heads in prayer."

The monsignor, pretending to be in reverence but really only looking down at a cracked tile floor, began to recite the "Our Father." Upon concluding, he added, "I also wish to thank Sister Mary, our head of fundraising, and I have asked her to say a few words."

Sister Mary Dija seemed surprised that the monsignor called on her, despite that she had been briefed just prior to the start of the party. She was standing at an adjacent table, chatting with Father Jon and Tony Sacco.

Sister, in her always-cute Spanish accent, spoke up: "Thank you, Monsignor Clark. You know, I so excited to tell of good news. This morning I receive a call from Gary Lee's father."

Gary Lee, the AD, waved to the staff from a distant corner of the room, perhaps on his father's behalf. He was standing with Jimbo Carns, the physical education teacher. Jimbo had the reputation of a village idiot, clearly at the college to save the school a real salary. He was, however, part of Gary's staff and had been known to gravitate to his boss at these types of events.

Sister Dija continued. "Kip, I promise him I call him by his first name," she said, giggling. "So, so generous. He offer to pay for our party today, and he wish that I announce this and say everybody have fun. He sorry he not here, but too many fish biting in Florida. I no understand but he tell me he safe from the fish and make me promise him I tell you."

The now fairly crowded room roared in a combination of laughter and applause.

Failing to see much humor in anything these days, the monsignor cut into the room's good time and said, "Thank you, Sister. I also want to welcome our school's chairman, who so generously found time in his busy day to join us. Mr. Sacco would also like to say a few words."

With that, Tony Sacco stepped toward the president and received a nice applause from the group. From the back, nearest to the beer keg, Adrian Kenny let out a loud "YEAH, TONY!" The dean, one of the first to get to the restaurant, had not left that spot since his arrival, clearly more interested in refills than mingling with light-hearted conversation.

The monsignor instantly showed his displeasure with the dean's catcall, swiftly nodding at his assistant and aggressively motioning her toward Mr. Kenny. Ms. Flopalis immediately responded with an understanding head gesture and began to mosey toward the keg and Mr. Kenny, already thinking of her intended words in cautioning the dean to behave himself. Rather than walking around all the tight-fitted tables, a more easily accessed path to the keg, Ms. Flopalis decided to take the more direct route through the table area. She began her critical assignment with a series of *excuse me's*, moving eagerly to please her boss. Only a third of the way to AK and the keg, the space between the tables was shrinking, making her now rely on a few members of each table to squeeze themselves tight to the table to allow her passage. Sensing most eyes on her, she became mortified when, peering up, she realized that Mr. Sacco was consciously delaying his talk until she reached her destination. Easing the moment, Mr. Sacco said, "Take your time, Jenny, we are in no rush."

With only a few tables left between her and the makeshift bar, the pathways shrank to hilarious six-inch aisles. Not being able to pass unless her body miraculously reverted some thirty years, she couldn't take the attention any longer, deciding she must turn back. Doing an about-face, the desperate assistant, along with her trailing dress string, took one step toward her start point before realizing… hmmm, bad decision. With no viable third option, she again decided to twirl in the opposite direction, now trying frantically to navigate through the final tables and make it to the keg. With several staff members giggling and smiling at her unintended obstacle run, her steps turned to quick and confusing stutters. Getting on her toes to raise her rather wide butt over the last few tables, her left shoe dislodged from her foot and lay lonely a mere few inches from the tips of her toes. With no way to bend down and retrieve it, the now unbalanced gymnast pushed onward, finally jerking herself around the final table. With a stance now temporarily leveled by one heeled shoe and one foot on its tippy-toes, she arrived at the beer keg with Mr. Kenny.

With all eyes now waiting for the judges to raise their score-cards, she sensed the need to give purpose to her adventure, and with her back to the crowd, she grabbed a red cup, quickly filled it halfway with beer, and still facing the keg took a large gulp…spilling a few drops down her chin onto the front of her dress, ludicrously pretending that the drink was her intention all along. With the chairman still silenced by the big show, she turned back to the group, hoping that the room's eyes were no longer on her. But of course, they were. Having no rock to crawl under, the confused assistant pretended she didn't notice the stares from around the room and looked back up to Mr. Sacco. In her favor, a beer foam line was now covering her out-of-place lipstick smudge between upper lip and nose.

Mr. Kenny, with half a load on, took a pitiful glace her way, shook his head laughing, poured himself a quick refill, and walked away. The monsignor, now in complete disgust, with a begging motion pleaded with Mr. Sacco to continue.

Mr. Sacco decided that the assistant had held the spotlight long enough and finally began speaking. "Quite a tough act to follow, Jenny, but thank you, monsignor, for graciously inviting me today. And thank you, Sister. You are always a breath of fresh air. Gary, please pass a special thanks to your father for his generous gesture." All eyes on him now, the chairman, as usual, was quite impressive. His fine light-gray suit, starched white shirt with presidential blue tie, and various finger bling showed both style and wealth. He was also more than comfortable speaking publicly. He continued, "You know my daddy, God rest his soul, always told me a man must always make time for his friends. And in this room I have many. With Easter approaching and summer right around the corner—" His words were suddenly interrupted by the sound of a cell phone ringing from within Sister Dija's long off-white robes. He paused to look the way of the sister. Embarrassed in interrupting the chairman, the sister simultaneously began reaching her hand through the robe's layers while scurrying toward the front exit in an attempt to limit her disturbance. Not one to pass on an opportunity, Mr. Sacco cleverly commented, "More good news to Sister, no doubt." The large gathering let out a loud laugh, confirming the chairman's well-placed humor.

Reaching the small lobby at the front of the restaurant, the sister scrambled into the coatroom, only to realize that her phone had stopped ringing. As she flipped the phone's cover to see the detail of her missed call, the words of Mr. Sacco could now barely be heard from the main area of the restaurant. Staring at her phone, the sister heard the faint sound of groaning, seemingly coming from the coatroom's back office. Her attention swiftly shifted from her phone as she strained to hear curious sounds. Louder groaning caused the young nun to freeze as her listening intensified. Peeking toward the back office, some ten feet away, Sister noticed that the door was half open but on an angle preventing her from seeing into the room. With no further sounds from the restaurant to interfere in Sister's attempts to hear, more groans reached her, this time in the form of low grunts and soft words that protruded from the space made open by the angled door. The little nun was mesmerized by the whispers and grunts of pleasure. Afraid but captivated, she quickly glanced back at the entry to the coatroom, so as to make sure she was alone and not being watched. Seeing no intrusion in her space, and overcome without choice, Sister crept through the coatroom to the office door. With a look far too interested for a woman of the cloth, she peeked into the open doorway. Coach Dolly Jackson was bent, facedown, onto the far-side desk, her skirt raised above her waist and her red panties dangling at her feet, kept off the floor only by the length of her high-heeled shoes. Sister was hypnotized at the sight of Ms. Jackson's naked black bottom, so much so that she was momentarily oblivious to the presence of Dolly's partner. Still, as Ms. Jackson's moans and grunts continued to intoxicate the woman inside of the nun, Sister took notice of Shane Ferrigno, who was rocking his partner from behind with steady and slow hip movements. He was almost fully dressed, only pants down, exposing his white buttocks, as they moved to and from Dolly's dark, dark rear. Sister's stance in the doorway was well hidden, confident that neither party to this scene had seen her. Then, without warning, Shane let out his own man grunt as his motion slowed, finally coming to an exhaustive halt. Sensing end, and now fearing being seen, the nun jumped back, toward the coatroom door and without looking exited quickly toward the restaurant, back to the party. Entering the main room, she quickly headed toward Father Jon's table. As she approached, flushed and eyes down, Kevin McMatty quickly saw the approaching nun and all too eagerly jumped from his seat next to Father Jon. With intentions that appeared stronger than simple courtesy, Mr. McMatty pulled out a chair for the sister, who plopped, more than sat, into its steel seat. It would take a few minutes for her female temperature and moisture to subside to normal.

As the hours passed, it was now a little after 4 p.m., and many had left the gathering, with that number increasing by the minute. A few others were standing around, one by one recognizing the time and near end to the festivities. Mr. Sacco was long gone. The once-full tables now sat only the remaining stragglers. Tabletops were littered with half-filled cups and finished plates. Empty or half-empty wine bottles were scattered throughout the large room. Most of those who had left were no doubt regrouping at home, making decisions on the rest of the day and night that only come from those times where alcohol plays a part in one's afternoon. Ms. Flopalis, determined to leave her mark on the day, was using her *haven't-been-washed-in-hours hands* to place uneaten food from the long-abandoned buffet table onto paper plates and covering each with cellophane wrapping. She was offering them to guests slowly moving toward the exit. Except for Coach Sully, the owner of an almost-always-empty kitchen refrigerator, all were respectfully declining.

The monsignor was still present, seated at an end table, farthest from the restaurant's front door. He was speaking in low tones to Patty Simon, the college's performing arts director. From afar, she seemed generally moved with the conversation, exaggerating the interested look on her face. The monsignor, almost whispering, gained an excited look from his tablemate. "So my idea Patty is to refurbish our theater with much needed amenities as it has been ignored for some time now. "You know, perhaps, new curtains, dance floor, backdrops...that sort of thing."

Thrilled, but surprised, Patty answered, "Monsignor...thank you, such good news. I have wanted to come to you for some time now, but with the challenges that face our school, particularly in light of this morning's report, I thought it not appropriate of me."

"Nonsense, Patty," chimed the priest. "Nonsense. One must offer a more attractive setting to recruit high school talent. Remember, my dear, enrollment is the key to this and every other school. I believe this will be a wise investment."

Of course, Patty gleefully concurred. "Oh I agree, monsignor, this makes me so happy and excited. I will get on it right away and present some proposals for you and Ms. Davidson to review."

"Well, I'm afraid it won't be that easy," responded the monsignor. "You see, Patty, at Pious revenue is very low. My thought was to secure a short-term loan from our friends at the Savings and Loan. They have been good to our school, and if presented correctly, I am certain they can be convinced. After all, our art students must see our commitment to the program, and as ambassadors, these students should serve as recruiting assistants to your goals for increased performing arts program enrollment."

An overly agreeable director responded, "*Oh*, I do agree, sir. I will wait to hear from you, and in the meantime I will search for best prices. Unless there is anything else I can do to help."

"Well, yes, Patty. There is. You see I envision this as a summertime project. While the money can be secured now, I think the work should wait until the conclusion of our spring semester when the school is less populated and your time is more flexible to manage the refurbishment effort. I have arranged a meeting over the Easter break, Wednesday at 10:00 a.m. in fact. I will be meeting with Mr. Correa from the bank to discuss our plans and request the loan. I want you to be there too, you know, talk the talk that you arts people are so elegant at. You will be a big help. I also want to discuss this with Mr. Sacco. As you know, he is an associate of Mr. Correa. Perhaps he also will put in a good word."

Enthusiastically, Patty responded, "Of course. Of course, monsignor. I will be there, prepared of course. Can I ask, for research sake, the amount we are looking to commit to this upgrade?"

With the restaurant now almost completely empty, a stoic-looking monsignor, now showing a posture more resembling his old self and back in the game, coyly replied, "Ten thousand. I think ten thousand will do it!"

Chapter Five

Easter-Break Eve

THE STAFF PARTY was now in the rearview mirror. For those who genuinely cared about the college, like Father Jon or the athletic director Gary Lee, they couldn't help wonder if today's affair would be their last. The changes at the college were all too evident, so far beyond those that could be seen on a financial statement. Gone or declining was the crystal-clear purposefulness of the school that had been so obvious at the turn of the century. Through the twentieth century, even in the early 2000s, pride filled the college hallways. The staff was family oriented. For those who had worked there, the school represented more a calling than a job. People used to arrive early, stay late, with seemingly endless college happenings occupying portions of most weekends. Those that craved the old days couldn't help wondering how the college got to its current state. Some just conceded that today's school environment was simply a sign of the times, akin to the decline of the Wildwood Beach town or to the nation's poor economy. Others blamed more philosophical or social trends like the deterioration of the Catholic church and the moral deep dive of both those who ran it and those who attended it.

The once-elevated employment standards of Pious College had given way to merely accepting those available or to favors…even granted to poor-performing employees. Employment standards were not alone in their slick slide downward. Student-applicant rejection lists, typically filling several binders in the nineties, were a thing of the past. The school still talked tough, at events like open houses and parents' nights, about the required high criteria of grades and leadership for those accepted to Pious. The truth, however, was that the school would now accept anyone willing to pay tuition, and those in the know could no longer deny this fact. Worse, the declining caliber of both staff and students was evident not only in the look and feel of the place but also in measurable stuff like college rankings, average acceptance scores, student GPAs, and postgraduation employment statistics. For the few good people that worked at the college, it seemed like the only thing pointing up at Pious was the number of student arrests during late-night havoc at sleazy Wildwood bars and nightclubs. Problem was, now most people at the college couldn't give a damn, and for these types, today's staff party was only a prelude to the much-anticipated night number one of Easter break.

The break was traditionally the beginning of the money time in Wildwood Beach and its crest. For those vendors willing to stay open during the winter months and for those who were about to reopen its seasonal doors, the spring and summer seasons represented the opportunity to fill cash registers and rid their shelves of inventory that mostly lay dormant over the last several months.

For the college's academic dean, Adrian Kenny, Easter break was an opportunity to keep drinking. And while the time off did little to curtail the next morning's hangover, it did eliminate the additional headache of dragging himself to work, a requirement becoming more and more difficult.

Adrian had not gone home after this afternoon's party. Failing to convince Coach Sully to barhop down the boardwalk straight from the gathering, he had gone it alone, agreeing to meet up with the coach later at Ziggys, a degenerating sports bar at the far end of the boardwalk. Sully had mentioned something about the need to study for a few hours, interpreted accurately by the dean as time for the coach to decide on tonight's bet. It was a little after eight that evening when he joined up with Mr. Kenny, instantly recognizing that he had quite a bit of drinking to do to catch up with a dean that was already very drunk. It was not uncommon on days off for Adrian Kenny to start drinking early, like he had today and continue until he either passed out or was kicked out of some drinking establishment, told in no uncertain terms that he had drank enough.

Ziggys called itself a sports bar on its faded pinstriped sign hanging a bit too low over its entrance door. Long full window shades covered the bar's large front windows, preventing look-ins from any boardwalk passersby. The place's best attribute was that it stayed open all year long, and its patrons really didn't change much with the seasons. Back in the day, it was a place where it was not unusual to see its customers made up of couples or friends from both genders. For some time however, the worn and always-dark facility mostly contained older men looking to free themselves from the confines of the missus or those just wishing to tie one on. Adrian liked the place for obvious reasons, while Coach Sully put up with it, knowing that the bartenders would align the room's TV choice squarely with that evening's wager.

Sully, feeling unusually confident, had guzzled his first two large draft beers, and now was making his third disappear. It was only a matter of seconds before he nodded the bartender's way for his fourth. With football workouts cancelled for the week, he too was looking forward to several straight days of sleep in.

The Knicks were up three at the half, and if they could just hold on in this pick-um of a game, he would be out; the term used by heavy gamblers when a winning bet eliminated the large debt to the not-always-so-kind bookies. Of course, if the Knicks lost—well, let's just say he didn't want to go there, of being placed in bookie purgatory, cut off from betting until all matters were settled in full. He looked down the bar, past his buddy AK, whose drinking continued to defy most things good. The dean was amazingly still knocking down bourbon, neat from a rocks glass. Sully caught himself grinning the way of a far corner booth, as he amused himself watching another very intoxicated biker guy kissing the neck of his somewhat resistant tattooed girlfriend. The jukebox was playing an old tune by the Beach Boys, fortunately not loud enough to overwhelm either the TV or any conversation he might have with the drunken academic dean. He remembered what tonight's mid-aged male bartender, an acquaintance more than a friend, had once told him—to spend any real time in this dive of a bar, one had to grow his ability to shut out the crap of it all. Be thankful, he had said, simply to either be working the bar or drinking at it.

There they sat, drinking for the next hour, Adrian beginning to slur his words and Sully caught up in every basket, foul, and loose ball. In the end, the Knicks blew it, changing instantly a wonderful night into a nightmare.

Coach Sully could not contain himself with the loss. "Fucken' Knicks! You think it would be too much to ask if they win just one fucken' game. They suck! And the damn coach just sits there. Another miserable losing night."

Adrian, sarcastic and slow, responded, "For the Knicks or for you?"

"For goddamn both of us," an almost screaming coach blurted out.

With this, the bartender took a step toward the anything but inconspicuous duo, put his index finger to his mouth, motioning for Sully to *shhhh* with the tirade and bad language.

In no mood for rules, the coach reacted to the bartender's gesture. "Shit. Okay, okay I get it. Give me another beer," he said as he gulped the remaining contents of his mug. Shaking his head from side to side, the bartender reluctantly stepped over, grabbed Sully's mug, and put it under the spout for a refill. Sensing no need to even address the academic drunk, he looked straight at Sully and said, "Neither of you guys better be driving tonight." He reached under the bar, pulled out a card and tossed it between the two men's drinks, and continued, "Taxi number. Be smart and use it tonight. That's all we need in here. Guys jamming us up with DUIs."

Adrian, somewhat shocking the coach that he was even listening, chimed in, "Yeah, yeah we're not driving." Turning to Sully, he said, "See that's why I don't bet on sports. These guys don't care. They win, they win. They lose, they lose. In the end, they have their millions, and guys like you don't mean shit to them. Why don't you smarten up and stop with the bets? You can't win. Even a guy not into sports like me knows that."

Sully, not about to be lectured, replied, "Fuck you, Mr. Dean! Tell you what, you stop with the booze, and I'll stop with the bets."

The bartender smiled at his two patrons and, although seemingly somewhat amused by their banter, moved his hands from up to down, clearly gesturing for them to calm down. The conversation now turned quiet.

Sully, looking to make the final point on the matter, reacted to the sudden silence, "I thought so. Stick to your books, Adrian, and I'll keep coaching. We all got our fucken' vices."

Adrian Kenny, slurring and moving on, said, "Well, after today, maybe we all better start thinking of something else to do. This school's gonna close. No doubt, with that guy in charge."

Coach responded, "What guy? Sacco?"

Adrian, now acting like an annoyed drunk, replied, "No, you idiot! The sleazy monsignor. He's the incompetent one who's driving the school into the ground. Shit, look at his secretary! He can't manage a mass, never mind a college."

Coach Sully, not so sure, said, "I don't know. The guy's a landmark here."

Without hesitation, Adrian responded with a slurring but rather coherent message, "Yeah an ancient landmark! Time has passed the guy by. Don't worry. Nobody should worry. I got a plan, and it's a plan that's gonna work."

"What fucken' plan? What the fuck are you taken about?"

With that, the bartender pretty much had enough with Sully's foul language, "Okay, guys, that's enough. Why don't we call it a night? You've both had enough."

The two men said nothing, each guzzling the remaining contents of their glasses.

Sully was quick to say to Adrian, "Let's go. Leave the man a tip."

To the delight of the bartender, the two men rose from their barstools. Adrian, clearly the less stable of the two, reached into his pocket and pulled out a few mangled bills and some change. Too drunk to look closely or care much, he tossed the money on the bar and, using Sully's shoulder, advanced himself past the coach. The two men headed for the door, Adrian in front and Sully behind him, smirking and shaking his head at his friend's wobbly walk. "Easy there, big guy," he mumbled to no one in particular.

Now somewhat stumbling side by side, the two men began to walk down an almost-empty boardwalk and turned right down a boardwalk ramp and into a parking lot. The lot was dark, only lit by a few overhead lights at the very far end, close to the cross street.

Coach Sully spoke in the direction of his buddy. "Leave your car here for the night. I'll drive you home. You're way too fucken' drunk to even fake it."

Adrian Kenny, feeling little relief from the chilled nighttime air, replied, "Yeah, whatever."

As the two men approached Coach Sully's beat-up Ford pickup, two other men, very young, perhaps in their early twenties, approached. The taller of the two men stepped between the truck and the coach's extended arm, reaching for the truck's side door. The young man put his right hand out, palm upward.

Coach Sully responded to the man's gesture, saying, "Not now, tough guy, not tonight."

From around the truck, the second man spoke up, "Sorry, Coachman, been way too patient. Another fucked-up, double-down disaster tonight. Pay the man now."

With no means to accommodate the young bookie's request, Coach Sully declined by saying, "Tomorrow. Come see me tomorrow."

Not agreeable to the coach's rejection, the second man nodded to the first. Getting his okay, the man standing with the coach grabbed Sully and violently banged his head against the truck. The coach fell to the ground at the man's feet. The strong youngster began kicking Sully repeatedly in the face and upper body. The coach was reduced to a fetal position in his attempt to cover up against the violent boot of his attacker. Adrian, slow to the rescue, attempted to intercede but was blindsided by a forceful blow to the side of his head. The punch and his still-drunken state caused Adrian to fall, banging himself on his way down on the front steel bumper of the truck. The young leader of the bookie duo leaned down to a very bloody face Coach Sully. Softly, he whispered to the Coach, "Do us all a favor, pay the money. It's twenty-eight hundred. And growing. Don't make me come back again. It's bad for my business. See, it works like this. You call on me, I don't call on you."

The two tough guys, mission accomplished, walked into the night as quickly as they had arrived. Coach Sully, using the edge of the truck as his crutch, slowly rose; his face was now a mess of cuts and blood and his body bent from the many kicks it had just received. He struggled to Adrian, slowly dragged him to the back driver's-side door, and managed to deposit him in the back seat. With a similar struggle, he forced himself into the front seat, thinking he'd give it a few minutes before attempting to reach into his pocket and find his keys.

On a night that started so promising for the two mid-aged guys, it was now clearly over. By the time the clock struck 11:00 p.m., Adrian Kelly lay in a drunken unconsciousness on his apartment's sofa, and Sully, still fully dressed, was sprawled out on his bed, bags of ice cooling a damaged body and spirit. The town's action, however, was far from over. Like most places for the young of age and heart, eleven o'clock was just the start of a long night's fun.

In a small two-story bungalow on one of Wildwood's obscure side streets, the party was just starting. Cory Penstar, head lifeguard, had rented the place on a three-year cheap. At the time of the trans-action, the landlord had conceded to most of Cory's requests, as the seventy-year-old two-floor box had sat vacant for years. Really, *bun-galow* would have been a complimentary term for this place as it actually could best be described as a little more than a tall shack. For Cory, though, and his lifeguard crew, it served its purpose. It was a place to hang out and crash. For those not much into the career path of it all, the lifeguard crib served to allow its dwellers shelter from the storm. The white-paint chipped doorway represented an entry for Cory to eat, sleep, drink, and have sex. This evening was no exception.

There was a party going on, and it was beginning to draw the usual cast of young night-lifers; girls paired up in groups pretending to have each other's backs and boys all looking to create true guy stories to be told over tomorrow morning's hungover beach setup. The downstairs open floor plan, where kitchen, living room, and front-porch closet was one largely unfurnished space vibrated with the latest pop sounds. The crowd was growing, all drinking, dancing and carrying on. In the far corner, Dylan McMatty, student council president at Pious and son of Provost McMatty, had pinned in a young and somewhat receptive female. With his arm extended to a corner banister and the girl temporarily trapped between him and the staircase behind her, he was laying it on as thick as she would have it. The room was loud and chaotic. Directly behind them, kids were passing an assortment of bong pipes, joints, and tequila shots. No worries. Several others were milling around a boisterous game of beer pong. For the moment, Dylan's only interest was acting on his inherited hormonal genes, so reminiscent of his self-taught playboy dad.

Dylan, trying not to scream but inducing a decibel loud enough to be heard over the room's music, said, "You know, if you play your hand right, I can help you with that transfer from Statton. Make things real easy for you. Get you the schedule you need. Even get your aid package to the top of the pile."

The girl, now more interested, said, "Oh you can, huh? And how might you do that, big shot?"

"Actually, my dad's the big shot. All I need to do is say the word, and it's done," Dylan responded. Rushing matters, he leaned into her, stealing a far-too-lengthy glance down her provocative shirt line. Not feeling the resistance that often comes from such a move, he bent to kiss her glossed-up lips. Quickly, the lass turned her head toward the banister, rejecting his way-too-soon advance.

"Listen, big shot," she interrupted, "I could use the help, but you know I'm seeing Cory, right? Have been for a while. You know that! Not sure he would appreciate you hitting on me in his apartment."

Not too deterred, Dylan continued his cheesy rap. "Nah, this is private like. Just me and you. Besides, Cory's not even here, probably up to no good. You ever think of that? I'm not looking for a permanent thing anyway, just two students making a deal. You're a business major. You're down with deals, right?"

Without much conviction, the girl questioned his feeble, but attractive, reasoning. "I don't know, Dylan. Sounds too easy."

A now-confident, half-the-way-there Dylan continued to push. "Tell yer what. I'm gonna go upstairs to use the little boy's room. Too much beer tonight. I'll wait in the spare room. Three minutes. You come up and we get down." The proposal received only cute giggles from its recipient.

He continued his pursuit. "It's easy. I wake up tomorrow, talk to the Provost first thing. It's done. Your call, lovely girl. Three minutes. Oh give me an extra minute to allow my quick pit stop."

Feeling he'd done enough to seal the deal, Dylan pulled his arm from above the girl's shoulder and sidestepped around the few kids sitting on the bottom step, started climbing, and disappeared at the top of the stairs. The girl, now down with the transaction, took a step toward the stairs, paused to look around, deciding to take on her unexpected transfer ticket.

Upstairs, Dylan headed down the short second-floor hallway toward the bathroom but became distracted from his urinal run by the low sound of some action coming from the floor's lone bedroom. Pissed that his love space was occupied, he approached the door and strained to listen. Faintly, he could hear a guy's voice, although he couldn't quite make out the words. Straining with his ear against the door, he heard an equally faint but understandable response from the room's female: "No, not tonight, please not tonight." A few seconds of silence went by, followed by a female letting out an "ooohhh" sound. The room's action was about to start. As he strained to listen, the transfer student from downstairs, who was now more than willing, interrupted his focus on the room's audio show. Seeing her, he put his index finger over his lips to convey the quiet sign and followed with a pointed finger at the closed door to the bedroom and a big smile. With both now listening, an unexpected "Cory, no... please" was heard from inside the room

With inquisitiveness turned to fury, Dylan's almost-partner let loose. "What the fuck!" She barged past Dylan and pushed the door open to witness the unmistakable scene. Cory was lying on the bed, shirt off and pants halfway down. He was leaning over Verona, the fifteen-year-old foster child of Darlene Davidson. Verona's shirt was fully unbuttoned. As on the beach, she was braless. Her full women breasts were out for all to see. For a few seconds, all four youngsters seemed shocked, just staring, silent.

The silence didn't last long, however, as Verona frantically jumped up, let out a screaming "SEE, I TOLD YOU!" and, using one hand to pull the sides of her shirt together, ran out of the room, down the steps and out of the bungalow. Cory, now sitting up on the edge of bed, could only stare sheepishly at his girlfriend intruder. Dylan and the girl stared back, each with very different expressions. All three appeared frozen, paralyzed in another Wildwood memory gone bad. "ASSHOLE" was the young lady's single blurt to break the ice.

Further down the beach, on a night filled with endless tales of alcohol and romance, a different story was unfolding. In the far end of town, Ocean Avenue and the beach were interrupted by a large mansion-like convent, the home of Sister Dija and a handful of older, very fortunate women of the cloth. On a bench, next to a prayer garden, sat Britta Holland, the performing arts assistant at Pious College and her new lesbian lover, Rae, a local real estate agent from nearby Cape May. There, huddled together in the chilled night air, each gazed forward into the landscaped garden filled with religious statues and prayer kneelers.

Britta broke the silence. "I know it's quick, but financially it makes sense. My job at the college doesn't pay me much. I'm living month to month, barely paying the bills. You're doing well. You just said you closed a deal on that big house, you know for that couple from New York and you said you have a few more ready to close. You just said the commissions are great. Why won't you even consider it?"

Pretending to be annoyed, Rae responded to her lover, "That's why you want me to move in, bitch. 'Cause it makes sense financially? Brit, that's not me. I don't give a shit about money." Rae emphasized her point. "If I did, I wouldn't be with you."

Britta let out a loving smile, gently punching Rae's arm.

Britta objected, "That's not what I mean, and you know it. You know how I feel about you. I know it's only been a couple of months—"

Rae interrupted, "Six weeks."

Britta continued, "Okay, fucken' six weeks. I want to start and end every day with you. Tell me you don't feel the same way. I go out of my mind when you're not around."

Rae interrupted again, "A real team, huh?" Britta smiled, put her arm around Rae, and continued: "Please consider it. You know I love you. Please. Besides, I need help with the spring show. It's only a few weeks away. You did always say you wanted to get into show business."

Both women laughed, then kissed long and deep, truly looking like fresh lovers.

Rae reverted to conversation. "Tell you what...let's go back to your apartment, end the night with a glass of wine, and who knows what else, and I promise to think about it. *Fair?*"

Britta smiled. "Okay, fair."

The two women rose from the bench and, holding hands, began walking down the long narrow sidewalk that traced the lengthy front side of the nunnery. It would be a quick two-block walk to the apartment and another chance to set the night on fire.

In a side window of the impressive nuns' state house was Sister Dija's room. As with all nights, she ended it alone, often thinking how nice it would be to share her upscale living with another. She was lying on her bed in the room dimly lit and soundless. Softly, she was pleasuring herself, careful not to make the sounds that she so dearly wanted to echo. Her mind was obsessed with the memory of Dolly Jackson and her naked dark behind. Envisioning herself in this afternoon's scene, her hand was now moving swifter, eyes closed, breathing deeper and louder with each passing second. Briefly, her thoughts shifted to the possibility of being heard by the other nuns in the rooms adjacent to hers. Only now, those thoughts served only to excite her and increase the uncontrollable, urgent passion. Thoughts of being caught roused her to an erotic brink of uncontrollable pleasure. Her moans intentionally become louder, begging to expose her need for a partner. Burning, her whole body began shaking and then exploding with the forbidden juices of a nun.

Chapter Six

Request

EASTER WEEKEND'S SUNNY weather now gave way to an overcast, gloomy Monday morning. Gone was the air of optimism around the college town, brought on through the weekend's bright and sunny climate. Today, Monday's calendar included a meeting meant only for gamblers, as its outcome posed the very real risk of backfire, and the monsignor knew it. The cloud producing gray and rather eerie skies aligned well with this morning's agenda. Other than the president, sitting nervously in his dimly lit office, the administrative quarters were vacant. Over and over, the panicky priest rethought yesterday's late-day decision to reach out to Tony Sacco, indicating only that an urgent matter needed to be discussed. Struggling throughout Easter Sunday's hours, the monsignor had reached little solution to the problem that he feared would burst onto the Wildwood newspapers at week's end. In the morning, he had missed mass altogether, not leaving his college residence and determined to create a surefire plan of blackmail escape. It was only yesterday's dusk, and still without answers, did desperation set in: a day-end condition that he had ultimately realized as inevitable within an unchangeable roadblock of facts and truth.

His inability to forge anything that resembled a clear way out had convinced him of his decision to seek the chairman's help. It was only now after a long restless night that he questioned his call to Tony Sacco. Yesterday's repetitive rehearsal of lies in explaining to Tony how and why he was being blackmailed now seemed less believable and more self-indicting. Only now did he wonder if his chairman could really believe his made-up version of this mess, or even if he could be anything that resembled convincing while privately hiding the hyperventilating image of a lie-detector bar screaming a dark, black angle off the page with each passing sentence of his explanation. Overcome with self-doubt, the monsignor had but two hours to master his fabrication before the arrival of his requested guest.

Studying his watch, the priest forced himself to relax in his high-backed leather chair. Convincing himself that two hours would be enough time to right his frame of mind, he loosened his suffocating white collar and closed his old and tired eyes. He allowed himself to recall the Easter breaks of his first years at the college. So much younger, he had already secured the envy of his clergy peers. Soaking in the prestige that came from being college president, he would stroll the campus seeking the deserved ring kisses from the few who remained at the school during Easter. Intoxicated by his newfound power, his persona had been fit and strong, and oblivious to the conflict it created to his once-noble, white-collar mission. Strutting the school's impressive grounds, he had acted as if he had become the made kingpin, untouchable in his decisions to decide the fate of whomever crossed his path.

Momentarily stuck in time, his mind oddly drifted to the love affair with his then-young Greek assistant. So drunk in desire for her slim and curved frame, he had tirelessly pursued her passion. As with most outcomes back then, his thirst for pleasure and power was quenched. He soon became her master and she his willing slave. Proudly, he had once again awarded himself the right to forgo the forbidding limits of his vocation and follow his thirst for dominance. His affair with Jenny had represented an escape from his abnormal preying of young boys, and at the time gave him a very warped, yet refreshing, sense of righteousness. He recalled Jenny Flopalis's naked and ripe body, so willing to please and pleasure him as his private deep throat, skilled at each of his sexual desires. So willing was she to keep secret her dominated role, with a reverence that portrayed and demonstrated his powerful position and its hold on her womanhood.

Thinking back was therapeutic for the once proud man of the cloth. But today's visit to the past would have to wait, as the precious time to prepare for Tony Sacco's visit was dwindling rapidly. He took out Steve Summers's press release from his top locked drawer, the one that was scheduled to be turned over to the newspapers in a few days. He read it for what seemed to be the one-hundredth time. It had not changed. It told the story of Jesse Kane as a thirteen-year-old rectory worker many years ago. It told of the priest's advances and boy's fear to stop him. It detailed graphically the vile and inexcusable crimes of molestation and pedophilia. It explained how the priest used this first event to threaten little Jesse that he would tell everyone what had happened. The press release described his sick promise to keep it a secret if the boy simply allowed it to happen a few more times, ultimately convincing Jesse that this was his best and only real option. God's way of keeping his priests happy, he had rationalized to the boy. The release told of Jesse's eventual bouts with depression, drugs, and attempts at suicide. It spoke of his switch to a gay lifestyle and how only Mr. Summers's help to arrange years of therapy allowed what was now a marginal ability to lead a normal life. It cautioned the forever instability in Jesse's psyche, and his constant fight to keep from harming himself. It was graphic; it was insanity, and worse, the priest part was all true.

It was not a document that could ever be shared in today's meeting or with anyone, ever! No, today would have to be a different kind of blackmail story. Today's story would include a blackmailer's threats to fabricate improper advances by the monsignor, but clearly and solely a fabrication, a lie, by an ancient acquaintance of the monsignor who held an old ax to grind and moreover was in desperate need of money. He would beg Tony for entry into the world of quieting those who could damage one's reputation, a world that he knew Tony held a say-the-word key—a world that existed but was never spoken about.

The monsignor had little to offer in return for such service, but he would be open to all things…if he could just make this go away forever. He had come to the conclusion, after much thought, that a simple ten-thousand-dollar payment would be merely followed by another one and another after that, forcing him to this path anyway, somewhere down the line. The monsignor was old and getting frailer by the day. He needed the help of someone who was strong, powerful, and not of character to shy away from such indiscretions. He needed someone like a young Shawn Clark, a young Father Clark, someone who did what he had to do, someone who wasn't affected by the morality of it all.

As was becoming all too common in the priest's emotional roller-coaster ride, President Clark was suddenly bolstered by a swift kick of confidence. He buried the release under a stack of desktop papers and lit a cigarette. Any nonsmoking rules were imposed only on others. He was President Clark, and the rules were his to apply or discard at his discretion.

The opening of the front door to the reception area interrupted the monsignor's very temporary enthusiasm. He could hear faint chatter. While the voices were too low to decipher what was being said, he could hear that these were female voices. It was not something that he had anticipated, as any deviation or interruption from the already-daunting and upcoming meeting could only make things more difficult.

The monsignor rose from his chair and walked toward the voices. When he turned the bend, alongside the dusty bookshelves filled with old magazines and outdated paperbacks, he saw Jenny Flopalis and a young Spanish girl, someone he had recalled only by face and not by name. His assistant looked his way. Initially, as with most things these days, a look of confusion filled her face, under the exaggerated squint of her forehead and eyebrows.

"Oh, monsignor, good morning! We did not expect to see you here." Frazzled beyond the normalcy of seeing someone with whom she has worked for many years, and meaning to nudge the young girl into a polite hello, she exaggerated her tap of the hand on the back waist of the girl, instead issuing a rather terse slap on her behind. The young girl reacted with a short hop forward, not understanding the assistant's gesture nor very appreciative of being slapped in the ass. Ignoring both the monsignor's stare and the girl's reaction to her poorly located nudge, Jenny stepped directly in front of the girl, as if now intending to hide her, forming a straight line of all three in the room. The monsignor, now impatient with the lunacy of his assistant, called out to his unexpected guests. "Jenny, what are you doing here and whom is that standing behind you?"

Jenny Flopalis turned her head quickly over her left shoulder, incredibly seeming to be surprised at the girl's presence, letting out an out-of-place "ohhh!" With that, she awkwardly skipped to the right to display her young guest to the monsignor.

"This is Veronica, monsignor."

"Verona!" interrupted the young girl.

"Oh yes, Verona," continued Jenny. "She is the new foster child of Darlene, you know Ms. Davidson."

The introduction drew a rather nasty stare from Verona and an immediate reaction from the monsignor. "Jenny, not a very nice way to introduce our guest. I'm sure Verona is the pride and joy of her new family. Yes, I do recognize you, young lady, and please know that you are now every bit a part of the Pious family as well." Immediately back to the point, the monsignor turned to his assistant. "Jenny, why are you here, as I have an important and rather private meeting shortly. I did not expect anyone to be in today."

Ms. Flopalis responded, "Oh yes, monsignor, but Darlene was so nice to offer her daughter's help today. Don't you remember? We need to stuff and mail the Easter-break letters to all of the students' families this week."

Frustrated, as he was with most of the college's tasks these days, the monsignor somewhat rudely responded, "Yes I do now remember. Jenny, can you gather the materials and work from the library, as I wish to conduct an important and private meeting in my office this morning."

With repetitive and overstated nods of agreement, Ms. Flopalis quickly walked by the monsignor and into his office. Now awkwardly alone with the young girl, monsignor did his best to conduct small talk. Somewhat ironic, and as if practicing for his morning meeting with the chairman, the monsignor used the time alone with the teenager to fabricating an overblown opinion of the job being done at the college by Verona's mom. Truth is, the monsignor didn't think much of Darlene Davidson's performance nor her way of communicating the school's financial status. To the monsignor, Ms. Davidson was a subpar CFO, and frankly her financial reports always seem to be relayed with a bit too much of a self-serving tone. At this moment, however, his exaggeration of the CFO's performance served as a suitable prelude to the forthcoming lies he would swear to, in his pending discussion with Tony Sacco.

With the monsignor growing impatient and tired to temporarily occupy the young girl and Verona equally tired of her fake, plastered smile gazed at the monsignor, Jenny Flopalis finally reentered the hallway. Her arms were extended, holding bundles of papers, topped with two large boxes of envelopes. Sensing an opportunity to break from her smile-stare at the monsignor, Verona rushed to Jenny and lightened her load by taking hold of the two boxes. The monsignor couldn't help but take notice that the youngster's quick movements had caused her young breasts to bounce within her soft white T-shirt, the young lass showing her all-too-confident way of allowing others to recognize that she was braless. His manly arousal, however, quickly reverted to this morning's dilemma as he gently nudged his assistant toward the door, looking to free the area of their presence and return to his thoughts of the pending encounter with the chairman. Taking the monsignor's cue, the assistant blurted out "Follow me, Veronica" toward Verona, and both quickly exited out of the main office quarters and down the long hallway toward the school's library.

Before he could fully reenter his office, again the opening of the reception-area outer door disturbed the monsignor. Turning quickly with intentions to be firmer with his assistant and the absolute need for his privacy, he was surprised to be met by Tony Sacco. He had arrived unexpectedly early for this morning's meeting. The chairman, half in and half out of the reception area, was straddling the outer doorway, busily shaking an umbrella and keeping its soaked droplets of water from entering the college's administrative area. Looking up, he saw the monsignor who greeted him without words, only a brief and cordial smile. "Good morning, monsignor," he said as he entered the space. Mr. Sacco first shook then extended his wet hand toward the priest. The monsignor took hold of it and, without emotion, responded, "Thank you for coming, Tony." Letting go, he turned quickly away from his guest and moved toward his quarters.

The monsignor slowly led Mr. Sacco through the reception area and into his office. His mind was racing. His thoughts were incoherent. His body language fought against the inclination of complete and unmistakable defeat. It was showtime for a priest clearly needing a bit more time in his dressing room.

The door to the president's office would remain firmly shut for the next two hours. The only sound in the outer reception area was the windblown rain against the unshaded glass that separated in from out, and the drips of water entering from the window's cracked upper frame. Causing a small puddle on the window's inner ledge, the water would continue to pool during this torrential storm, ultimately spilling itself onto the tattered and stained old carpet.

It was now approaching early afternoon, and the rain and windstorms had dissipated to a mild, cool mist throughout Wildwood Beach. Local kids, off from school, saw the break in rain as their opportunity to make their way back to the boardwalk. Dog walkers and joggers could again be seen throughout the town. Merchants began to slowly line their storefront porches with an assortment of products for view and sale. Even the Wildwood pier rides were now being wiped dry by the eager workers looking to make up for the lost proceeds from a very wet morning. The town seemed to be coming alive again with the hopeful promise of late-afternoon activity and nighttime adventures. Locals could actually visualize these things in Wildwood. If you hung around its beach town long enough, you could just sense and feel the increased buzz throughout the streets, parks, stores, and boardwalk. Only at Pious College did the morbid and sullen air remain.

Finally, and without warning, the door to President Clark's office opened. Without any noticeable words or gestures of goodbye, Tony Sacco passed out its doorway, though the reception area and out the door. Within a minute, the monsignor could hear the sound of the chairman starting, and then revving, his always-new-looking black Porsche. Seconds later the car sped off, returning the campus to an eerie and, for the monsignor, threatening quiet. The monsignor leaned back in his chair, stoic and without energy. There was no expression in either face or body. He closed his eyes and temporarily drifted away.

Gradually returning to thoughts of the present, the monsignor decided yet again to read the threatening release of Mr. Summers, perhaps to better compare its message to that just communicated to Mr. Sacco. His desk was sloppy, covered in papers not in any order. He opened the drawer where he had thought he placed the letter, but it was empty. Remembering he had reviewed it prior to his morning interactions, he searched the top of his desk, but it was not there. Becoming more frantic, he repeated his picking up and putting down of desk papers several times, to no avail. He searched under his desk and through its trash basket. The damaging press release was gone. The monsignor slammed his open hand on the top of the desk, then thought better of his next move and sat back, deciding to rethink the steps since he last read the damning release.

Suddenly, it hit him like a winter's wind on an empty Wildwood Beach.

Without thinking, he had let Jenny Flopalis enter his office alone, not remembering that the release was out on the top of his desk. He had not expected her and clearly did not conduct appropriate tidy-up before rising to see this morning's intruders. She had left, arms full of papers, letters, and Lord knows what else. He had been so distracted. Knowing Jenny and her failing ways, he was convinced that if the release was removed from his office it was unintentional, and most likely unbeknownst to his assistant. *Dear god*, he heard his mind scream out. Could she have seen and read the letter in the library? Could the young teenager have seen it? Could his dimwitted assistant unknowingly stuffed the release in a parent letter? *My god!* He rose with urgency to head to the library, hoping to find them still there.

Rushing, yet of enough mind not to seem panicked in case he was seen by a cleaner, maintenance worker, or anyone else who might be in the building, he moved in the direction of the library. He barreled through the wooden double doors that separated the administrative offices to the adjacent hallway. He walked quickly by a few classrooms, made a left, and increased his pace past the walls lined with portraits of the current pope and bishops. *How pathetic*, he thought, somehow finding energy to remain in character with his typical outlook on most things Catholic.

Finally, he arrived at the library, flung open the door, and quickly passed through a vestibule into its main area with conference tables, workstations and case after case of periodicals and books. Arriving at a point to have clear vision throughout the space, he peered into the entire large room. It was empty. The tables were clear of any papers or signs of this morning's task. It was as if no one had been there since it had been cleaned late last Friday, the day referred to by Catholics as Good Friday, the day Jesus was crucified.

Chapter Seven

Winner Take All

"I KNOW IT's a lot to ask, Gary. Believe me, I do get it. I have no right to be here. It puts you in an awkward position and clearly threatens everything for me, my job, my reputation, everything. But I have no other place to go. As you can see by my cuts and bruises, these guys don't fool around. I just want a chance to get out. I'm done with this shitty way of life. I want to pay them off and then no more gambling. I promise you. And I will pay you back within a few months. I swear!"

Having uttered the spiel of so many degenerate gamblers before him, Jerry Sully sat quietly in the closed-door athletic director's office, anxiously waiting for a response from AD Gary Lee. It was Thursday, the week after Easter. School was still on recess. Coach Sully, with so few options, knew that Gary had plenty of money and would be in his office working. As one of the few conscientious staff members at Pious, Gary acted most days for the right reason. He didn't need money. He had a hefty bank account, a portfolio of blue-chip investments and a Wildwood Beach estate, envied by all in this down-trending beach town. Gary Lee wanted really hard to believe in Pious College. Most months, he didn't even pay attention to the biweekly direct deposits that hit his account, the evidence of a paltry and not-needed Pious salary. He also knew that someday his already-wealthy status would reach stratospheres that few ever enter. His widowed father was a multimillionaire with expansive accounts and fine properties, and Gary was his only child. Unless one wanted to think about multiple generations down the road, there was not much need for financial planning by Gary Lee. Besides, Kip Lee, the dad, employed a stable of advisors. As for day to day, Gary had more than he could ever spend.

Looking from across his desk at his unexpected visitor, he responded, "I don't know, coach. You're really putting me in a tough spot here. Quite frankly, saying that your request is crossing the line would be understating it. I mean, Jerry, you report to me for goodness sake!" Gary Lee sat back; the conversation temporarily paused by both men. The AD was not one of the cronies riding the Pious gravy train, content in the school's spiral toward bankruptcy. He genuinely believed in his job and in coaches who represented the leaders of young men and women.

Thoughts of suggesting the coach's firing to the monsignor was clearly reasonable based on the gall and utter insensitive desperation of the school's football coach. The practical side of any quick reaction and the implications of any knee-jerk decision also crossed the AD's mind. The fact was, announcing the departure of one of the school's key coaches, regardless of his unsavory ways, could be too much for an already-struggling athletic program to handle. Always smart and often kind, Gary's thoughts also flashed to the possibility that a denial to the coach's request could result in something even more serious for Jerry Sully, something perhaps worse than the obvious beating he took. The AD sat motionless, in thought, peering at the bluish purple bruises and scabbing slits over most Sully's face.

Angered by the position he was being put in by this less-than-stand-up guy, the AD broke his normally calm and professional demeanor. "How much?" he blurted at the coach.

"Well, Gary, you see—" started Coach Sully, only to be aggressively interrupted now by a man who was clearly pushed over the edge of his usual cordial nature.

"Listen," Gary Lee said with a clear intent to intimidate. "I want no stories! I want no damn details! I have little respect and certainly no patience for grown men who risk everything because of degenerative vices. Listen and listen good. If I do this one darn time, it will be *against* my better judgment. If you don't shape up, I will never help you again. In fact, I will do everything I can to rid this school of your sorry, pathetic presence. *How much?*"

"Three thousand," sheepishly uttered the coach.

With that, Gary Lee rose and walked to the side of the room with the old-fashioned four-drawer cabinet, ripped open the top drawer, and returned to his desk chair with a brown rubber-banded checkbook. Angrily, the AD scribbled three thousand dollars in the amount box, forced the makings of his signature, and disdainfully pen-scratched one word, *Sully*, on the check's payee line. He pushed the check toward the coach and, without words, rose and disgustedly left the room. The coach lifted his body, sore but coming alive, and grabbed the check; secured it in his front pants pocket; and quickly left rat-like, first the office, then the building. As he headed for his truck, his battered face showed a simple expression and one that defied any natural tendency toward self-assessment or guilt. Expression best defined? Mission accomplished.

One thing about those who live obsessively, drawn to unrelenting urges and addictive behavior, common sense has long left their respective mindsets. Addicts of any kind live in the moment only, incapable of focusing on anything beyond their next fix. In Sully's current moment, he saw himself with a warped sense of newfound luck. Hopping into the truck with an enthusiasm and adrenaline that ignored his aching, beat-up body, he drove directly to the town's seedy check-cashing storefront. Sully knew the place well, as it was his first stop leaving the school each payday. He was the only Pious employee still receiving his pay by check, without direct deposit. His crude and uneducated way of thinking had convinced him years ago that the less he could be traced by IDs, accounts, social security number and the like, the better. His old account at the Wildwood Savings and Loan, containing only pennies, had lain dormant for years. With its neon *Check Cashing* sign flashing and blinking, the one that only made sense during daylight as more than half of its bulbs had long since burned out, Coach Sully urgently flung the door open and entered. He signed the back of the check, paid the well-worth-it fee for service, and quickly left with most of AD Lee's donation, in cash of course.

Pulling away, now with a pocket full of money, the thought of going to visit the muscle-head bookies and make good never crossed his mind. Instead, he flicked the blinker left, crossed the bridge that connected the beach town to the highway, and headed north up the tree-lined Garden State Parkway. At eighty miles per hour, he would be at Exit 38 in no time. The exit placed him square on the Atlantic City Expressway to his favorite casino, Caesars, a straight run from the expressway to its front-door valet parking stand. Pulling in, and not bothering to turn off the engine, he jumped out of the truck and gave a quick *come here* with a tasteful head nod to the kid working the valet stand. Slipping him a twenty, he convinced the boy to keep his truck off to the side in the driveway, as he would only be a few minutes.

Caesars, once a prideful establishment that attracted high rollers, fine women, and even a celebrity-filled nightlife, was only a shell of its former look and feel. Patrons of wealth and self-proclaimed class had long been replaced. The daytime was filled with mostly out-of-work chain-smoking vagabonds, begging or blowing their few bits of monthly welfare. There they sat, pulling on slot arms, while trying to convince the very suspect waitress staff that they were real players and deserved free drinks or coffee. It being 2 p.m. in the afternoon, the joint was still hours away from nighttime when it was mostly frequented by very old teenagers or very young adults, many of whom were there to get drunk or pose as wannabe gangsters. For the most part, these dropouts would be either way too happy courtesy of the night's ecstasy pill or far too drowsy and stoned, the effect of too many bathroom-trip hits on crack pipes. Because of this seedy night crowd, the evenings' few casino winners always needed to be real careful leaving the building as security was, let's say, somewhat depleted as casino profit levels went further through the floor.

Single-minded, Sully wheeled through the revolving entrance/exit door. He headed straight for the center-room bar. With his left hand buried in his pocket to secure that day's wager, his right hand pushed the two very-available stools to the side, giving him free passage to stand cozy-like to the bar. The tender was an older lass with overdone lipstick and hair curls that resembled either a bad wig or some type of mixed marriage gone bad. Clearly, what little charm the place held onto was reserved strictly for the evening staff.

Sully ordered a double Wild Turkey, straight rotgut bourbon, threw a twenty at grandma and proceeded to gulp the brown juice in two large swallows. Smacking the bottom of the empty short glass on the worn wooden bar like some wrangler asking for another after tending to the herds all day, the coach licked his lips and ever so briefly closed his swollen eyelids. He didn't want another. Sully liked to drink, but it was a distant second to his one true passion.

He nodded to the tender as if to say thanks and headed to the table that he long decided would be that day's winner take all.

In the afternoon, no one would have ever described the place as crowded. The casino, clearly in a cost-control mode, didn't spend unneeded salary coin on dealers standing around waiting for players. Most of the tables were unlit and closed. Management had decided that during weekday afternoons their establishment would only light up and staff a few tables, those that represented the more frequented games of choice. Passing the darkened blackjack tables with twenty-five dollars and up betting only, he sidestepped around the open one with a minimum five-dollars-a-hand action. The table had only one patron who seemed more interested in the coach's tattered jeans then the dealer's one-down/one-up blackjack hand. Her interested look was clearly a sign of availability to do just about anything the coach needed. At the moment, though, Sully found it easy to ignore her very-special face design of black lipstick and overdone blue eye shading. Not being totally unmanly, he did throw a quick smile her way as he glanced admirably at the creature's large and mostly protruding breasts, which were barely held in tow by a netted red tank top, clearly a size or three too small. This tiny piece of cloth must have been a no-brainer for this starlight when she initially picked it off the rack. Its see-through netting allowed a clear view of her dark, large, and inviting nipples. One could wonder if such a display may have violated some township code controlling nudity in public places. On this day, however, Coach Sully had full control in accurately prioritizing his vices. Without hesitation, he kept on walking.

In the distance, some thirty or so feet away, he saw his table of choice. The dimly lit roulette table was the only one of four that was open. Although on this day, at this hour, patrons were given no choice as to which wheel to choose; at least it offered unlimited betting to those willing to gamble on their favorite number. At the time, the table served only two players. Looking like a couple that may have consummated their passion sometime back in the fifties or sixties, Sully only took quick note of the Chinese man and woman standing over their piles of gray-colored chips with red border. Tourists might have been a good bet, given away by the camera around the guy's neck and the gold liquid Hawaiian drinks, complete with little red umbrellas sitting snugly on each of their coasters. No problem on this or any other day, however, as roulette was not a game of competition. Players were simply looking to align with the little white ball spinning in the wheel. In fact, when a table got crowded, it was rather common for more than one player to gamble on the same number. Other than the inconvenience of less-than-adequate elbowroom, or perhaps the undesirable cheap body odor of the player next to you, it didn't matter how many people one shared the table with. Besides, Sully would be there for only a single spin.

About ten feet away from the table, Sully stopped in his tracks and glared up at the lit board, which displayed the table's previous twenty winning numbers. Only the coach wasn't interested and in fact wasn't even looking at the numbers. No, Jerry Sully was there for one-shot, winner-take-all *red* or *black*. Picking a number was rather difficult, although somewhat easier than, say, a game like lotto, simply because a winner needed to correctly pick only one number. If the ball landed in the slot for that number, you were a winner. The payout, however, a nice thirty-five dollars for every dollar bet, was a good indication of the odds and the difficulty in the success of one's choice. Unlike the strategy of the cute oriental tag team, Sully had no desire to spread his wager on several numbers for the one and very critical spin of the wheel.

Conspiracy theorists in the gambling world would often wonder if the casino influenced the winning number through a magnet system, controlled by some eye in the sky and a guy positioning the magnet from some small, dark, and remote back office. The theory promoted the idea that with a magnet, the establishment could make the ball land anywhere it wanted to, ensuring that the happy little white ball never landed on those numbers with large bets on the line. Sully had thought of that, though, fully aware that such an internal control was more reserved for players who were hot and willing to risk more than they should. In fact, the conspiracy theory also recognized that such a devious system would usually let (or even make) a guy win a few times to get his very naive confidence level up. By that time, Sully had figured, he and his prize would be long gone.

The coach's stare at the winning-numbers board, on this day anyway, didn't require one to have had taken statistics in college. Three-fourths of the twenty previous winning numbers had been red. Despite these last twenty numbers, Sully was a veteran in such matters. He knew full well that playing red or black was slightly less than a fifty-fifty chance. The *slightly less than* was caused by what Sully had always thought of as the two annoying green numbers at the top of the roulette wheel. Zero and double zero, painted bright green on the wheel, was the game's way of sweeping both red and black bets into the casino's coffers. While the odds were clearly not on these two numbers, one might be surprised how often players got wiped out when the white ball landed in the very small green slots. So as not to have these numbers be blatantly offensive to players, the game actually let you put your chips on zero or double zero, as if betting on any other number. You just did not have the choice of green when playing colors; it was either red or black.

Sully's decision was made. As with all derelict gamblers, he never, ever considered the very real shitstorm he would enter should he lose. Sully strolled to the tip of the table and emptied every cent from his pocket on the game's green felt surface. The red-vested man charged with that afternoon's spins quickly counted it up. As a player could request any breakdown of chip values, Sully was proactive in slicing through the suspense. Knowing it didn't matter and further knowing that the dealer would soon find out why, the coach looked into the eyes of the worker and spit out two words: "Large chips."

With that, the dealer counted the almost three thousand in chips and slid them in front of the coach. Jerry Sully, never bothering to count or pick up any, pushed all of them back toward the dealer, stopping their movement when directly residing on the rectangle red box. In a zone where only true gambling addicts enter, the coach's body language screamed *Let's go*. The dealer glanced up at Sully with no particular expression. To a veteran dealer, desperate players were commonplace and largely ignored, sort of like the old lady cashier tending to those winners who were looking to cash out. She stopped thinking of it as money a long time ago.

With all bets down, with his right hand, the vested worker grabbed the wheel and gave it a hard spin and then like a real pro whirled the little white ball around the wheel's perimeter. After a few seconds, and with the same right hand, he waved over the table and said the only words that would be heard until the ball stopped and the wheel ceased spinning: "No more bets. No more bets, please."

Sully's left hand was buried deep in his left jeans pocket, the one where only minutes ago was filled with the AD's generous loan. His right hand clenched the brim of the table's corner. If you looked real close, his fingertips were an exaggerated shade of white from the pressure of his grip. The ball bounced around the innards of the wheel that showed no signs yet of slowing. The Chinese couple, seemingly in unison, sucked on their mai tai straws, staring at the bouncing, rolling, and unpredictable white ball. Finally, the wheel began slowing; the little ball seemed to want to settle first in a red slot, then black, then another black, then red, and finally came to stop. The dealer's words aligned quickly with the latest number now showing on the board. "Red 35, red 35," sang the man behind the wheel. Sully took his left hand out of his pocket and put a loosely clenched fist up to his lips. Frozen in that position, he glowered at the table, mesmerized as the dealer counted out his winnings. When pushed toward him, he put both hands behind his back, as if touching the large pile of chips might spur an action that was not part of the plan.

"Cash out," he said affirmatively, now feeling that his words told all who could hear, including himself, that he was done. He gathered all but one of the smaller valued chips in one large scoop, made eye contact with the dealer, and closed the session with a very happy "That's for you." He turned without much emotion, confirming that for gamblers the thrill before the outcome far outweighs even winning. With part two of the day's plan clearly accomplished, Coach Sully walked directly toward the only open cashier window.

Approaching, he couldn't help notice the girl with the striking blue eyeshade. She was leaning on the closest slot machine to the cashier, watching him. Cashing in his chips, he deposited his large bills, amounting to almost six thousand, in the same left front pocket of his jeans. As he headed for the door, the lovely creature approached him and in her own form of desperation, uttered softly, "For one large bill, I will make you very happy." Sully, tempted but unusually and uncharacteristically intent on sticking to a plan, gave a smile and responded, "Maybe next time, sweetheart," and continued his stroll to the casino exit.

A deep breath accompanied his hand-push through the revolving door. Feeling a sudden and unneeded propensity to be conspicuous, he purposely showed no smile and no emotion. He casually handed the valet kid another twenty, hopped in the truck, and pulled away. On instinct, the vehicle moved toward the sign for Parkway South. His thoughts were calculated and calm. *I'm back in*, his mind repeated over and over. It would be a quick pit stop to see his bookie friend, hand over 2,800 dollars, and head out to get a newspaper to start reviewing tonight's games. It was nice day, he thought to himself, springtime sunny and mild. Perhaps, he thought, he might even do his homework on the boardwalk; yeah that sounded good, bench facing the ocean of course.

Chapter Eight

Passion

SHE STRADDLED HIM as he lay on his back, comfortable in his over-sized bed. His hands softly held her hips, guiding the slow rhythm of her rocking bottom. He stayed silent so as to hear fully the sound of her humming and groaning. His eyes refused to look above her neck, content on gazing at her breasts and her light, small, sex-filled nipples. He held back his thrusts, letting her movements dictate the timing of their mutual and orgasmic ending. But he envisioned her as another. The thought of his lust for the little nun Mary Dija, her neck, her breasts, the feel of her wetness, threatened untimely orgasm in this early morning sex. Sensing explosion, he violently grabbed his partner's lovely breasts, pinching hard her nipples, forcing her to burst into orgasm. He did the same, spew after spew after spew of his manhood as he joined in her screams…until both of their bodies were empty.

She rolled off him, her young bones aching and exhausted; the drips of her sweat tasting salty on her lips and her tongue. Her glance at her partner brought her back to the day. "Amazing," she whispered, breaking their entry into the present.

"I should go, Kevin, so much to do today." Patty Simon felt awkward. She hadn't intended to spend the night with Kevin McMatty. He was almost twice her age and a coworker. While finding him ridiculously attractive, she didn't know him all that well and, frankly, most times was somewhat put off by his come-ons. She needed to escape, to gather herself and to think about how she, about how they, would move on from this somewhat surreal scene. By no means was she repulsed or even in any way convinced that it was a mistake. Who knows, by day's end, she might even consider the possibility of a relationship with the school's provost. But now was not the time for decisions, nor did she wish to solicit his views on last night, nor on this morning.

"You don't have to leave, Patty. You know that, right? We could relax. It is Friday, our last weekday off before the little brats return on Monday. I'm told my breakfasts are rather tasty."

"I'm good, Kevin, really. I don't eat in the morning," she responded as she quickly began to throw on her clothes. She sensed his man-gaze, perhaps admiring the latest notch in his belt.

"I hope you don't feel bad about this, Patty," Kevin said, "or even embarrassed."

"I'm a big girl, Kevin. You don't need to worry. Christ, you sound like my dad! The only thing I feel right now is hungover from too much damn wine."

"Sorry. Okay, okay. No worries. Maybe we can talk later. I need some coffee," he responded, as he stood up, standing on the opposite side of the bed, facing her almost-frantic moves to finish dressing.

Sensing herself giving the impression of being way too quick in her exit, she stopped, took a deep breath, and faced him. Forcing herself to relax, she looked at him and smiled. Naked, he smiled back, clearly feeling no awkwardness in fully displaying his hairy broad chest and now fully spent penis. Finally making eye contact, he put out both arms and broadened his smile, inviting her to him. Fully dressed now, she casually walked around the bed, leaned up, and kissed his lips.

"Bye, Kevin, off to see the monsignor. I had fun," she said confidently and lightheartedly as she quickly turned and exited the bedroom. Headed for the front door, she stopped only to bend for her shoes in front of the couch. Careful not to slam the door behind her, she stepped down the few porch steps and headed for her car. With her back to the house, she couldn't help but slightly shake her head, hearing her lips instinctively and softly utter the word "Asshole."

She hopped in the car and quickly squashed the very temporary thought that the word could equally apply to her. Over it, she drove off looking for the first coffee shop she could find.

After devouring a Columbian bold sixteen-ounce cup and a large chocolate-glazed doughnut, she sat motionless at the corner table in the Ocean Avenue Dunkin' Donuts. She debated whether to go home and shower before intruding on the monsignor, planning to find out why his e-mail did not explain the reason for cancelling Wednesday's meeting at the bank to secure funds for her department's refurbishment. She briefly thought back to this morning's sex and her quick departure from the provost. She caught herself smiling, thinking first of the pleasure that was so long overdue in her life and then of their brief conversation. She giggled out loud, thinking about the truth. Eating in the morning might be her most favorite thing to do.

After a quick shower in her modest, but comfortable, second-floor apartment nestled in the Wildwood's south-side neighborhood, Patty Simon sat quietly, focusing her thoughts on her intended visit to President Clark. She didn't have an appointment and frankly liked it better that way. She had been a bit taken aback by Tuesday's very brief e-mail from the monsignor cancelling Wednesday's meeting at the Wildwood Savings and Loan. Initially she was angered. She had wasted a good part of Easter Sunday researching materials and prices to fit the ten-thousand-dollar request to the bank for performing arts improvement. She considered it rude that the e-mail came without explanation, particularly given that the monsignor himself initiated her attendance. Since then, that anger had turned more to concern about the overall state of her department and its place on the list of the college's priorities. Budget constraints at Pious were causing her to have some doubts about the feasibility to produce an upcoming spring performance that was up to her standards. Longer term, Patty was beginning to question whether this college was a place where she could grow her department into something special or even whether it represented the smartest employment choice to advance her career. Never overassessing her own worth, the pretty young director recognized that the less-than-premier stature of the program at Pious played into the school's decision to offer her the position in the first place. Typically, such positions were off-limits to someone of such a young age. She would not have been considered for such a post at universities with established and well-regarded programs. Likewise, however, she also didn't want a résumé that placed her at the top of a failing program. Like with everything in the field of education, funds were needed. Robust budgets, if managed correctly, translated into well-equipped programs and that in turn allowed the ability to attract talented young students. Similarly, with sports or even academics, recruiting the best and most talented students from high schools was a key element to growing any college program. Recruitment, however, required desirable facilities, attractive events, and an established track record of accomplishments for its graduates, none of which were evident at Pious. It was time for Patty Simon to get some honest answers from the monsignor. Remaining timid and shying away from confrontation was not a formula that was working all that well. The period of gratitude to the school for offering her the directorship now needed to transition into fighting for her program and for the funds it would take to improve it. Heck, she thought, look what going a little out on a limb last night had gotten her: the best sex she had in years.

Patty's drive from her apartment to the administrative building at Pious College was a short one. She thought it a good bet that the monsignor and his assistant would be in today, given that school and all its classes resumed in full force on Monday. As she pulled into the nearly empty parking lot, she decided that prior to speaking to the monsignor, she would ask Jenny Flopalis for the performing arts expense report for last year. Better, she thought, to first take a quick look at last year's spending before approaching the monsignor. Through Easter, she hadn't spent much at all this year. If she could convey with some specifics that, over the last sixteen months or so, her department had toed the line over costs, perhaps the monsignor would be more accepting of her request to loosen the school's purse strings to improve her program. Perhaps then, also, they could have a meaningful discussion about performing arts; at least he would feel inclined to explain his decision to forgo his request for funds from the town's bank.

Entering the building's dimly lit lobby, Patty approached the main office entrance, passing numerous boxes and what looked like a week's worth of mail sitting under the reception window. Odd, she thought, that nobody was processing the mail—a task, she would have assumed, that someone continued when school was not in session. She confidently walked past the obstruction, pushed open the office door, and walked in. With a good view forward, she saw Jenny Flopalis sitting at her desk appearing to be either deep in thought or sleeping. The monsignor's office door was shut, not a healthy sign that he was around.

"Good day, Jenny," she said, hoping that her words would bring life into the groggy assistant.

Opening her eyes and slightly jumping in her seat, the assistant ignored any attempt at greetings and said, "Oh, the monsignor is not here. Haven't seen or heard from him since Monday. Quite strange really and no answer to my e-mails. Quite strange."

"That's okay, Jenny. I guess it can wait. Listen, while I'm here, I was hoping to get a quick copy of last year's expense report for my department. I'm doing some planning, and I need a summary of costs to complete it."

The monsignor's assistant, as was all too typical these days, seemed flustered by the request. Her face blushed, and rather than responding, she began rustling through a number of single-page sheets of paper that were scattered on top of her desk.

"Jenny, I wouldn't think last year's report would be on your desk," Patty said, now somewhat confused by the assistant's response to her request.

Jenny Flopalis still did not respond verbally, but quickly pulled her hands away from the papers, as might a child who just got caught touching something that was off-limits. She sat motionless, still no response, but now shifting her eyes in quick, repetitive, dart-like glances downward. From where Patty was standing, she seemed to be fixated on either her legs or something below her desk.

"Is everything okay, Jenny? Are you all right?" Patty questioned.

With that, Jenny let out a long sigh, stood up, pushed her chair backward, and proceeded to get on one knee, reaching under her desk. Patty stepped around the desk, now eager to see what the assistant was reaching for, her bewilderment made clear by the cute, but quizzical, expression on her face. Ms. Flopalis arose holding in both hands a six-inch-deep aluminum pan, the kind used for baking or storing food. It was filled three quarters high with sudsy water, now spilling slightly on each side, as the assistant was having trouble balancing the awkward water-filled pan. As she tiptoed ever so slowly away from her desk, struggling with the heavy-looking pan and toward the office's kitchenette, water was spilling from all sides on the carpet. Patty, looking down, saw the naked feet of the assistant, now realizing that she had been bathing her feet, and clearly embarrassed to let on her midday foot soak. After Jenny turned the corner into the kitchenette, Patty could hear her dumping the water in the area's undersized sink. A look down from desk to kitchenette displayed wet footprints mirroring the assistant's path on the light, pale carpet. The performing arts director, attempting to play along with Jenny's refusal to verbally address the scene, just softly smiled upon the assistant's return to the desk and said, "The expense report? Do you have it? May I get a copy?"

With that, Jenny Flopalis, shoeless, walked across the room and opened the middle drawer of a three-drawer file cabinet. Squinting, she began nodding her head up and down in a yes motion, pulling a thin manila folder from the drawer. Turning, she smiled at Patty and offered her the folder while hiding one bare foot behind the other, as if Patty hadn't noticed that she was shoeless.

"So grateful. Thank you, Jenny. I will return the papers by Monday. Please have a great weekend."

"You tooooo," chimed Jenny.

Most who had the need to interact with the monsignor's assistant these days usually departed with one of two impressions. Either you felt disgusted and annoyed that such a klutz manned the school's important Radar O'Reilly-type position, or you felt sorry for the aging woman who clearly had seen sharper and better days. For Patty, her mood tilted more toward the latter. Besides, there were more pressing matters to occupy the performing arts director's mind this day. She would head home, prepare for her discussion with the monsignor, and maybe even give her assistant Britta a call to solicit her input on the matter. Also feeling much better about this morning's escapades, she might even place a quick call or e-mail to Kevin, even if that decision was more inspired by budding estrogen levels than anything that resembled common sense. Nothing all that harmful in giving the old guy a fair chance, she thought, as she strolled through the parking lot toward her car.

Her ride home was a short one. As much as she wanted and needed to focus on her career and the need to confront the monsignor, she couldn't do it. Her mind was filled only with sex. She tried to persuade herself that it was Kevin who dominated her thoughts, but that didn't work. It was only the sex, not the partner. It had been so long, not only the act but also the craving for passion to again be forefront in her mind. As she turned off the main road and on to her side street, she caught herself fantasizing foreplay with Britta. Her visions of deeply tongue-kissing Britta's open and begging lips and mouth while caressing her large, ripe, oversized breasts and nipples made her legs quiver as the vehicle neared the apartment driveway. Moisture turned to dripping wetness, bought on rapidly by her lesbian fantasies, something that also hadn't surfaced in quite some time.

She turned off her car and hurried into her apartment, urgent to lie down and satisfy herself. She dropped the folder on her coffee table, sat on its adjourning couch, and unbuttoned then dropped her skirt. Almost trancelike, her eyes gazed forward to the table, to the full cup of coffee she had made but not drank after her shower, to keys, a TV clicker, and the folder. With her hand about to enter her heated panties, her eyes met, and then read, the label on the manila folder's protruding flap: "Prior Year Soccer Team Expenses."

Patty broke out laughing. Her mood was abruptly ended. She stood up, now convinced of the pathetic state of the college, kicked off her skirt from around her ankles, scooped up the folder, and flipped it high into the air. With papers raining down in her tiny TV room, Patty headed straight to the kitchen, to the refrigerator, to be exact.

Chapter Nine

Helplessness

It was Friday, the end of the first week back after Easter break. The week had been a quiet one, with most acclimating themselves back to the routines of work on a college campus. Early in the week, one got the feeling that the staff somehow didn't quite share the springtime enthusiasm so noticeable within its students. Young minds always seemed to perk up when the weather turned warmer, most turning to visions of summertime. There were internships to be pursued, vacations to be planned, the excitement of new romances and an anticipated end to the rigors of schoolwork and tests. Of course, there was also a whole class that was graduating, looking to begin their entry into the real world. On this Friday, the vacation hangover for some Pious employees seemed to be giving way to cracks of smiles and pleasantries that usually preceded most weekends.

Typically, other than the springtime musical, this was a time of year where activities at the school decreased. Sports teams, losing ones at that, were done. Next year's paltry incoming class had been registered and this year's not-enough tuition had all been collected. Administration began to busy themselves with coordination plans for graduation. Over the next few weeks, under the leadership of Father Jon, the school would look to organize graduation day and the many administrative tasks that preceded it. The young priest was quite capable and most times genuine in executing an event that made parents and students alike feel that their accomplishments were of the worthy kind. Father Jon was crafty in convincing families that their heads should be held high as they were leaving a place that was perhaps larger and nobler than what reality had seemed to present over the last four years.

For the underclassmen, the cold nights huddled in and around dorm rooms had ended. They were replaced by daily routines where most of them left the campus after their last class to gather at the beach, the boardwalk, or in the town's bars. These students were versed in gravitating to those establishments that went through the motions of carding but seemed just fine with accepting almost anything that resembled IDs, fake or otherwise.

In the main office, the college's leader plodded through his week with a quiet, uneasy presence, arriving early as normal, but ending each day ahead of that which was usual. The monsignor's demeanor was obvious to those working or visiting the office, an attitude that conveyed an unspoken *do not disturb*. He seemed content to stay out of things, allowing his dimwitted assistant the role of a make-busy operative, exaggerating her tones of busyness and stress, but inwardly relishing the joy of acting as if she was in charge. Her obliviousness to her boss's posture was, for this week anyway, a blessing to the monsignor. And while thinking of it often, he had not conjured up the energy to speak to his assistant about the threatening press release letter. Recognizing that ignoring the letter's disappearance could turn out disastrous, the old priest also knew that raising the issue brought an equally undesired focus by an assistant that was capable of inadvertently bringing light to a very dark subject.

On this Friday, President Clark planned to dismiss himself a little before 3:00 p.m., deciding that he would head straight back to his residence. The lack of any communication from Tony Sacco continued to force angst with every door knock or phone ring. As the week had moved from Monday to Friday, so raised his penchant for doubting his strategy with the chairman. He wondered more and more if Mr. Sacco had seen right through his fabricated and urgent tale of unwarranted blackmail. While he had done almost nothing the entire week, the monsignor's internal strife left him exhausted. Each day seemed to make him years older, each thought of his past made him frailer, each breath seemed to further sap the dwindling supply of his once-formidable and combative tendencies.

He had started each of this week's mornings with a stop at the school's confectionary, demonstratively to pick up a coffee, camouflaging his purposeful glance at the newspaper headlines that still sat in a bundle, not yet prepped for sale by the store's student worker. His daily relief to find that he was not the news of the morning was short-lived, quickly replaced again by the tense nervousness that accompanied the unknown. Today's consideration to reach out to Tony Sacco was squashed, as it had been the previous four days, knowing that such action could only be interpreted as desperate. Still, he was desperate. His fears of public humiliation, ruination, and even indictment had brought the monsignor to a place of sobering helplessness. For the first time in such a long time, the priest was overcome with loneliness. His life's poor decisions had carved who he now was and landed him so very far from his calling. His call to serve the church meant nothing to him now. His pathway of godliness, once the mainstay in his life, had long been replaced with seedy perversions, aspirations of power, and a penchant for manipulation and self-gratification. It was too fatiguing to even contemplate how he arrived at his present state. But he knew well that no road led back to his once-proud conviction of faith and the simple vows of priesthood.

As the monsignor made his way to his residence, the campus spilled out, contrasting vibrations to the slump-shouldered old priest. The sun warmed its grounds, smiling its bright rays on a small group of freshmen tossing a Frisbee on the grassy portion of turf that lay adjacent to the student center. Among them but one boy, chest out and so content with his four female companions. He flirted laughter at their lack of athleticism, but remained patient with their willing but uncoordinated attempts to catch and hurl the spiraled bright-orange disc.

In the distance, past the row of parked bicycles that lined the walkway to the college's dining hall, was the Pious theater. The outdoor vestibule to the theater's front entrance was active with laughter and chatter. The monsignor noticed the scene, but continued in the direction of his residence, never considering a stop to observe the preparations for the upcoming musical. Past the theater, students sprawled on the large lawn chatting, eating, or just relaxing. Some wore earphones, producing no doubt the best of songs from playlists and trending tunes. The campus was a happy place this day, and the monsignor knew well that he didn't belong in such an atmosphere. He stepped through his front doorway and flipped the door backward, closing his connection to the peaceful, sunny day that seemed reserved for those without pain, those that were young and good-looking and carefree.

Inside the theater, among the various sections behind and on each side of the venue's seating, groups of student actors and in-charge types echoed sounds of busyness. Workers, on ladders, readied cables and lighting stanchions. Off to the corner of the stage, dancers stood in an informal circle, practicing two steps, helping each other master the show's routines. Stagehands, all volunteers, filled the stage's broad wood flooring while they placed the finishing touches on the play's Georgia settings.

Patty Simon had decided that her young troupe of actors would perform *The Color Purple*, first a powerful novel written by Alice Walker in the early eighties, and later brought to Broadway in late 2005. It was the story of sisters Celie and Nettie over the course of four decades in rural Georgia at the first half of the twentieth century. These two black young ladies were forcefully separated and kept apart, subjected to inhumane abuse. The play depicted their collective struggle to reunite and survive their offensive circumstances of racism and sexism.

Patty originally chose the play because it was among her favorite musical scores, only now beginning to realize the timeless nature of the story's underlying themes. Frankly, as she learned more and more of the play, she privately questioned if her program was up to the task of producing such a compelling and provocative performance. Her assistant, Britta Holland, remained positive that it was the perfect selection for the college; African American student numbers garnered a greater percentage of the overall student population with each passing year. The play's selection also seemed to draw enthusiasm from various, unexpected members of the Pious community. Dolly Jackson, the African American women's basketball coach, offered her help in tutoring some of the troupe's black actors, and while no one knew if she had any experience that would warrant such inclusion, her help was gladly accepted. By her side was, typically, Shane Ferrigno, the football coach. At Dolly's request, Shane had recruited several of the football team's black athletes to agree to be extras in the play, an addition that provided authenticity and realism to the script's serious theme.

Britta's partner, Rae, also became a welcome face at rehearsals and late-night recap meetings. What first had earned Britta's gratitude that her friend was warmly welcomed, was lately however transforming to a bit of skepticism as the days drew closer to opening night. It seemed to Britta that Patty was being a bit too friendly to Rae, a notion she had communicated as *lesbian insight* to her partner, who was still rather new. Rae pretentiously waved off such a notion as ridiculous, despite privately having Patty's slender and sexy frame occupy more and more of her thoughts and unspoken fantasies.

Standing next to seat one, row one, Patty Simon gazed around the theater. Eager to get on with today's rehearsal, she spoke loudly, "Okay, PEOPLE, LET'S GET STARTED! ACT-TWO ACTORS...TO THE STAGE, PLEASE." With that, Patty took a seat, stage front, and began jotting some notes in the yellow pad that had seemingly become part of her hand over the last several days. As various students made their way to the stage, Britta and Rae followed down the center aisle. Rae, trying not to be obvious, made sure that she was to Britta's right and first to the sharp right turn that would get her quickest to the seat next to Patty. Britta, following Rae, watched her partner turn swiftly and plop onto the seat directly next to Patty. She stopped short of taking the seat next to Rae. Standing directly in front of the now-seated Rae, she stared down at her, frowned her lips, and shook her head side to side. "What?" Rae said upward. "Would like to sit here?" Britta ignored the question and sat down, intentionally leaving an empty seat between herself and Rae. Rae's hand reach to Britta was equally ignored as she stared down at her phone, refusing to launch her anger and contribute to any additional unease within the trio. *What a fucken' mistake*, she thought, reflecting on her insistence to invite Rae to join the play as a volunteer.

Act two began with Celie, hunched against a wooden bedframe, carefully reading letters about her sister's whereabouts. Celie was being played by freshman Kadeejah Hall, a pretty young African American, and one of the few truly talented performers at Pious. Dolly Jackson was standing off the stage, to its left. Her body language displayed the posture of an interested coach, intently watching the student perform. Her expression gave away her exaggerated, self-appointed ownership of the young girl's performance. Alternating her glances from Kadeejah to Patty, she was obviously looking for the director's reaction to the young student's performance (and as she perceived it, her tutorage).

With the lights dimmed low, and the spotlight on the stage's young actor, Patty found herself privately distracted by Rae's perfumed violet fragrance. Her thoughts drifted from the play to Rae. Sensing that the physical connection she felt toward Britta's partner was mutual, the intoxicating scent of Rae's perfume spurred Patty's willingness to discard the professionalism required of the moment. Her urge to communicate her passion to her assistant's lover, once beyond anything that she would normally do, was overwhelming the moment. That Britta was but a few seats away added to the insanity of her emotion. Rae's powerful scent was forcing her thoughts to run wild. All morning, she found herself staring at Rae's body, her hips, her lips, and her large round breasts. As if without choice, more and more she was ignoring the common sense that cautioned her. She felt herself sliding down in her seat. The heat between her legs seemed to first seep, then gush, into and through her panties. Too strong to ignore, she began to lean toward Rae. Her mind, rapidly distancing itself from the stage's activity, was now focused on her almost uncontrollable urgency. A brief second of caution forced her to consider that there were those behind her who may be watching her and not the stage. She pretended to jot something in her notebook and looked back at the stage. As the actor continued in her performance, Patty's body language intentionally overstated her interest in the performance, even pointing toward the actor, pretending some previously discussed direction between the two. Convinced that her movements were now fully promoting her involvement in the rehearsal, she quickly leaned into Rae's shoulder, positioning her face toward her ear, to begin a whisper. As quietly as is possible, ensuring that even Britta, only a few seats away could not hear her, she whispered in Rae's ear, "I want you so badly." Rae's reaction was motionless and silent. She was frozen, paralyzed and consumed fully by Patty's come-on.

Patty and Rae were snapped back to the moment quickly and unexpectedly as someone had flipped on the lights to the theater. The darkish theater that presented ambiance to the rehearsing performers, and privately added energy to the passion of the two front-seated romantics, was now completely lit. The change in setting immediately halted the theater's action.

Patty stood quickly, turned, and looked left in the direction of the square black lighting panel located on the sidewall, next to the stage and a few feet from the front left corner of the theater. There, staring back at Patty, was the school's CFO, Darlene Davidson, her right hand still placed on the switch that had disrupted the theater's goings-on. Her left hand clutched the shoulder of her pretty Spanish stepdaughter. The young girl wore an expression of nervousness, superseded only by the grave and urgent stare of Darlene toward the trio in the front aisle. Without words, the CFO, pulling Verona by her side, began advancing toward Patty. With quick steps, she walked across the walkway that separated the stage from the front row of theater seats. Finally reaching her destination, she spoke up. "Patty, we need to speak. Now. Verona, please stay with Britta, I will be right back." With those terse words, Darlene with Patty following exited the theater, front right, to the small office and changing room located through the hardwood door that displayed a large poster from the original play, *The Color Purple*.

Once alone, Darlene sat on the worn beige love seat that sat adjacent to the office's small desk and office chair. She whisked the papers that lay on the two-seated couch toward its far arm, saying calmly, "Patty, please sit." Now fully engulfed in the tension of the moment, Patty sat down, saying, "Sure, Darlene. What's the matter? You're scaring me! What's going on?"

The CFO looked squarely at Patty and said, "I have bad news. Shocking news. Verona was just at the beach. There was a crowd next to the rock jetty. You know, the one across the sand from Milligans on the boardwalk. Verona went to see what was happening. Patty… there were two bodies…DEAD! Two men."

"OH MY GOD! Darlene, what happened? Do we know them? OH MY GOD? Who were they?"

Darlene Davidson took a deep breath, looked down and then back up. She placed her right hand over her mouth; her eyes were filled with tears as she chokingly said, "Verona said one them was the dean…AK…Adrian…Adrian Kenny is dead."

Chapter Ten

Knock-Knock

FROM HIS UPSTAIRS sitting room, the monsignor heard a soft knock on his front door. It was approaching 6:30 p.m., and the light from the day's stubborn sun shone brightly through the room's dual windows.

The priest was seated in the inner portion of the room in a rather uncomfortable, hard chair, upholstered tightly in navy blue fabric, with curved wooden arms. Next to the chair was a small round table, strewn with books and pamphlets, mostly unread, mostly outdated. It was not often that the monsignor had visitors, and when he did, they were almost never unexpected. In his current state of mind, the knock on his door instantly threw the clergy into an anxious posture.

With his old and tired legs, he stood and wobbly moved toward the window, the one that showed a clear vision down to the house's front door. Apprehensive to almost all things these days, he expected the worst. As he approached the far side of the left window, he positioned his body against the wall to ensure that he would not be seen in case the door knocker was purposely glancing upward to the second floor. Now fully positioned, he leaned his head slightly past the frame that separated the wall from the window and glanced down. His body was instantly overcome with nausea and panic. Standing patiently outside his front door were two Wildwood Beach police officers. Their police car sat intimidatingly in front of the house.

They were alone, with the immediate surroundings of the residence void of any others. Again, avoiding the obvious doorbell in front of him, the police officer knocked on the front door with three hard raps.

The priest, now convinced that the worst was upon him, struggled back to the sitting chair. He sat down, unsure of his next move. Should he ignore the visitors? Pretend he was not home? Could he answer the door with any attitude that resembled normalcy? Should he react to their accusations with shock or even with anger? He felt himself nauseous and convinced that he was about to throw up. He rose and moved his shaky legs quickly to the small bathroom, located a few feet down the hallway outside the sitting room. Deciding he could not coordinate the bending of his body down to the bowl, the priest succumbed to vomiting into his smallish white porcelain sink. Bent over, cramped, he managed to force the single water handle upward, allowing a strong stream of water to wash and drain most of his sickness. For the next minute, the monsignor stood at the white basin, balancing himself with a right-hand grip on the towel stand that sat upward next to the sink. When his stomach had eased a bit and his breathing rid itself of the shiver that only comes from overwhelming fear, he grabbed a used hand towel from the silver stand and wiped his teary eyes and sick, odor-filled lips. Dropping the towel at his feet, he returned slowly to the sitting room, heading straight for the wall to the left of the window. Bracing himself with his hand on the white sheetrock, he again peered through the window downward. The police and their car were gone. He gazed beyond the street in the front of his house, and all appeared normal. There was no one to be seen. He noticed the beginnings of dusk in the far-end portion of sky that stretched beyond the trees on the west side of the campus. For minutes, he stood there confused, uncertain of almost everything. He was empty, a hollow frame of a man filled only with an exhaustive fear and regret, his body sullen and his emotions consumed with sickening remorse. He wandered back to his chair, sat, and began to quietly sob into his hands. There he stayed for over an hour convinced of no direction that was worth any energy. His age helped him now as fatigue allowed him to doze and then sleep, still sitting straight up in his chair. The light from the window gradually faded and dimmed as daytime turned to night. The warmth of the Wildwood spring air turned quickly to a biting beach-town chill.

94

Chapter Eleven

False Alarm

THE CHIRP OF springtime robins faintly squeaked through the closed second-floor windows like a peaceful chime, awakening the bent body of the aged monsignor. The temporary peace brought on through sleep, a peace so desperately needed, was gone. Forcing his eyes open, he struggled against the chair's firm, wooden armrests to end his slouch and sit up. His old body ached from a deep sleep in a seated position. Despite his predicament, his overwhelming fatigue had allowed a rare and unexpected full sleep throughout the night. Awake and without choice, his mind instantly invited thoughts of yesterday's end and his temporary avoidance of his unwanted visitors.

It was a few minutes after 6:00 a.m. Rays of early-morning sunlight slowly rose over the town's ocean, bouncing off the priest's residence and igniting the window's view on the opposite side of the room. To others, this day was the beginning of a beautiful spring Saturday. Today, those in charge of their beach-town households could fill the day with optimistic errands, those busy work chores that had been put on hold until winter eased and finally left town. All through the town, screens replaced storm windows, deck furniture reappeared from storage, hoses were reconnected, flower gardens were readied, and covers were pulled off green water pools. For the young ones, garage doors could finally be left open, granting free access to the tricycles, sports balls, and skateboards. The town's merchants were actively anticipating the sounds of their cash registers opening and closing throughout the day.

For the monsignor, however, there was only trepidation. Rising, he slowly left the room, purposely avoiding a glance into the mirror that hung picture-frame-like on the far wall. He moved down the hallway into his bedroom where he undressed himself naked, kicking his clothes toward the hamper in the corner of the room. He consciously decided that bending to place the clothes in the hamper would have to wait. It was a time where he needed to place normalcy on hold. The typical sense of a tidy room now seemed senseless. The monsignor was in a very bad way, his body language reeking of surrender.

Careful footsteps carried him through the doorway into his master bath where he turned the shower on hot. Prior to stepping in, he picked up a plastic bottle from his sink tray and swigged a large mouthful of green Scope. In the shower, his frame stood motionless under the hot water, letting the mouthwash seep from his lips down his chin over his fat belly to the waiting drain on the shower's floor. As the waterspout drenched over his thinning gray hair he abandoned thoughts of reaching for the soap, feeling that his arms were too old and tired to exert themselves. It was there he stood for many moments, until he could feel the water turn from hot to warm. Turning the silver handle, the flow eased then stopped as he grabbed a towel from the shelf that rested within arm's distance of the shower exit. He decided on socks, underwear, his black pants, and a white undershirt as that was all he could muster for today's wardrobe.

As his thoughts moved to today's decisions, he heard a soft knock downstairs on his front door. The noise was unlike yesterday's, not nearly as forceful or threatening. He moved as quickly as his body would take him to the other room's window and glanced down to see the identity of his visitor. It was Jenny, his assistant, facing the door and holding what he recognized as a local doughnut-shop bag and a newspaper.

As he slowly moved to and then down the stairs, he surmised that she was there to tell him that the police were looking for him.

No one ever came straight to his residence. He knew that yesterday the cops must have first stopped at his office, where Jenny would have been working late, finishing the bits and ends to the college week. He expected the newspaper's front page to scream his guilt. Approaching the door, his mind swiftly crafted his intended denial to his assistant.

Reaching the door, he opened it, stared at his visitor, and waited for her to begin the exchange. Strangely, his all-too-often frustrations with Ms. Flopalis were now replaced with the comfort of being with someone familiar and nonthreatening.

"Good morning, monsignor. I apologize for bothering you so early, but I have been up all night. I wanted you to hear the news from me, although I am sorry to be the one to have to tell you." Not allowing her to continue, the priest interrupted.

"Okay, Jenny, okay. Come in. Is that coffee in the bag? I very much need some coffee."

"Yes, monsignor, from the doughnut shop, the way you like. I also have a doughnut, the sticky kind, I am afraid. I thought better of it only after I bought it."

Jenny, following the priest's lead, entered the home's living room. The priest took a seat on the couch and began clearing the clutter on the adjacent coffee table. Taking her cue, Jenny sat next to the monsignor, placing the newspaper facedown on the table, with the bag next to it. Without speaking, she removed the coffee and handed it to the monsignor. Not thinking, she removed the sticky doughnut from the bag and placed it directly on the newspaper. Realizing that her placement was somewhat less than sanitary, she tried to pick up the doughnut but with it came a page of the paper, now messy and stuck to the doughnut. Realizing that the monsignor was watching, she quickly dropped both the doughnut and paper on the table, saying, "So sorry, let me get a plate from the kitchen."

"Never mind, Jenny, never mind," said the priest. "I am not hungry. I just want my coffee." As he began to remove the lid from the cup, he noticed that Jenny was holding her right hand up, like a one-handed surgeon who had just scrubbed her hand prior to surgery.

Realizing again that the monsignor was on to her predicament, Jenny began to lick her fingers, finally saying, "So sticky, I should never have brought this stupid doughnut!"

"It's okay Jenny, go wash your hand in the sink. I will just sit here and enjoy my coffee."

Jenny quickly rose, shuffled to the kitchen, and washed both hands in the sink using the blue dish detergent that was sitting next to the coffee cups and utensils that were resting in the sink rack. Sure that the monsignor was not looking, she dried her hands on opposite sides of her dress and quickly hurried back and sat in the same place next to the monsignor. She noticed that the monsignor had not touched the newspaper. Unknowing to her, the monsignor could not bring himself to turn over the paper to see its front-page headlines, as fear had won out over any curiosity to confirm his daunting suspicions.

With the tomfoolery that had become all too typical of a Jenny Flopalis interaction now concluded, the visit turned serious and started with a tone of resignation from the monsignor.

"What is your news, Jenny?"

The assistant, now free of distractions, visibly became shaken. Her eyes welled up with tears as she turned her focus downward and away from the monsignor. With her hand shaking, she pushed the sticky doughnut aside and reached down to pick up the paper, a source that apparently provided the answer to the priest's question.

As if the forthcoming answers were in slow motion, the monsignor readied himself for his world to crumble. He felt his body turn tense, thinking that his secrets were finally about to surface. In a strange way, like others that he had read about that committed acts of pedophilia, he was overcome with senses of both shame and abstract relief that his sickness was revealed, that his torturous secrets were released. Somehow, the overwhelming fear that had gripped his very being with the thought of being exposed had left him. If it had to be, then at least it was with Jenny, a sorry old soul, but someone who he knew genuinely cared for his well-being. Jenny would always remain his past partner in a relationship that he had come to lean on over the years, thinking of it as the normal portion of his life's sexual experiences. Despondency overcame him, and he placed his palm on the inside of Jenny's thigh, looking to communicate that his feelings for her remained and that he wished to ease and lighten her discomfort. The gesture made clear that it was okay for Jenny to continue.

Slowly, Jenny picked up the paper and turned it to display its front page. Its headlines were met with shock rather than despair, then with possibility rather than submission. The two aging, old, once good-looking lovers sat silent, staring down at the bold black letters:

COLLEGE DEAN AND LOVER FOUND DEAD

The monsignor grabbed the paper, pulled it to him to allow his fading eyesight to see clearer. Under the headline appeared a photo of a sea of cops standing around two body bags in the sand on Wildwood's Beach. The caption read:

> *Police cordon off the area of the north-end section of Wildwood Beach where the bodies of Adrian Kenny, Pious College Dean and his apparent lover, Steven Summers, were found dead, pinned to a rocky jetty.*

The relief of learning that this was not his tragedy, that his blackmailer was dead, along with the dean of his college was too much to absorb by the monsignor. He could not control his overwhelming emotions. He was confused. His mind raced with only pieces of full thoughts:

> *Tony Sacco? Adrian Kenny? Lovers? Jesse Kane? Yesterday's police visit?*

The monsignor let go of the paper and covered his face with his hands. His body was shivering with relief, yet convulsing from his perceived role in this news. Without warning he burst into tears, an emotion that had been building for years. He made no attempt to control himself. His crying released scream-like yelps, helpless and harder than he could have ever imagined possible. Decades of torture, of deceit, and of guilt poured out of every pore of his body. Trembling and weeping, he collapsed into the arms of his assistant, his weight pushing her against the corner of the sofa. He was a wrecked, wimping example of a man who was just temporarily brought back from destruction.

As his body calmed in her arms, he lay silent, soothed by a contact he hadn't felt in many years. His eyes remained closed, shutting out a world that had become unlivable. He felt her stroking his hair, both of them content to stay in this position forever. As the moments passed, again he dozed into sleep, accepting of the compassion that is gifted to those of old age.

After hours he awoke, finding himself alone with a blanket strewn over his body. He had no answers, only that, if given the chance, he would be kinder to Jenny. His thoughts quickly shifted to the early-morning news. Wishing for further information, he remembered that he had yet to read the story in the newspaper, so he forced himself to sit up. He flipped the cover page of the paper, which was unmoved from the coffee table. The article took up the entire inside cover and his eyes jumped to the bold print at the bottom of the page. It read, *continued on page 12*. He focused and began to read. The bodies had been found midday yesterday on the portion of the beach that ran parallel to the busy end of the boardwalk. Inside the jacket of Steve Summers, the police had found a love note from AK, apologizing for their lovers' quarrel the night before. His reading paused a few seconds, as he tried to reconcile AK as gay. No one, he thought, ever considered the dean as a gay man. There were quotes from a few teachers who expressed shock as they praised Adrian as a good man without any known enemies. Steve Summers was described as a newcomer to Wildwood, with no known occupation or history in South Jersey. The article quoted a police sergeant as stating that the men had been shot and autopsies were occurring to determine the timing of their deaths. The article labeled the investigation as *early*, but noted that the police considered this a homicide, ruling out the possibility of double suicide. The monsignor finished the page and decided he would jump to page 12 in the kitchen, brewing a hot pot of coffee. Coffee seemed to be his only meal of choice these days.

His tired legs strained to pick his body up from the sofa. He used his left hand to grab the arm of the couch for balance, as his right hand clutched the newspaper. He was halfway into the kitchen when he noticed an envelope on the kitchen table. Jenny must have left it, and as he moved closer, the scribble on the envelope became readable.

Forever our love secret, it said in handwriting that the priest clearly recognized as his assistant's.

The monsignor picked up the envelope while laying the newspaper down on the edge of the table.

Strangely, for now, he chose Jenny's note over the rest of the newspaper article. He felt overcome with a youthful anticipation. All the memories of his affair with Jenny, so many years ago, seemed renewed, or perhaps he just needed an optimistic force. It had been so long since he felt energized by anything. Suddenly, Jenny wasn't the aging, mindless assistant. Rather, she was his loyal friend and lover. He was eager to read her love note. It had been so long since someone, anyone, made him feel worthy. He quickly withdrew the envelope's contents. The feeling of anticipation from a positive interruption to his morose world excited him.

Immediately, his ray of brightness turned dark. His heart raced, and again its vessels filled with fear. He recognized the paper immediately. It was the press release, the one that disappeared from his office, the one that the now-dead man had thrown at his feet.

Chapter Twelve

Lost Soul

AT NIGHT, WHEN one was alone, houses on the beach could get a bit eerie, especially when a troubled mind prevented anything resembling reasonable thinking. The rather complex mix of a quiet stillness clashing with nature's sounds might seem peaceful and natural during the day, certainly much less ominous when with others. But for now it was unnerving and scary to the young man pinned to the sofa. It was only ten forty-five in the evening, a long way until the sun would peak over the water and hopefully bring a bit of warmth and maybe even a little sense to the other day when all that represented his world, Jesse's world, was lost with the murder and death of his partner.

The house, a summer rental, was a simple but well-kept single floor ranch tucked neatly on the outskirts of Wildwood. From Ocean Avenue, access to the large front yard and open porch required one to negotiate the quarter-mile sandy dirt road that ran from the beach town's main road. More like a wide path than a road, it led straight to the private section of Wildwood Beach, which bumped nicely against the house's back deck. Often Jesse and Steve would leave the car in the spacious pebble-filled driveway and walk into town to enjoy the day and then head back to their little hideaway. Past the bumpy sand dunes they would stroll, carrying bags of treats purchased on Ocean

Avenue, or their arms would be filled with boardwalk treasures to fill the well-ordered pastel-painted rooms throughout the house. If their arms were unoccupied, they would just hold hands.

Jesse recalled the day that Steve had told him about this fabulous sanctuary, as he liked to call it. He told him that it was a perfect spot for them to relax all summer. He told him that it was an ideal spot to carry out their plan in making the evil priest pay for his sins against Jesse. The residence was going to be temporary, their own private hideout where they would be happy, and maybe even safe from the nightmares that continued to plague his young and handsome thirty-two-year-old partner. In this manipulative relationship, Jesse was the adherent disciple, following his partner's lead and content to live as and where he was told. Never questioning, Jesse had fully accepted Steve's conclusion that the events of his childhood had left permanent damage beyond what any psychiatrists could do to help. Over time with Steve, Jesse thought less and less for himself, leaving almost all matters to his conniving but somewhat faithful partner. He saw Steve as his friend, his guardian, his protector, and his lover. Steve said that Jesse should agree with his intent to punish the bad priest. So he did. He had convinced Jesse that the results of the priest's actions left him unable to take care of himself. And although he didn't know, or as Steve said, "He didn't need to know" what the actual punishment plan was, it would be over by the end of the summer. Then, Steve said they would move away and get on with their lives.

With Steve now gone forever, all of that was now over, and Jesse was left confused and afraid. More and more, he found himself feeling anxious, staring at the front door in the harsh realization that his only partner in this world would never reenter. Tonight's sound of waves crashing, the chirps from the darkness's sand-dune crickets, and the occasional flapping of the colorful flags that hung on the back deck's railing did nothing more than add to the night's unease.

Neither dumb nor slow, Jesse was just not very trained or experienced in adulthood. There were times when he couldn't remember his life before Steve, and when he could, he was more instructed than advised by Steve not to, hearing over and over that those memories were not good for him. He remembered his family as not very close, and his parents were now strangers in a town far away. For all he knew, they could have passed since it had been many years where he even thought of reaching out to them. He had no friends. Sure, there were people who Steve had introduced him to, but always making sure they never got too close and continually being reminded that his guard toward others needed to remain up. According to Steve, he was the only one who Jesse could fully trust. Over the almost fifteen years since his parents had chastised and then abandoned him for expressing that he might be gay, it was Steve who had cared for him. It didn't take much at the time for his new father figure to convince him to move in, allowing the proper care that he needed. While they moved residences a lot, their homes were always in somewhat remote towns and never where Jesse could fully develop himself. He didn't work, never even learned to drive, and his interaction with the outside world was always with Steve nearby. "The world is a mess," Steve would say, and he was there to make it right for Jesse. Jesse's mentality, over time, became severely handicapped. Almost thirty-three, his perception of the world, one that was crafted by his partner, was limited and his potential opportunities in it were unknown, foreign, and defying his strong physique and rather good looks.

Jesse sat motionless. Despite a kitchen full of food purchased by Steve the night before he left the house for the last time, he hadn't eaten much since the cops showed up at the door. He hadn't done much of anything, just sitting in the house, confused and alone. His mind kept drifting to that awful and unexpected visit. If not for the old rent receipt inside Steve's jacket, Jesse still might not know what happened to his partner. It was the police's lead back to the house.

Jesse remembered being numb as the older cop explained what happened to Steve. He was asked for something, anything that verified Steve's identification, finally remembering and handing over Steve's old Florida driver's license, the one that he kept in the old shoebox along with various other aged trinkets and papers. He recalled his ride in the back of the cop car and the constant questions by the police. He remembered his frustration with his inability to respond to most questions, noting over and over that *he just didn't know.* He remembered even having trouble explaining who he was and describing his relationship to Steve. On the day of the murder, he told them that he hadn't left the house, that it was too hot and so he had stayed inside all day watching his movies on the little TV and VCR that Steve had set up for him. It only now, without his partner, struck him as abnormal that he had few answers for what he did for a living, finally halting the questions with the exasperated response that "Steve takes care of my living." He had felt intimidated, unprepared, and ill-equipped upon being forced to identify Steve's body. Before being dropped back at the house by the cops, he had agreed to stay in the Wildwood Beach area, never fully explaining that he really had nowhere else to go. Only after sitting for a while back at the house did it dawn on him that maybe the cops thought he had been involved in Steve's murder. He was completely blank on suspecting anyone who would do this to Steve. He didn't know Adrian Kenny as he had told the cops three or four times, as they insisted on asking about this man over and over again.

When asked about enemies of his partner, Jesse had explained to the police that Steve really had none. And he meant it. Fact was, all through the years there weren't many relationships to talk about simply because there weren't many relationships, period. Asked if Steve or him had any long-standing grudges, problems, or concerns with anyone from Wildwood, he had simply responded no. It was only now that he thought that maybe he should have told them about the evil priest. Many thoughts raced, then gradually slowed, in Jesse's head until he dozed to sleep scrunched on the couch, his body covered by Steve's tattered bathrobe, an article that he had clung to earlier to help ease his anxious frame of mind.

Chapter Thirteen

Facing the Music

Too PARANOID TO move through his typical routine of a morning coffee stop at the campus confectionary, the monsignor slowly left his residence, heading directly to his office. It was early on the day following the shocking news of murder. As he crossed the path adjacent to high trees that lined the campus's entrance to the administration center, he purposely stayed in line with the trees' shadows as an attempt to block others from seeing him. The once-powerful kingpin that ruled the campus kingdom had been reduced to hiding and lurking behind trees. So appropriate, he thought to himself, that he now took on the characteristics of how most think of pedophiles... slippery, disgusting old men, slumped over and hiding in the shadows. He temporarily considered turning around, maybe even ending it all, feeling a disdain and disgust for himself and for the position that he had put himself in.

He wondered what he would be walking into. If he had a choice, he would skip the day entirely, slip back to the silence of his residence, empty his tortured head, and wait for news, any news to come to him. The priest knew, however, that such a move was impossible given his position at the college and the expectation of others. He would be looked to for guidance on how the college was to deal with this tragedy. Staying away, he knew, would bring only curiosity and suspicion.

Across the lawn, with the administration building's front door now in sight, he quickened his step through the parking lot to avoid any potential contact or communication with the scattered students and adults milling to and from and now within earshot of his pathway. He took a deep breath, reminding himself that the guilt and the fear was at this point only privately in him, that others with the exception of his assistant and the chairman knew of no connection between himself and now-dead blackmailer. As he walked by several parked cars, approaching the brick stairway leading to the double door that would access the first-floor vestibule and hallway, he was summoned by a familiar voice from behind. His legs quivered as he slowly turned his head. There standing, grinning an odd and sinister expression, was Tony Sacco dressed in a full black tuxedo with shining bling adorning each of his fingers. His diamond cuff links were pinned to a starched white shirt and reflected into mirrorlike black shoes. The monsignor approached him cautiously, thinking that perhaps he should walk him to the side where they could talk privately. As he motioned a head nod to his right, signaling his chairman away from the now numerous passersby, Mr. Sacco stood still and began laughing. From several cars, doors opened and stepping out were various members of the college's staff, led first by Coach Sully and Shane Ferrigno. There was also Darlene, the CFO holding the hand of her scantily dressed stepdaughter. From a distance he recognized Gary Lee, side by side with his wealthy father, also walking toward him. From his blind side, he heard footsteps, and turning his head he saw the two policemen who had been to his house. They were approaching rapidly. Mr. Sacco was now giggling, hand over mouth, and acting bizarrely happy. From the building, the group was joined by a running Ms. Flopalis. Unlike the chairman, she had tears streaming down her face. Yet despite her broken demeanor, she seemed young, with a face that reminded the monsignor of his once-sexy and dominated lover. Confused and now sweating, the monsignor stood frozen. Tony Sacco spoke up, almost chiming, almost singing, "SHE DID IT, MONSIGNOR! SHE DID IT. SHE KILLED STEVE SUMMERS!" With that the two policemen grabbed the monsignor's assistant, ripped her arms behind her back, and handcuffed her. As they dragged her away, Tony Sacco pointed and focused now on a young boy running to them from the opposite side of the parking lot. He was sprinting, literally almost running out of his pants. As he got to the monsignor, he grabbed the priest's hand, placing it softly on his cheek. The young Jesse Kane was sobbing, and the monsignor's hand filled with the boy's tears. The priest fell to his knees and hugged the boy, now both weeping in each other's arms.

Unconsciously sensing what it was, the priest ripped himself from sleep, bending his body to force a back-aching shimmy up the bed's headboard. Sweating, exhausted, and out of breath he felt old, ugly, and defeated. It had taken all his energy to thrust himself from his nightmare, flinging him forward like a rag doll to rise and face the day.

Chapter Fourteen

Reflection (Holi)day

USING THE SCHOOL'S emergency-alert system, morning cell phones, those of both students and staff, vibrated and chimed throughout the college. Motivated to decision-making in the strange absence of the monsignor and spurred by a genuine and caring effort to address the situation, the e-mail came from Father Jon at 6:32 a.m.

> *In Honor of Adrian Kenny*
> *Friend, Mentor and Dean*
> *The College reverently recognizes his passing*
> *A time for reflection*
> *May he rest in peace.*
> *All classes and activities are cancelled for today.*
> *We wish to invite all students and staff to attend*
> *tonight's service at Luke's Funeral Home, 7pm, at*
> *1620 Ocean Avenue in Cape May. Tomorrow's Mass*
> *will be held in the Campus Chapel, 10am, followed*
> *directly with Burial Services at Saint Matthew's*
> *Cemetery in Wildwood.*

As with all things, Father Jon meant well. With his unsuccessful attempts to reach the monsignor and with the dean having no known family, he had taken it upon himself to make all the arrangements. Declining Ms. Flopalis's offer to organize a cupcake-and-coffee get-together in the school cafeteria, Father Jon was gifted in his knowing and willing ability to do the right thing. Honestly, he didn't care much for AK. Fact was, almost no one did. AK's often-rude and coarse attitude was not real conducive to friendships. He didn't seem to want friends, just some occasional company as he slowly drowned himself in liquor. Father Jon found him to be another of the college's lost souls, no doubt overtaken through his addiction to drinking and aided by his understanding that there wasn't a very high bar to live up to at Pious. What had irked the father most about AK, however, was his penchant for the lazy and superficial approach to his job as dean of students. Father Jon was as humane as they come, but no one would ever mistake him as shallow or stupid. He knew exactly who Adrian Kenny was. But the good father, today as with every day, was intent on doing the right thing. He was the kind of guy who would stop in a one-hundred-degree desert, dismount, whip out his saddle shovel, and dig a respectable hole to bury the stagecoach robber who was shot, killed, and left behind after a failed attempt to make off with the rider's valuables.

Father Jon had seen so much crap at the college and witnessed firsthand the less-than-noble leadership of the good monsignor. Driven to a place that ignored the school's chain of command, it didn't faze him should his decisions to close the school and establish services be questioned. After all, look at his alternatives: an AWOL president and a dimwitted-led cupcake gathering. Good lord!

Father Jon saw that there was more to the dean's death than met the eye. He didn't believe for one moment that AK was gay. No, this was a story that had some unraveling to do. Father Jon, however, wanted no part of any investigation. He was content to leave that to others. He would simply drive the respectful services for a now-passed associate. In his heart, he believed that all humans were children of God, and with that, each was deserving of a right to dignity in both life and death. Heck, there was a time not too long ago when most people at Pious College shared Father Jon's penchant for goodness. He knew, however, that those days were long gone. Deep down, he knew that most of the staff at Pious and almost all the students were happy to just get a free day off. Father Jon knew that most people couldn't give a damn about anything but themselves, especially those who would feel it self-serving to show their face at tonight's services.

Much like the sullen atmosphere around campus, the day was an eerie one, cloudy and damp, void of the activities and usual pace that a normal school day would bring. At the far edge of town, on a white bench facing the uninterrupted crash of each ocean wave terminating on the day's raw shoreline, Sister Dija sat motionless. Gazing at a perfectly straight line made by the far end of God's ocean, Sister's mood was unusually serious. The layer after layer of light-brown robes kept her body warm from the damp, chill air and her tight-fitting habit shielded her ears and much of her face from the shoreline wind that resembled more a late autumn day rather than the beginning of spring. It was not often that she thought further than the day ahead. Almost always Mary Dija lived in the present, typically keeping busy at one thing or another and seeming happy to most. It was only as she grew in years had the nights' loneliness made her question her chosen vocation to service and celibacy. Once an unwavering calling, most nights now ended in doubt and anxiousness. Given the school's financial plight, only recently had she begun to dread the possibility that, at any time, she could receive notification from her order transferring her out of Wildwood and drastically changing the nature of her daily service.

The beach in back of the convent was always mostly empty, although there was no known rule that reserved the space for the dozen or so nuns who called the luxurious convent their temporary home. Fact was, it was quite a walk along the shoreline to get to the convent, with the end punctuated by a rocky jetty that extended from the water all the way up the sand to the far side of the nun's hotel-like structure. Unlike the populated beach spots, frankly there wasn't much that happened at this end of the beach, save a few of the local residents figuring out that it was a undisturbed spot to let one's dog tire itself out in the very early morning, initiating another day of mostly carpet sleep while its master enjoyed the outdoors of Wildwood's beach and town. Occasionally during mealtime, the sisters would comment on the extent of that days' footprints in the sand, a boring and mundane topic even for the uneventful, unexciting lifestyle of the convent's habitants.

Death had a way, as Father Jon had suggested, to force reflection in most thoughtful souls. Mary Dija seemed to fit that category. Gazing where water met sand, the sister sat mesmerized by the spill of each dying wave onto the thousand of pebbles that lined the seashore. Through death and its darkness, the world would keep spinning, a fitting thought as she watched each wave meet its demise, only to be followed by another. Tonight would be hard on some, she thought, as would tomorrow's service, but like the waves, more days were sure to follow. Contemplation of a world without end served to calm Mary Dija, convincing her that her peace and true identity were near. Revelations filled her, now assured that her usual urgency and trepidation to find herself was self-inflicted and that God would eventually show her the way. She committed herself to living one moment at a time, an approach filled with positive thoughts that would ultimately reveal her destiny. That is God's way, she thought, thrusting herself in the loving arms of his mercy.

Overcome by the newness of her peace, she closed her eyes, loosened and rid herself of the habit that now seemed to be suffocating her face, and let the ocean's wind sweep through her hair and neck. One with all things good, Mary Dija drifted to sleep, alone on the edge of the beach.

After a time, moisture's breeze awoke her. Neither knowing nor caring how long she had slept, the sister sat still. Finally freeing itself from the sky's gray clouds, drizzle replaced the damp air, raining down on Mary Dija. Lifting her hand to wipe the rain from her brow, she felt the increased weight of the layered robes that draped her arm. The rain was increasingly soaking her clothes amid the thick, humid beach air. Reaching through the slits in her robe, she giggled to herself, knowing that unlike her elder peers in the convent, there was no small hanky stuck in her garments. Always feeling too young for such an accepted routine, her hand searched for the small round pocket watch that hid as usual within her cloth garment. Pulling the watch to eyesight, it said 2:10 p.m., confirming her unusually long stay on the hardwood bench. As the droplets of rain now ran down her face, and over her top lip, sister seemed to relish her solitary afternoon, free to taste the raindrops, uninhibited to be drenched through to her cotton T-shirt and panties. As she tilted her head back to allow direct hits of rain to splash off her young and pretty facial features, she had found a new experience, so much longer and so much more enjoyable than the short bench stints on hot and sunny days. The rest of the day could wait as Mary Dija stayed frozen in the moment, even looking forward to its ending when she would strip from her soaked robes and stand naked under a shower, with water as hot as renewed flesh could bare. Seriously considering the unthinkable, right here on the bench, *outside*, not knowing who may be watching, the good sister closed her eyes and eased her hands gently through the slits in each side of her robes.

Looking right and left to ensure she was alone, Mary Dija's spell was abruptly broken. To her right, where the rock jetty exited the water, cut through the sand, and formed a border to the beach's end appeared a young man. Oblivious to the sister's quiet presence, he slowly strolled through the rain toward the ocean. The sharp, jagged rocks appeared to act as a magnet as each of the man's steps pulled him closer to the rocky, rutted service. Seemingly without much thought, he stopped, perhaps ten feet from where each wave met its end. He plopped himself in a sitting position in the sand, resting his back against the rugged jetty wall. Lifting his vision down the broad, endless shoreline, his body language echoed a strange submission.

Although some fifty sandy yards separated the two lonely beach souls, the sister could recognize the man being of tender age, and despite his slumped, seated posture, he seemed fit and handsome. With her isolated, warm, and wet comfort now replaced by the day's chill, the nun's soggy robes and drenched hair felt out of place and awkward. Giving in to her curiosity, Mary Dija rose from the bench, deciding to see if the man was in need of help. She slowly stepped from the wood platform into the sand, beginning her walk toward the stranger. With each step, more and more sand attached to the bottom of her wet robes and her summertime sandals. The man, still oblivious to her presence, sat motionless with head bent between his knees, shielding his now-hidden face from the continuing drizzle. Now but only twenty yards from the man, the sister felt her lips utter the words "Hello," forcing Jesse Kane to look up and recognize the presence of his intruder. The sister smiled an expression of reassurance toward the man, not fully calculating that the picture of a wet petite woman of the cloth would be far from threatening to anyone looking her way. The man's face oddly showed no expression that his isolation had ended, seemingly staring through the nun and down the long-and-empty shoreline.

"Is everything all right?" spoke the nun.

"I guess" was the man's only response.

In her cute and own mastery of the language. she spoke up. "My name Sister Mary. I live here." She pointed away from the ocean and toward the large convent behind the white bench. "Me no want to bother you. It just no happen that anyone sit on this end of beach, not in rainy weather." As if on cue, the rain suddenly became more steady and harder. The man smiled briefly in her direction but said nothing. Again, she broke the silence. "Anyway, I want to make sure you okay. Is anything I can do?"

Turning his head toward the ocean, he responded, "No, thanks, sister." His curt words bought Mary Dija her unfortunate reality. For a brief moment, she had forgotten her appearance. Her words were that from a young woman speaking to a new and strange man.

She felt her body slump as forced to accept the apparent perception by the young man. "Okay, you need get out of the rain. You get sick sitting here." With that she turned, closed her eyes tightly as to forbid any notion of tears, and slowly walked back toward the convent. As she approached the wooden bench and to its right the sandy planked wooden walkway that led to the structure's rear entrance, she gazed back toward the young man. Still motionless, he sat unfazed by the now-steady drops of rain that fell straight down from the gray sky that engulfed the beach and its Wildwood neighborhoods.

As she moved toward the back vestibule, she remembered that she was to be alone well into the day. She had earlier refused her peers' offer to join them in their drive north, up the Parkway to the Barnegat nursing home, where they would spend the day tending to the elderly inhabitants that called it their home. She recalled her apologetic declining of the offer, stating that she would need to ready herself to arrive early at tonight's service, helping with any of the last-minute tasks in support of Father Jon. She expected the other nuns to be gone all day as the hardest part of such a noble routine was leaving, seeing the joy of the town's old folk dissipate as they realized that their guests' visit was over, again to be left alone with only the reality of their loneliness and their age. As she stepped through the doorway, she realized the inadequacy of the small square mat that sat just inside the room, too small to keep the wetness and sand from releasing itself from the bottom of her robes onto the fine white-tiled floor. Rather than adding another sweep up chore to her day, Mary Dija decided to begin undressing in the spot just inside the doorway, allowing the various garments to fall helplessly onto the mat at her feet. Now down to only her normally very comfortable underwear, she felt chilled as her damp T-shirt and panties clung to her body. Purposely, she moved slightly to the right where should could see herself in the oval mirror that hung to the side of the convent's entrance into their massive, country-style kitchen. The vision of herself briefly shocked then interested her. Her body was reminiscent of a magazine picture that she had once locked her eyes on. She had confiscated it from a young male student in the back of a classroom, his attempt to pass the time from her boring lecture in an early-morning religion class. Her frame was slender and curvy. Her legs, save the goose bumps from the chill, were more of a young beauty than of a nun of humility and chastity. Her torso appeared more X-rated than humble, her shirt soaked and stuck to her frame with wet, inflated nipples and small round breasts displaying a see-through image that screamed opposite to her life's calling. Her face and hair were pretty, that of a model who had just removed herself from a shower or pool. There before her was confirmation, a newfound validation that her hidden feelings of want for passion and mating were more powerful and uncontrollable than simply those that came from her mind and thoughts. It was who she was. It was whom God had made her to be. Aroused but controlled and oddly confident, she stripped herself of the remaining clothing that covered her body and her spirit, dropping them to the floor. Slowly, and with a joy of inner freedom, she walked into the kitchen naked, convinced that her truth was being revealed. Finally, her soul and body were coming together as one, freed from the cages of guilt and fear and limitation.

As she stood in the shower, letting the warming water douse the chill from her bones, she lathered her hand with soap, beginning her rubbing first slowly, then more swiftly between her legs. She allowed her thoughts to drift to that day's stranger, fantasizing his presence with her in the shower. She envisioned the stranger pinning her to the shower wall. Her mind filled with the imagery of his manhood entering her over and over again as she begged him for more. Eyes closed, her fingers entered her vagina as her body exploded. She heard herself screaming and groaning. Purposely she yelped louder, hoping that the stranger remained nearby and could hear her.

Without drying herself, she stumbled to her room and threw herself facedown on her bed. As the shower's water dripped from her body to her sheets, she lay motionless with naked bottom protruding up, drying from the warm air in her quarters. Exhausted, she fell into a daze-like sleep as her revelations took hold within her. Her peace, however, was quickly invaded by a rapping on the convent's back door.

Chapter Fifteen

An Unwanted Visit

IT WAS SLIGHTLY after 4:00 p.m. The monsignor sat tucked in his residence, staring at the TV. The volume could barely be heard, rather the sound of sizzle permeated from the kitchen. There barefoot, draped in a worn housedress she had packed in a plastic supermarket bag, Jenny Flopalis was frying a hamburger. She had arrived early that morning and had long abandoned her proper attire to drape on the maid-like garment. Her goal was simple this day. She was there to take care of the priest, to make sure he ate and readied himself for tonight's service. As she had expected, her presence was welcomed, continuations of her recent visit whereby she and the priest had obliterated the many-year pretentions that there wasn't something special between them. Conversation was sparse, with neither of them looking to promote any relevant banter. For the monsignor, he was stuck in submission, acceptant of any future fate and an approach that he had decided to play out. He had convinced himself that his predicament was beyond anything that he could control. Resigned to its unknown ending, he simply hoped that any punches his way would be soft as both his body and soul were weak and brittle. The assistant, well, she was as usual devoid of any answers other than her natural instinct to be subservient to her master. She held no other purpose in this world. He had seen to that many years ago with a dominance that would last a lifetime. Her intelligence was far too low to see it any other way. Like a family pet, she simply bided time waiting for the next instruction, hoping that her master would pet her head and talk kind words. On this day, *pathetic* was too kind a word for the occupants of this residence, a sad irony for the master who once felt that his domain wielded indefensible power and direction over all that would be.

As with just about all that she cooked, the burger was almost inedible, burnt, a lifelong reaction to being scolded as a child for serving undercooked meat to her equally dominant father. He was an old-fashioned Greek who viewed women as God's placement to serve men.

Placing the blackened burger on a dish, she poured a morsel of roasted peanuts on the empty side of the plate. Never thinking that the combo may be inappropriate, she knew that the monsignor liked peanuts. As she walked through the kitchen, plate in hand, a few of the round hard nuts rolled off the plate and onto the floor, rolling in different directions. Unable to coordinate plate with bend down, she decided to serve the monsignor and reserve peanut pickup for later. As she placed the less-than-scrumptious meal on the coffee table in front of the stoic priest, she realized she had provided neither napkin nor utensils with her delicacy. Quickly heading back to the kitchen, her bare right foot stepped squarely on one of the fallen nuts. As her favorite pastime of foot bathing had softened her feet more than most, the peanut did not get crushed; rather, it stuck, sticky-like to her sole. Rather than simply reach down to dislodge the unwelcome foot ornament, the assistant hopped on her left foot to the kitchen sink. She steadied herself with right hand on the edge of the counter and reached down with her left hand to retrieve the peanut from her sole. With her mission within arm's length of success, the nut broke free and again rolled along the floor until its energy ended. There it sat center, squarely within the middle of the checkered linoleum floor. Frustrated, Jenny Flopalis headed back into the living room and plopped into the chair, which sat diagonal from the monsignor's place on the couch. About to ask him how he was enjoying his meal, her glance at his plate reminded her that he still was left only with bare hands and shirtsleeves to serve himself and wipe his aged lips. Her panicked decision to begin the second attempt at her daunting retrieval of fork and napkin was interrupted by a hard rap on the front door.

The monsignor shifted his vision from the TV to his assistant. Unable to muster any thoughtful response, Jenny stared back, neither making any motion to move toward the door. Knock number two was even louder, as if to signal a stronger urgency that someone inside should answer. The raps of front-door noise felt like quick, sharp daggers to the chest of the shaky priest. Accepting that this intrusion could no longer be avoided, the monsignor slowly rose from the couch, attempted to steady himself, and walked to the door. With little resolve of confidence, the priest could exuberate only an old set of slumped shoulders that begged for mercy as he reached for the doorknob. Opening the door exposed two young police officers seeming to be spotlighted and sparkling from the late-afternoon sun that had broken through the gray and rainy skies. There was no need for the priest to begin with any opening comments.

"Good day, monsignor. I am Officer Crockatolli, and this is my partner, Officer Archy. May we come in?"

"Certainly. Please come in. Certainly," responded Monsignor Clark. "Can my assistant get you some coffee?" With that, Ms. Flopalis, standing on the edge where kitchen met living room, turned toward the kitchen and began to exaggerate an eye scan of the counter for the offered beverage ingredients.

"No, sir, thank you," said Officer Archy. "We just need to talk to you briefly. We won't be staying long."

"Fine," said the priest. "Please have a seat," he said, motioning the officers to the room's sitting area. "Do you know Ms. Flopalis? She has been with the college for some time." Jenny, hearing the introduction, bowed both head and torso down toward the officers, a motion reserved more for greeting a Japanese ambassador than two intruding Wildwood Beach cops.

The two officers sat together on the edge of the couch, with the monsignor on the chair diagonally facing them. The assistant, having scurried away with the burnt burger, decided it best to stay busy, as she bent to rest on both knees on the kitchen floor. Proceeding on all fours, she began to crawl around, searching for and retrieving the handful of peanuts that had fallen earlier. Refusing to delay or interrupt the conversation that was about to start, the inwardly distracted monsignor pretended not to notice his assistant dog-walking in the kitchen. The two officers, given their seated positions on the couch, backs fully facing the kitchen, remained oblivious to Jenny's retrieval tricks.

The officer who had introduced the pair at the door began. "Monsignor, we are here to speak about the two men found murdered on the beach."

"Yes," the priest responded, "terrible thing. We at the college are still in a state of shock. How can I help?'

"Well, sir, we are here to inquire any knowledge you may have of anyone who may have presented a danger to your dean. We want to also discuss what you know about Mr. Summers or for that matter of their relationship together." The cop continued. "Monsignor, whoever did this was not an amateur. This has every marking of professionals, and unfortunately these types leave few clues. Without someone coming forward with information, our unit has little to go on. Our interviews to this point have revealed very little. There appears to be no direct witnesses…never is with pros. But, sir, no one gets murdered for no reason. There is an enemy lurking somewhere. Once we identify that motive, it typically points us to some evidence, hopefully more than circumstantial. As the head of the college, you must have known Mr. Kenny well. Yes?"

The monsignor sat back, pretending to think in a way that would be helpful. Rushing through his mind, however, was that the authorities had nothing. Quick thoughts confirming Tony Sacco's involvement were supported by the cop's description of the killers. Professionals! The monsignor knew of only one professional, and it was his chairman, the man who he had gone to for help! Buoyed by the officer's opening statement, the priest was overcome with relief.

"Well, Officer, I knew AK. Mr. Kenny, that is, as well as any other at the college. A good dean, he was. Perhaps afflicted with personal demons that led to his propensity to drink a bit too much, but

I found him to be neither a violent nor dishonest man. I know of no one who held a grudge toward him." The monsignor felt his confidence growing. "He had no known family, as we all will be able to attest to tonight at his service. I am committed, Officer, to helping, but I'm afraid I can offer little to the information that hasn't already been provided."

With that the officer turned toward the kitchen to find Ms. Flopalis now glued in the closest chair, listening attentively. He spoke up. "And you, ma'am? Do you know of anyone who would be inclined to bring harm to the dean?"

The assistant, sitting awkwardly on her hands, felt the vibration of them starting to shake. With pressure from her thighs, she pressed on them with the weight that would hide her panic. "No, Mr. Officer!" she snapped. "I didn't know the dean. Well, I knew him…but I really didn't, if you know what I mean."

Ignoring her disoriented logic, the officer turned back to the monsignor. He looked at his partner, and on cue the other officer spoke up. "How about Mr. Summers, monsignor? Have you ever met him?"

"No, Officer, I have not," responded the monsignor.

"So you have no knowledge of their apparent relationship?"

"No, Officer, I do not," again responded the monsignor.

The officer expanded on his question. "Funny thing about the man. He is not known by anyone in the area, a newcomer by all accounts. His only connection to the area is his membership at Club Eighteen. Just joined. We haven't been able to talk to ownership at the club yet. Tony Sacco has been out of town. Due back tomorrow we are told. We are scheduled to ride out to see him in the morning. You know Mr. Sacco, yes, monsignor? We hear he maintains an affiliation at the school."

"Yes, Tony? Yes, a good friend of the college. He is a generous man who sits on our board. Away you say? Thought I might see him at tonight's service." The monsignor glanced down at his watch. "Oh my, look at the time. It's after five. Will there be anything else, officers? Afraid I must get ready for tonight's service for our dean. Will be a difficult evening, I'm sure."

With that, the officer rose, followed by the other. "No, monsignor. Not for now. Hopefully something will break, and we may need to speak again. Thank you for your time. We will see ourselves out. Good day, sir." And turning toward the kitchen, he said, "Good day, ma'am." Jenny signaled a quick wave at the two officers.

"Okay, officers, good day," said the monsignor, "and good luck."

With that the two officers made their way to the front door and exited, gently closing the door behind them.

As for most of the day, the monsignor and the assistant said little. As he headed up the stairs, deep in thought about his just-ended discussion, he uttered, "Change back into your clothes, Jenny, we will be leaving for the service shortly."

Jenny Flopalis, resembling some cartoon character making a mockery out of the sheer seriousness of the situation, placed the back of her wrist on her forehead. Sweeping it across her forehead, she looked up at the monsignor, now approaching the top of the steps. "WHEW, THAT WAS CLOSE!" she spewed.

Chapter Sixteen

An Unlikely Pair

THE CFO SAT silent on the edge of her king-size bed. She wore a dazed expression, the aftereffects of her first romp in the soft white sheets in quite some time. A woman tending more toward routines then passion, she could now check this week's orgasm box. Half-smiling, it had been some time that her weekly let-go was satisfied by a man, rather than by the typical mind-forced fantasies and her two petite fingers. Turning her head, she viewed sheets falling off the sides of the bed in every direction, and strewn clothing littering various parts of the worn hardwood floor throughout the room. A pair of men's boxer briefs partially covered the top of each number five on the small black alarm clock that rested on the bed's far-side end table, evidence of her unlikely late-afternoon session of sex with an even more unlikely partner. It was 5:55 p.m. AK's memorial service was scheduled to begin in a little over an hour. Soon her foster kids, both Ash and Verona, would return from unknown whereabouts, look-ing to devour their six thirty dinner, another routine in the CFO's mundane daily lifestyle. Darlene Davidson would have to quickly usher her guest out of the house and begin her search of refrigerated leftovers to serve her two not-very-particular kids. While not inten-tional, the CFO had come to appreciate, and often took advantage, of her children's acceptance to eat just about anything that was put in front of them. Unlike the spoiled little brats who resided in most homes, her foster kids came from very little, and the bar for food was set fairly low. Most poor kids, she had come to realize, grew up on fast food and small portions of what could easily be garnered. Tasty, healthy home-cooked meals were not very high on a foster child's expectation list.

The door from the master bathroom finally creaked open. *What in God's name was he doing in there?* she thought. Quickly resisting the temptation for negative thinking, her eyes fixed on the opening. Still no entrance by her afternoon knight in shining armor. She decided to be nice, yet firm, in her intent to rid herself of his presence. After all, she thought, it was her who had declined his texted invitation to grab a bite to eat at Wildwood's local diner, rather suggesting that he stop by for a sandwich. It wasn't his fault that the sandwich plan was quickly replaced by a few shots of Johnny Walker Black, some awkward foreplay of the living room sofa, finally leading to some very consensual fornication on her bed. Frankly, it was about time that the soft double mattress served for anything more than sleep. Finally, the football coach appeared.

"You know, Darlene, we should do this more often. It's not normal to ignore the obvious chemistry between us."

"Now what would someone who majored in tackling people know about chemistry?" she replied.

"Hey now, young lady! You showed quite the talent for tackling yourself a few minutes ago. All I'm saying is that I enjoyed this. And I think you did too."

"You're right, coach. I did. But I have to ask you to leave before Ash and V get home. They are due any second. I'm trying hard to set a good example. Wouldn't want them wondering what the football coach was doing here on our day off. They're young but far from stupid. Please dress quickly. Anyway, we both have to get ready for AK's service. It starts in an hour, and I still have to feed the kids."

The coach quickly began putting on his clothes, although in slow motion compared to the time it took to take them off. "No problem, Darlene. I'm outta here. I did want to talk a little about AK, though. Maybe we will get a chance later."

The CFO noticeably slowed the pace, thought for a second, and responded, "I don't know. What's to talk about? The whole thing is a fucken' nightmare."

The coach hurried his response. "Of course it is! But I keep going back to something he said to me a few weeks back. He was very upset with the college. Told me he had a plan that would change things at the top. Never really got into the details. To tell you the truth, I thought it was the liquor talking. Its only after the murder that I thought about it."

"WHAT? What plan? Who was he talking about? Jesus, coach! Did you tell the cops any of this?

The coach, now fully dressed, made his way out to the living room quickly followed by the CFO. Turning to Darlene, he leaned forward and kissed her on her cheek. "Listen, don't say anything until we have a chance to talk. I haven't mentioned any of this shit to anyone. Will tell you one thing, though. There was many a night where I sat with Adrian in one bar or another. I would bet my house that he didn't have a gay bone in his body. I would have seen it. That whole thing about the note between him and the other guy who got killed is bullshit."

"My god, yeah let's talk later," replied Darlene as she gently pushed him out the front door. "See you at the service, coach." As Coach Sully walked briskly to his truck parked directly in front of the house, Darlene Davidson couldn't resist. She poked her head outside the front screen door and said rather loudly, "Hey, coach, by the way…you don't have a house!" Coach Sully grinned without responding, jumped in the truck, started the engine, and pulled away. As he turned left at the first corner, he saw Darlene's two kids making their way up the block adjacent to their home, quickly navigating the sandy sidewalk. He slowed the truck as he passed the two teenagers. His eyes were glued on Verona, whose open shirt showed the skimpy top of her purple bikini. "Damn!" he uttered as he drove off toward the late afternoon's falling sun.

Chapter Seventeen

The Service

Luke's Funeral Home, a pretentious stucco structure opposite the boardwalk in Cape May, bristled with activity. Cars, unwilling to wait in line for the slow valet service, struggled to navigate into the cramped parking lot. Others rubbernecked past the building's entrance, hoping to find street parking in a town where parking was always more of an adventure than a simple routine.

Ocean Avenue was alive at 7:00 p.m. on this almost-summer evening. Most beachgoers, kids, and families paid no attention to the crowd forming in and around the town's only funeral parlor. While AK's murder was a big deal to some, especially at Pious College, like most stories that hit the airwaves it rapidly lost its headlines and soon would be long forgotten. Locals and visitors to this tail town of New Jersey's shoreline were busy either ending their long afternoons or merging them into the fun of nighttime, a connection without interruption, a transition one could get good at. It had been a few days since the murder, and most radio and TV stations had moved the story down toward the bottom of their playlist, replacing it with the newest tales of woe in a world where there seemed to be an endless supply of affliction and calamity. Most people at the beach were there for a good time, an opportunity to tune out work and life's struggles. While at the beach, visitors intentionally stayed oblivious to the downtrodden newscasts describing the world's inconceivable tragedies. Even the newscasters themselves seemed to stop hearing themselves a long time ago, as they would jump from a harrowing disaster to…say…the latest lotto winner or some kid's profitable lemonade stand. Tragic events in today's society were often without widespread impact, sort of reserved only for those unfortunate souls whose number had been called. It was especially like this when you visited the beach. Sound from speakers came in the form of music, not news. A TV was reserved mostly for a big game that you could enjoy while drinking, maybe even gambling. Who the hell had time to feel miserable?

The day's clouds and rain were long gone, unveiling a gorgeous early evening that engulfed Cape May. Now sunny and warm, Ocean Avenue's shops, bars, and restaurants were brimming with chatter and laughter. The boardwalk that lined the beautiful beach was active with walkers, strollers, pets, and teenagers on the lookout for memory making. The mood of the town seemed to be contagious to those approaching Luke's Funeral Home.

Cape May was widely recognized as an upscale Wildwood, a beach town at the most southern part of New Jersey. Its restaurants were thought of as a bit nicer, a little classier than those of its northern neighbor. Its shops contained upscale goods and were frequented with clientele of elevated income. Even its bars and liquor stores served to a swankier population of drunks. All of this was reflective in the rentals in Cape May, where the prices clearly exceeded those in Wildwood. This pristine beach town was sometimes described as *Wildwood without the riffraff.*

Father Jon considered none of Cape May's above-average reputation when making tonight's arrangements. Fact is, he could have done without the almost twenty-minute drive south. It was just that the lone Wildwood funeral home didn't answer the phone upon his several attempts to contact them. Frustrated with the all-too-common lack of service displayed by his town's entrepreneurs, he had dialed Luke's in Cape May and immediately received courteous and prompt help.

AK's body continued to be held at the police morgue as the police continued with their ongoing investigation. With no family members soliciting claim to the corpse, there it would remain until the examiners were through with it. Father Jon decided to simply set a picture of the Dean on a small table at the front of the room. The funeral home had provided two small kneelers a few feet in front of the picture for anyone wishing to prayerfully show their respects. The priest had asked that the funeral home provide some flowers in the room, wishing to call on no one for their help. Only Gary Lee had called around 4:00 p.m. that afternoon, asking Father Jon if he needed help with tonight's arrangements. The priest had declined requesting, however, that he could use someone to ensure that the college chapel was presentable for tomorrow morning's mass. Of course, the genuinely caring athletic director had agreed to Father Jon's request.

Other than his alert system communication to all faculty, staff and students, Father Jon had e-mailed only the monsignor earlier in the day. He had asked the head of the college to arrive early, noting that he had reserved him a chair in the first row of seats. In the e-mail, he had mentioned that given the Dean had no apparent family, the monsignor should be there to greet those who made their way to the kneelers to pay respects. Father Jon had received no response from the monsignor. While the monsignor's incognito approach to the past few weeks was recognized as odd by most, his lack of an e-mail response was typical. Often the monsignor would not respond to e-mails, leaving the sender baffled and wondering if he hadn't seen them or perhaps was just ignoring the content... another head-shaking abnormality that was simply accepted by those within and around the college.

It was slightly after 7:00 p.m. when the monsignor and his assistant opened the door to the front entranceway of the funeral home. Their ride down the parkway was closer to a sermon than conversation. More than once the monsignor had instructed Ms. Flopalis to remain near him during the evening as he wished to use her presence to escape any unwanted conversations with those in attendance. He also anticipated that he would have to be the one to say some prayers, thus advising his right-hand pal to help him quiet the room when he gave her the high sign. Mostly, he had warned her that he may wish to leave early or even quickly and that she needed to mirror his exit pace, or if not, she would have to take a ride back to Wildwood from someone else. Jenny had assured him that she would be by his side, making it clear that her presence was aimed only to please. Being the monsignor's pawn never fazed the hypnotic assistant, as she was elated to be in the refreshed and spellbinding graces of her master.

Upon entering the wake, the monsignor was overtaken by the size of the crowd. The packed room was filled with the all-too-familiar faces of the school's faculty and administration. As he gazed right to left, it was apparent that everyone knew everyone, and for reasons he wished to leave unanalyzed, the aged clergyman felt repelled by the sight of the gathered school staff. As the size of the gathering began to cause some to spill into the adjourning hallway, the group's chatter increased in volume. The scene was beginning to take on the feel of a night out rather than a somber and respectful event. The monsignor could only stand back and witness the coldness and inappropriateness that in large part had developed under his frosty leadership. Despite his earlier plan to fabricate an exaggerated sadness, his expression could only muster an insensitive smirk of indifference, while his black heart beat to a "let's get this over with" body language. Little did he know that this scene would represent the best part of his night.

For those in the room with quick and perceptive aptitudes, it was hard not to notice that, other than Dylan McMatty who was no doubt dragged there by his provost father Kevin, there were no students at the service. Not that anyone was surprised with the failure of students to respond to Father Jon's invitation. Most had long since recognized the farce that had become a Catholic education at Pious. Compassion for others or simply doing the right thing was contrary to the typical self-centered Pious College student. Student decisions to take a powder on this event also confirmed the unpopularity of the dean with the young people on campus. AK worked hard to consistently validate his reputation of being uncaring, a somewhat nasty drunk who had little time or patience for those he was employed to serve. That students' opinion of AK was one that was shared by most in the now-loud, less-than-gloomy chamber. Of this pack, only guys like Gary Lee and Father Jon would feel the sorrow of the moment and the sheer apprehension that comes from the unease of an unsolved murder. Most others couldn't see past what they wanted to do when wake class was let out.

As the monsignor nodded and smiled his way to the front of the room, he had bumped into Father Jon, quickly thanking him for organizing the service and then leaving him abruptly in an obvious attempt to forgo conversation. Father Jon, a decent human being, showed no body anguish, which would clue others of the monsignor's latest diss. Time at the college had numbed the good priest to the general rudeness of it all.

The room, when empty, appeared to be of decent size for its intended purpose. At its center were several rows of padded folding chairs, capped in front by a single row of hard cushioned chairs with wooden armrests matching stout wooden legs. The room's borders were lined with couches that matched the fabric of the front-row chairs. The back of the spacious quarters was intentionally indented with doorless closets displaying wooden coat rails and a series of hangers. Tonight's weather would render this space somewhat useless. The warm, comfortable evening had eliminated any need for overcoats, assisting all in attendance to come and go as they please, a welcomed perk that one didn't have to display their entrance or exit by either hanging or grabbing a coat off the rack.

Rather awkwardly, the monsignor stood motionless at the front of the room, his back to AK's photo and the hired kneelers, simply gazing apathetically at his numerous Pious College servants. Over and over he was forced to offer his hand to a member of the Pious community circling around, right to left, then stopping briefly at the front of the room to pay their respects. Angled to the monsignor's right, Jenny Flopalis had taken a seat in the front row. With her eye level squarely at the monsignor's belt buckle, the assistant was acting like she was following the instructions of some old-time basketball coach demanding that his player keep his eyes on the midsection of his opponent in an effort to stick with him and mirror his every move. If observed by another, say from across the room, one might swear that the assistant just couldn't keep her eyes off the monsignor's groin area.

On one of the back-corner couches sat Patty Simon and Britta Holland, neither on this night wishing to invite nor deal with Britta's girlfriend, Rae. The news of AK's death had resulted in an unspoken adjustment to the tension being caused by the rather voluptuous performing arts volunteer. The last time Patty had seen Rae was during rehearsal when the lavender-scented lesbian had gotten her drunk with horniness as Britta sat seething but a few chairs away. That rehearsal's interruption by Darlene Davidson with the news of AK's murder had squashed any real path for an imminent confrontation between the three of them. Play rehearsals had been put on hold after the news of AK's death, and any subsequent conversations between Patty and Britta had become more like those between a director and an assistant than an oversexed bisexual and a jealous, but always willing, lesbian. With Britta, Patty had decided to take a "*that never really happened*" approach to the electricity between her, and Rae and Britta continued to play stupid about the obvious attraction between her boss and gal pal. Except for a few private and powerful three-some-fantasy masturbating orgasms, Patty had stuck to her thoughtful decision to pretend Rae's very real come-on hadn't occurred.

In the opposite back corner of the room stood Coach Sully. His get-lucky romp with the CFO only but a few hours old, the coach was staring at his phone as the 7:00 p.m. start to his latest bet had gotten underway. Too consumed with his wager to act the part of a grieving friend, the most Sully ventured off his iPhone screen was to check the room for Darlene. He wished not to waste the blue pill he had gulped down right before leaving his apartment, rooting for the possibility of a daily double with the CFO. Figuring that Darlene would want to hear more about AK's comment that he had some sort of plan, Sully intended to offer some conversation and, of course, round-two intercourse back at his place later, once the wake show was over. What the football coach didn't notice was that Gary Lee, the AD still awaiting payback from Sully's recent borrowing, sat still, staring at the coach. His annoyed expression seemed to evidence his awareness that Sully was back to gambling. More disconcerting for the AD, it confirmed his own gullibility that his previous generosity would somehow set the coach straight, away from his degenerate betting ways. Locked in on the coach, Gary Lee seemed to be ignoring the blabber spewing in his direction from Jimbo Carnes, his dimwitted PE instructor sitting next to him.

In a row of chairs toward the back of the room sat a lifeless Shane Ferrigno, passively staring forward. Other than having his right hand resting comfortably on his date's left knee, the assistant coach appeared to be one of the few not engaged in conversation. Ms. Jackson, his partner, sat equally indifferent, unmindful to the room's activity. From their expressions, one might have wondered whether the thrill between them was gone, or perhaps they were both engulfed in the thoughts of yet another losing and miserable sports season. Funny thing though, their demeanor was the closest thing to appropriate in the now-crammed in space.

Each passing moment witnessed one more handshake from the monsignor, one more forced smile, one more fake *thank you for coming*. As the line began to subside, the monsignor glanced at his watch. The wake had now entered its second hour. The crowd's open chatter was causing a noise level that was usually reserved for rooms in which all held their favorite cocktail. Having had enough, the monsignor looked down signaling to his assistant with a nod meant to communicate that he needed to say something to her privately. Rather than rise, Ms. Flopalis misread the priest's gesture and simply nodded back, as if to say, "All good, master, we have it covered." Frustrated, but not willing to call out to her over the many less-than-somber conversations, the monsignor nodded again to his assistant, this time more aggressively, angling his head from her to him, as if to say, "Come here." Again, this time mirroring the priest's accentuation, the assistant nodded back smiling, seemingly content of her job well done. With his frustration moving closer to anger, the monsignor stepped toward his seated assistant with intent to pull her arm upward toward him, so he could whisper the remaining night's plan. Before he could, he was tapped, blind side, by Father Jon.

"Monsignor, I believe it now appropriate that you say a few words as our guests appear a bit unruly," said Father Jon.

"Yes, Father, I agree," the monsignor responded. "Jenny," he said somewhat loudly. "Can you please close the entrance door to the room and signal quiet so that we may get on with tonight's service."

"Of course, monsignor!" said the trusty assistant as she rose and hurried up the left aisle toward the double doorway that at the moment was open to the exterior hallway. A few feet from her destination, she observed a few faculty members who stood straddling the doorway entrance. "Get in! Get in!" she blurted, "I need to close the doors!" Rudely pushing her way through them, she grabbed one doorknob, partially closed the door, then made her way to the opposite doorknob and again partially closed the door until her position, back to the room, allowed her to grab both doorknobs and begin to pull them closed. Staring at Jenny accomplishing her mission, both the monsignor and Father Jon positioned themselves at the front of the room, readying themselves to address the crowd. As the doors were about to close, Ms. Flopalis felt a tug in the opposite direction. Someone from the hallway was trying to get in. Without any consideration for the stranded individual trying to enter, the assistant pulled harder, intending to force the doors closed. With but a mere six inches of gap in accomplishing the monsignor's request, her hands slipped off the doorknobs as the pull from the hallway continued.

Like a tug-of-war participant when the rope snaps, the aged assistant began stumbling backward until she crashed into the last row of chairs, lodging herself on the floor, stuck between two chairs and two rather shocked seated staff members. Those who immediately saw the action let out a collective gasp, but once Ms. Flopalis began to struggle to free herself and rise to her feet, gasps turned to laughter. As if led by the ghost of AK, the room's members started to clap until applause filled every corner. The monsignor stood aghast, staring at the calamitous scene. As those around the assistant moved to help her up, the cause of the mishap revealed themselves, as the entrance doors slowly opened.

The room's amusement instantly took an abrupt turn from hilarity to disbelief. There in the doorway stood a familiar face taking on however a very unfamiliar look. With her, holding hands stood someone unknown to this ever-increasingly offensive college community. Sister Mary Dija had arrived complete with a new persona and what appeared at first look to be quite the new friend. Without a single spoken word, her presence elicited shock and *can't-look-away stares* from every set of eyes in the room.

Gone was the plain complexion of the little nun. Her face glistened with dark eye shadow, soft glowing blush, and an even softer red lipstick. Her body had discarded the layers of beige robes in favor of a sleek black sleeveless dress, neckline to knees. The tight-fitting evening wear revealed the previously hidden curves that most women would envy and all men crave. Her shoes were simple black high heels, adding height to her incredible yet improbable newly revealed frame. Her fine brown hair was brushed back, held in place by a simple short nun's habit that did nothing to cover the gorgeous face, ears, and neckline of the college's new raving beauty.

At her side was a young man, handsome and athletic looking. He wore black slacks and a simple white-collar shirt that was covered by a nondescript sports jacket. His expression appeared less than self-assured but oddly determined to some end. After a closer look, he appeared to be more clutching than holding Sister Mary's suddenly very sexy right hand.

Akin to a group of soldiers under attack, bunkered down awaiting the next bomb to explode, the room became silent, instantly taking on an eerie, almost-surreal setting. Nobody spoke. Spellbound, most began to survey their adjacent space to take in the reaction of others.

Then, without cue and quite unaware that her movement would act as the icebreaker, Ms. Flopalis gathered herself, scurried past Sister Mary and her new boy accessory to the doorway, and pulled both doors shut. Single-mindedly, the assistant turned toward the front of the room and nodded affirmatively in the direction of the monsignor and Father Jon, as to say, "Please continue."

Ignoring any alternative that would include addressing Ms. Flopalis's circus act, the sister, her new look, or her new boy pal, Father Jon finally spoke up.

"If you would all please have a seat, I think it appropriate now to continue with our service for Mr. Kenny."

With more attendees than seats, and as if his action would satisfy an essential requirement to elicit his approval of the nun's new makeover, Provost McMatty popped up from his end position on the couch. Just a few feet away from the newly arrived duo and with an unmistakable gesture, he pointed to the open seat and said, "Sister, please!" When the nun's reaction to the offer was to head turn toward her guest, McMatty, ever the gentleman, quickly reached down and grabbed his son Dylan's arm, pulling him up off the couch, thereby making room for two. Politely and quietly, the sister thanked Kevin McMatty and, gently tugging the hand of her partner toward the open seats, sat down and focused on Father Jon.

With all eyes on the sister and her guest, no one in the room focused on the monsignor's reaction to the wake's new arrivals. The monsignor appeared to be in a state of shock and distress. Shivers filled every inch of his body. His hands and legs shook, his stomach turned nauseous, the ability of his brain to alter his movements ceased! He had immediately recognized the nun's partner. It was Jesse Kane, the boy he had so violated as a child. It was Jesse Kane, the partner of the murdered Steve Summers, the man who he asked Tony Sacco to take care of. It was Jesse Kane, the one individual in this world who, of one single thought, made him quake…made him cower…made him quiver.

The monsignor stood frozen in a nightmare that was real and directly in front of him.

Father Jon finally spoke. "Members of Pious College, we are here tonight to remember one of our own. Adrian Kenny represented many things both to our college and to each of us here tonight. He was our dean, our peer, our friend, and our fellow human being. May God allow him peace and eternal rest afforded through a place in his kingdom. We will miss him dearly."

Father Jon paused, then continued, "Before I ask the monsignor to lead us in prayer, I think it is more than appropriate to first offer each of you an opportunity, should anyone wish to speak of Dean Kenny."

The room immediately took on an unnerving silence. Nobody spoke. In fact, nobody moved. Father Jon had just thrown a curve that undoubtedly was not expected. Everyone slumped in their chairs, unwilling to either respond to Father Jon's request or make himself or herself the center of the room's attention. Except for one man. He had eventually found his afternoon partner and was seated next to her halfway down the room's left-side aisleway. He rose, slowly, but with the assurance of a man who had meaningfulness to his movements. Unlike the often-measured, agenda-riddled language from Coach Sully, this time his body language screamed with sincerity, indisputably absent of any intention to impress or showboat. The coach had something to say.

He briefly surveyed the room, finally fixing his eyes on AK's picture. He began talking first softly, then with a louder conviction and purpose.

"I am not a fancy speaker. Most times, my words sound more like a dog barking. I get that. I am also, despite my workplace, not a very educated man. I know football, big deal," he said, softly laughing at his own words.

"But I also know my friends…the few I have. AK was one of them. Maybe because neither of us will ever win a popularity contest on this campus, we understood each other…better than most, I think. Deep down, AK wasn't a bad guy, just a guy who got caught up in a shitty existence. Sorry for the language, Padre. He really didn't have anybody who cared about him…really cared about him. I think that's why he drank. A guy does what he has to…to find a friend, I mean…even if the friend is a bottle of booze."

The transformation of the room at Luke's Funeral Home was unlike anything close to typical at the college. The wake's callous shenanigans and laughter very quickly turned serious. Darlene Davidson sat next to the coach, motionless, save the squeezing of her two hands together so hard that you could see the hard-pressed bloodlines turn darker within each finger. Dolly Jackson's sniffling, as she wiped her teary eyes, was the only sound in the room. Father Jon stood somewhat awestruck in place. Gary Lee sat mesmerized, unmoving and expressionless, with Jimbo Carnes next to him, both hands fully covering his face. Even the monsignor seemed to temporarily put aside his awkward and potentially dangerous situation presented by the room's newcomer. He stared at the coach, motionless and attentive.

Sully continued. "I took your offer to speak, Father, as this reality has finally hit me. My friend is dead. And worse, someone killed him. And we're all sitting here laughing like it's some damn TV show that's not real. It's REAL! And we should be thinking about who did this to him. Helping bring justice…for AK…not for us." The coach paused again, considering if he was done talking. He decided not to be done.

"And one more thing. No matter what anyone says, that guy Summers wasn't AK's lover. I'd bet…" Coach Sully stopped midsentence. "Bad choice of words." His nonintentional humor seemed to break the room's concentrated tension, as a few chuckles could be heard. "*In my opinion*," the coach continued, "AK was not gay. Don't know what that note was about…but again *in my opinion*…that was total bullshit. Sorry again, Father."

With that, Sully sat back down. Before anyone could react or consider moving on, the group was presented with another surprise voice.

"I would like to say something about that, if I may?" Sister Mary's new friend shockingly spoke up, his tone somewhere caught between a comment and a question. Without getting an answer, the young man, now possessing a newfound boldness, continued. "I must agree with this man. Your teacher was not Steven Summers's lover, I was!"

The young man paused, and the room's reaction was predictable. A series of gasps could be heard throughout the cramped space. The monsignor, with no place to hide, leaned on the closest chair's wooden armrest to steady himself. Strangely, Sister Mary Dija sat still, without emotion. Her look seemed to tell others that this was not the first time hearing the revelation. Finally, the silence was broken by a single word response from the coach, "WHAT?"

The man continued. "Yes, I am Steve's best friend…his lover. I never met your AK…and I would have if the note were true. It is not." Without warning, the young man turned away from Coach Sully and stared in the direction of the monsignor.

"It's me, monsignor. Don't you remember me? I'm Jesse! Don't you remember me? Jesse Kane. From a long time ago. Don't you remember me? From the rectory."

The monsignor stood paralyzed in his spot. His trembling prevented any response.

"Monsignor, please! Help me! Steve said he spoke to you. About me! About me being here." He looked down at Sister Mary. "Sister, please! You said that the people at the college...the monsignor...they would help me."

Jesse's words had deteriorated from comment to a begging plea. He began to break down, shoulders slumping, tears welling up in his eyes. From across the room, Darlene Davidson could be seen grasping the forearm of Coach Sully. The room's inhabitants were dazed and more than a bit confused. Still, not a word was spoken by anyone in the room, certainly none from the shaken monsignor.

Sister Mary rose from her seat and placed her arm around the young man to comfort him. Half-hugging the stranger and half-swiveling her head to gauge the room's reaction, she finally let go of Jesse and turned toward the monsignor, seemingly about to begin speaking. Her intentions were, however, quickly and abruptly interrupted as the double doors accessing the room flew open.

With a purposeful entrance, two police officers entered the service, the same cops who had visited the monsignor at his residence. Following them was a tall older man dressed in a classic gray suit, white shirt, and light gray tie. He wasted no time in speaking. "I must apologize to all here for this intrusion. My name is Detective Cummings from Precinct 22 in Wildwood. Please excuse what must seem like an unforgivable disrespect toward your dean. It is not meant to be so. I'm afraid I must ask Mr. Kane to come with us."

"He arrested?" blurted Sister Mary.

"No, ma'am. He is wanted for questioning at our station house," responded the detective.

"Now?" Sister Mary inquired.

"Yes, ma'am, I'm afraid so." With that, the detective politely took the arm of a nonresistant and defeated Jesse and led him out of the room and out the building.

The drama-filled atmosphere was followed by a deafening silence overtaking the room. Sister Mary, now being comforted by the ever-ready Provost McMatty, sat back down. Coach Sully, with hand on forehead, also sat shoulder-to-shoulder with Darlene Davidson. Even Father Jon could not bring himself to continue, now aimlessly standing in the front corner of the room, staring at a bunch of funeral-provided flowers. No one knew what to do or what to say. No one wished to lead this congregation, which was now very leaderless.

Finally, Ms. Flopalis stood up from her chair, moved toward the monsignor, and leaning into him with the grace of a staggering drunk, whispered, "Come on, monsignor. Maybe we should go. Maybe it's time to leave." With that, she pulled his arm until he followed her down the left aisle, past one shocked and confused staff member after another, out of the room, disappearing from the wake.

Chapter Eighteen

Car Rides

THE FUNERAL SERVICE for AK had come to a startling end. Most of the people inside had begun following the monsignor's lead and were exiting the premises. A few remained, digesting the wake's events and avoiding being labeled as rude for exiting quickly. Absent of a casket containing the deceased, the lone picture of AK at the front of the room seemed to sanction all to simply leave without again striding to the front of the room to again pay their respects.

The fine brick walkway from Luke's Funeral Home split some twenty feet from the building's exit door. Left led to the curb on Ocean Avenue. On its sidewalk sat a shiny-finished wood stand with symmetrical rows of hooks and the keys of those who had used the facility's valet service. Right led to the building's parking lot. Given the single lane that represented both the lot's entrance and exit from and to the street, it would take some time for all the cars to begin their navigation homeward.

As the crowd from AK's service continued to drip out the funeral home's exit door, both paths resembled more that of trauma zones than simple passageways to one's transportation. Nonetheless, for those who had just experienced the drama of tonight's service and its unpredictable, even disturbing, ending, it was time for each

Pious College employee to find their cars and begin the ride back to Wildwood.

Before the night's revelations began, one would have predicted that a good portion of the gathering would use the hours after the service to continue their evenings in local Cape May restaurants and bars, maybe even with solidarity to raise their glasses to AK. Earlier in the evening, the mood was party-like, with the service creating a wonderful excuse to get to Cape May, step out on a beautiful spring night, and pursue those magical moments that seem to reveal themselves within a beautiful beach town.

For those in attendance tonight, however, those possibilities dried up swiftly, as the uplifting mood changed quickly with each rapid-fire-like eye-opener. The once-sunny day had turned dark. For many, the talk of murder left them uneasy and anxious. The thought of happily gallivanting through town now was far less attractive, almost frightful. Also, for many, tonight's surprises seemed to create as many questions as it did answers. No doubt, the evening's car rides home would produce many different opinions. It was not an easy night to figure. Most left confused and trying to take in and comprehend what just took place.

Being the first to leave, the monsignor and his assistant had already reached the entrance to the north side of the Parkway before most had even gotten to their cars. The priest, now a bit less queasy, began to question the soundness of his earlier decision to allow Jenny to lead him out of the room. In retrospect, it was only his dazed and stunned mindset that caused him to forgo any consideration on how that might look to the others who were there. In an effort to gain some sense of how his departure may have been perceived, he began to replay the events leading up to his early, rude, and most suspicious exit. He started his attempt to recreate the night's roadmap with a simple question to Ms. Flopalis.

"Jenny what happened after you stumbled and fell? Can you recall exactly what followed? Please be specific."

Although perhaps he should have known better than to ask for her help, the assistant's response was something less than what he was looking for.

"Oh, monsignor, I am so sorry for that. My hands slipped trying to close the doors. I almost had it, but someone was pulling from the other side. I am okay, though. Nothing broken. Maybe just a little sore in the morning."

With that the trusty assistant stopped talking, rotated her head forward, and gazed out into the darkness of the Parkway.

The incompetence of her response and her inability to catch on to the monsignor's concerns pushed the strained priest over the edge.

"GOOD GOD, JENNY!" the monsignor bellowed. "That is not what I'm *fucken'* asking or by the way the least bit interested in… Jesus, woman! Don't you see the *goddamn fucken'* position I'm in? Are you that goddamn stupid not to realize what leaving like that might look like? Do you not *fucken'* understand who that was in there? My god, Jenny…you are no help. NO HELP WHATSOEVER! Christ, what am I going to do? Please just shut up. SHUT UP! Let me think!"

Jenny Flopalis froze in her seat. Her lips began to quiver. The monsignor had never been so angry with her. Without any words to respond, the assistant began to cry, although remaining more than conscious to do her best to sob in silence, forcing herself to keep as much emotion in check as she could.

The monsignor glanced quickly as his loyal, however limited, assistant. The fatigue and stress of the last several weeks had reached its boiling point. He felt helpless in any ability to control anything. The weeks and weeks of his thoughts being dominated by blackmail, by Jesse Kane, by his dealings with Tony Sacco, by his loss on the grips of his job, and for that matter anything to do with the college left him broken beyond any foreseeable repair.

He was exhausted. And as if possible, to make matters even worse, he had zero confirmation from a suddenly AWOL Tony Sacco of what actually took place regarding the murder of AK and Steve Summers.

As the lit green sign on the Garden State Parkway cued *Exit 4, Wildwood, 1 Mile*, a few tears began to roll down the immoral priest's face. As the car slowed, the right blinker flashed on the darkened dashboard. The monsignor and his assistant exited the Parkway, neither attempting in any way to control or conceal their misery.

Neither driver nor passenger could gather much in the way of consolation for the other.

Meanwhile, further back on the Parkway, Coach Sully cruised his beat-up truck closer and closer to home. Next to him was Darlene Davidson. The coach had convinced the CFO to excuse herself from Patty Simon's car, her earlier ride. Unlike the monsignor and Jenny, their conversation was calmer, almost analytical. At Darlene's request, Sully had elaborated on AK's comment in the bar, the first night of Easter break, that the Dean had some plan that would change the deteriorating school, something to address the lousy job being done by the monsignor.

He explained AK's rather emphatic disdain for the monsignor and pathetic job that he was doing. He surmised that if his contention that AK was not gay was indeed correct, then someone must have planted the love note between AK and the other dead guy. Buy why? He had no answer.

Darlene, never the nonthinker, proposed some help to the coach's suspicion. "Coach, besides AK, we have no tie between Summers and the school...except maybe an indirect one. Think about when the boy was pleading with the monsignor to remember him, something about a long time ago at a rectory. Lord knows what that's all about. He said something that established a connection. Remember? He said that Summers had spoken to the monsignor about him...about him! The young guy Jesse. Remember? Seems to me that our good President Clark may know something. So far, it's the only link between AK, Summers, Jesse Kane, and the school."

Coach Sully stared deeply at the CFO. Turning his head from the road's view made the CFO a bit nervous. Pointing to the front windshield, she said, "Coach, please...the road...remember...you're driving!"

Taking a quick glance at the road, Sully turned back toward his copilot. "Wow! You are good! Jesse's comment went right over my head. I was so shocked that he called himself Summer's lover that I really heard nothing after that. Very good. Very, very good, Ms. CFO! Now, what's our next move?"

143

"Whoa, hold on, cowboy," responded Darlene, somewhat taken aback by the coach's question. "What do you mean *our* next move? Sorry, don't want to play in this game, coach. Not in a murder case. Let the cops do their job. Solving murders is way above my pay grade. I got kids to think about...a big, fat mortgage to pay. Nooo! Sorry. Not my cup of tea."

"Oh come on, Darlene! It's AK! We should at least tell the cops what we know."

"Coach, listen to me. I wasn't the only one to hear that tonight. If it's out there, the cops will eventually know too." Half-laughing, the CFO continued. "Shit, coach, they are interviewing this guy as we speak. Don't you think any communication that his partner had with the school will come up? Noooo...no f'n way! Tell you what, I'll make you a deal."

"A deal, Darlene?" said the coach. "Really? What kind of deal?"

Darlene shuffled in her seat to be a bit closer to the coach. She placed her hand between his legs, and her expression showed that she was instantly impressed with what she felt. "Let us novices stay out of the murder-solving business. Okay? Let's stick to what we know. And right now, coach, all I know is that I'm still hot from that speech of yours. What say we park it at your place, guzzle a beer or some wine...whatever you have in that crappy refrigerator of yours, and then ring the bell for round two today? Now that's a deal you can hardly turn down!"

Finding it ever so easy to revert to all things that come naturally, nobody had to twist Coach Sully's arm. "I do very much like beer!" He smiled with the coy grin of a man who knew his day was to end in a very pleasurable fashion.

With the driver content in the moment, the truck sped up, finding its most direct route to his apartment.

In her little Toyota, Sister Mary Dija sat alone on an adjacent side street to Luke's Funeral Home. It had been well over thirty minutes since she had left the building and entered her car. The made-over nun saw little reason to hurry home to the convent. Refusing a sinister-like invitation from Provost McMatty to stop for coffee on the way back to Wildwood, Sister Mary sat still, representing the last of tonight's gathering to leave Cape May.

It had been one hell of a day for the petite woman of the cloth. Her afternoon revelation to see clearly and give in to who she was had brought such joy and relief. And although her personal admission to be a woman first, with all other things second, exposed a future unknown, she was good with that. Her newfound entrance to self-awareness had come with a fresh and welcomed inner strength. She was amazed that her entrance to the wake, exposing her brand-new and expressive self, could feel so natural. Her ability to let go and be free served to rid herself of the restrictive chains that had been the root of so much of her doubt and unhappiness. For now, she would not abandon her vow to be a nun, deciding that today was a first step to allow her the freedom to explore her inner being, ultimately allowing herself to be true to who she was, to whom God had intended her to be.

Still, the late day's events had left Sister Mary uneasy. Her anxiousness, however, was not born from her decision to reinvent herself nor was it from the reaction of others upon her startling entrance into the funeral home. Her edgy frame of mind continued to revert back to Jesse. What had started as a simple, almost-playful infatuation and a lighthearted intent to save the day, to save his day, had now become far more serious. On the way to the wake, her new acquaintance had revealed to her the nature of his prior relationship with the monsignor. Although absent of graphic details, his story was enough to—at minimum—suspect and perhaps envision the worst. Beginning with Jesse's story and ending with his removal from the wake prompted a feeling that she must do something. It was she who had responded to his unexpected door knock that afternoon with warm, dry clothes and a genuine promise to help him. It had been a very long time since the sister had anything personal and meaningful to attend to. Her intent to help was as much a gift to herself as it was to Jesse.

As she gazed down the side street toward Ocean Avenue, a sports car slowly rolled past, its top down and its driver and passengers young, laughing, feeling the joy of the warm night's possibilities. The scene was the sister's invite to change her sullen mood. She took a deep breath and began to let her mind drift, envisioning herself as carefree and uncommitted to the vows of restriction. For the moment, her daydreaming eased the day's calamity. Content to stay in her fantasy, she leaned back in her chair, closed her eyes, and defused her anxiety. She would sit as long as the feeling would last. For the petite and now sexy nun, the moment would not last long. From the southernmost point in Cape May, Sister was jolted into the present by the loud shrill of an approaching ambulance. The alarm served to sharpen the nun's realization of where she was. Swiftly, her presence, alone on a side street in a town somewhat unfamiliar, felt uncomfortable and a long ways from the boring but safe routines that occupied most of her nights. With a paranoid purpose to beat the sirens to the stop-signed corner, she quickly sat up and started the engine. Yanking the shift arm to drive, she pulled the car to the corner. Without signaling, she aggressively made a left turn and sped in the direction of the entrance to the highway north. Without so much of a glance in the rearview mirror, she distanced herself from the sirens, from the funeral home, and from the daydreaming that suddenly felt so far out of place. She would return to Wildwood and to her room, a place where she could quell her anxiety, regroup, and recover from a day where her courage was out front and on full display.

Chapter Nineteen

A Notorious Day's Ending

JENNY PULLED HER tired and flabby body from the monsignor's car without words. Her self-image of a cleaned-up and nicely dressed executive assistant that left the house that evening now resembled more of a tattered, aging mess that only a good night's rest and a morning retry could improve. A half-hearted glance back through the passenger's-side window was all the good night she could muster. Walking toward her front door, her right hand awkwardly ransacked her pocketbook for keys. As she pulled out the clanging set of keys, resembling more of a custodian's arsenal than that of college president's assistant, her hand's exit from the purse caused several used tissues to seemingly jump out of the bag and float down, depositing themselves on the walkway and its grassy edges. The assistant either didn't notice or was too wrecked to care, so there they would stay until the evening breezes blew them to settle as bush trimmings or perhaps litter on adjacent properties in the very modest neighborhood that Jenny called home. Seemingly, as with all things in her life, nothing came easy anymore so when she stood in the doorway clanging the oversized key ring and searching for the front door key as if she hadn't done this in months, an impatient monsignor was not surprised. Eager to drive off, and in the foulest of moods, he did not abandon the many-year ritual of waiting until Jenny entered and was inside safely. While this once-chivalrous routine no longer held the same "ahhh" factor as in the old days, in some small way it still represented the unspoken loyalty between the two.

With his assistant secured for the night, the monsignor's short ride back to his residence on campus would be used to gather his thoughts, hopeful that his thinking would reveal his next move. He tried hard not to be overcome by the seriousness of his predicament; the dangerous potential of outcomes was all too obvious. There were too many pieces of the story that ominously led back to him and too many players that filled his world with risk. *There must be ways to simplify things*, he thought, as his foot gently applied the break to softly cross the small street-wide road bump that forced cars to slow down as they approached the campus entrance. *Too complicated*, again he thought. In too many ways his knowledge of the all the perils were gray and cloudy. How could he plan anything? He still hadn't heard from Tony Sacco and while he assumed the beach rubouts were the chairman's doing, he could not be sure. With Jesse now in the mix and actually interacting with the college's staff, the monsignor could easily think the worst. His fears were born from uncertainty, an unsure nausea of not knowing exactly who knew what. Still, the monsignor viewed taking action as a path closer to sanity than the torturous mindset of deciding to sit back and do nothing.

There was the coach, who very sudden-like and remarkably was displaying a level of intelligence and forthrightness that few thought he possessed. There was Father Jon, always bright and a man with a dangerous sense of righteousness that could force actions for which he would feel no choice. There was Jenny and while he was convinced that she would never do anything intentionally to hurt him, she was also dumb enough to say the wrong thing to the very wrong person. And of course, there was Sister Mary. Her new image left her far too unpredictable and her new association with Jesse…far too dangerous. Finally, there was the unknown: a cast of college and town characters that in large part he wielded very little control. *Simplify things*, he thought as he pulled slowly into his reserved parking spot in front of his residence.

As the worn-out priest entered his house, he dropped his keys on the foyer table, made a hard right, and sat in the chair next to the small black landline telephone, propped up on an antique end table with push buttons facing him, waiting to be played.

From the table's single drawer, he withdrew a pocket-size tan leather book. Opening it, he positioned his thumb and forefinger to keep the book opened on a flap simply labeled *D*. From his black short-sleeved priest shirt, the monsignor reached into its chest pocket and pulled out his narrow reading glasses and placed them squarely on the lower bridge of his nose and stared down at his book. Locating the desired number, he hit the speaker dial-tone button on the phone. Alternating his sight back and forth between the book and phone buttons, he started to press buttons, noticeably exceeding the three for area code and seven for the phone number. Still on speaker, a ringing began after a brief connection delay.

In a heavy Spanish accent, the female answering the phone greeted her caller, "Buenas tardes, Hermanas Dominicanas de la Caridad," meaning *Good evening, Dominican Sisters of Charity.*

"Good evening, Sister Angelina. It's Monsignor Clark from Pious College."

"Ay, monsignor, cómo estás? Me so happy to hear you! I so surprised!"

"Well, sister, it is so nice to hear you as well. Sister, do you have a few minutes? I have a rather unusual but important favor to ask."

Chapter Twenty

A Trepidatious Mourning

ON AN UNUSUALLY warm and humid morning, the gray Wildwood skies sprayed the town with a fine, moistening mist, making the decision of whether to carry an umbrella left to the choice of each outdoor inhabitant. It was seven thirtyish, and most of the college's faculty and administrators were awakening, preparing to ready themselves for the morning's 10:00 a.m. memorial service in the campus chapel. For most, what was once thought of as another school commitment forcing yet another required, yet undesirable, attendance, today's event contained the drama akin to the anticipation of one's favorite weekly television episode. Only everything about this morning was real. AK was really dead, murdered, and nothing about this tragic production could change that. Last night's Cape May sideshow was fresh in the minds of today's expected attendees. The wake's escapades, even for those who truly had no involvement in anything relating to the former dean, left each in attendance feeling cautious and uneasy. Last night, unlike most gatherings that mourned the passing of a friend or acquaintance, there was little to no post-wake chitchat. Most in attendance departed quickly with jaw-dropping expressions, left to decipher what they had just witnessed and each forming an interpretative decision whether the night was simply the height of Pious College buffoonery or something far more serious.

Coach Sully was in his man-cave apartment's kitchen brewing up two cups of hot coffee, one for himself and one for his CFO partner who, after last night's round two of less-than-thrilling sex, had decided to just roll over and sleep off her now-questionable decision for additional fornication. As the coach balanced the two overly filled cups of java, he strolled back to the bedroom, consciously keeping his arms close to his sides to prevent open air from throwing off his rather foul body odor. Approaching the doorway, he entered the room noticeably squeezing in his midlife beer-bulging stomach. To his delight, Darlene was preoccupied, somewhat feverishly texting her two foster kids like a mother who was feeling a bit guilty and several hours late in checking on the well-being of her kids.

Across town, Father Jon was already showered and dressed in his plain black outfit and white collar, a uniform that for him at least still meant something honest and good. He was sitting stoically at his bedroom desk scribbling his attempt at a eulogy for AK. Disgusted with everything to do with the monsignor and abandoning any reliance on a meaningful participation by the president at this morning's service, his intent was to keep his sermon and eulogy brief. His morning mood seemed to recognize that the ship had sailed for any real or genuine reflection by those expected to attend.

For the monsignor and his trusty assistant, while in separate locations at their respective residences, the scenes were eerily alike. Each sat at their kitchen tables, the priest staring aimlessly at the far counter and drape-covered window behind the sink. He was, as with most days, starting out tired from another restless sleep that did little to energize his aging and stress-riddled body. Once strong and purposeful, the monsignor was frankly a wreck of anxious tension, old bones and diminished power.

Jenny Flopalis, not feeling her usual misguided morning purpose, sat eyes glazed, gawking pointlessly at the table's half-eaten piece of dried toast lined with butter. The corner of her mouth and down halfway to her chin displayed a clear greasy-like streak of moisture, an apparent oozing of butter that both missed its mark and was left unwiped by an unaware and unmindful soul.

For the rest of the college's finest, the morning equally started without much joy, fanfare, or outward energy. Except, however, for Sister Mary Dija. The made-over nun was alone, sitting mindfully in the small room that attached the nun's kitchen to its main dining area. Within the residence, and when she was alone, it was perhaps her favorite space. She had departed her room outfitted unlike any other time she could think of. A small white T-shirt covered her bra-less top, causing her breasts' nipples to create two evenly balanced and (to the sister), rather sexy bumps. She had noticed this in her gaze at the bedroom mirror and somewhat consciously decided no cover-up was required. Her feet were bare, only soft-touched by the light-gray cotton sweatpants that hung from her curved young hips. As with her bra, she had forgone the need for panties, freeing her bottom's curves from any distortion. Amazingly, she found great comfort and ease in accepting her newfound womanhood, recognizing that with even the slightest attempt, her sexy presentation could arouse her.

As with the rest of the convent paradise, the room was impeccably clean and tidy. Each piece of furniture had been thoughtfully arranged. Each ornament, from the sofa's decorative pillows to the soft green end-table clothes, was perfectly showcased in place. Even the room's various religious knickknacks suggested premeditated placement not to be disturbed or angled from their carefully placed post. The nun sat alone, deep in her thoughts about the day's decisions. Without the slightest bit of guilt, Sister Mary had consciously decided not to leave with her nun mates to this morning's mass at the town's lone Catholic parish church, deciding that thoughtful contemplation, alone, better served the moment. Quickly she was learning that her freedom and willingness to explore both the world and herself represented a form of work and mindfulness that was not needed in her former way of thinking. With her prior lifestyle of pre-determined schedules and commitments now replaced with several daily decisions, her day required far more thought and a continued determination to find her true self. While her prior approach to life was clearly the easier and perhaps safer route, her current approach made her happy and free, two attributes that she was convinced were God's latest gifts.

Chapter Twenty-One

A Person of Interest

IT WAS A short jaunt from the monsignor's residence to the campus's chapel. With the early-morning threat of rain now giving way to peeks from the almost-summer sun, the monsignor pulled open the front door and exited the residence. He had decided to arrive a bit early for AK's service. While an early arrival increased the opportunity for Father Jon to request his undesired participation in the hastily crafted funeral plan, President Clark, at any cost, looked to avoid the feeling of *all eyes glued to him* should he enter a chapel full of faculty and staff.

Striding cautiously, the monsignor could see the chapel in the distance, adjacent to the campus's north-side student quad. The priest stopped next to one of the many small brown benches along the cement walkway. At a few minutes after nine in the morning, he gazed upward and let the early sun warm his face. From a distance, he could see that the courtyard to the chapel was empty. He had succeeded in his intent to arrive free of undesired pleasantries, or worse, questions or comments regarding last night's wake. He decided to sit a spell, just for a minute or two, and contemplate his words in the event that Father Jon asked him to speak. The brief task, however, brought on thoughts of AK, and for really the first time, the death of his dean hit him. For a moment, and a rare one at that, the priest was overcome with grief for someone or something other than himself. Briefly gone were thoughts of his own predicament. Momentarily gone was the pain and fatigue from scheming, from the ugly and distasteful smell of narcissism and self-importance. A man he knew well was dead, never again to taste the world's majesty. Sadness overcame the mixed-up priest. He had finally realized that AK's death was so much more than a plot's twist that he was being forced to deal with. AK, to the priest's knowledge, was never part of any of this mess. Only now did his murder and curious ties with Steve Summers bring thoughts that he, the president of Pious College, may have been indirectly responsible. Tears welled in the aging, tired eyes of the monsignor. If he could only go back, he thought, far back, long before this whole chaos, back to a time when he was young, to his rectory days. Given the chance, he thought, he would be stronger. He convinced himself he would have ignored the sick, loathsome, and vile temptations within him. *The child*, he thought. Jesse was only a child! The monsignor placed both hands over his face. Elbows bent forward resting on his thighs, the priest sat and wept. Into his hands flowed tears and into his mind crept the thought of divinity and his own mortality. He had so woefully let his Lord down, and his weakness had served to now ruin his life. He even contemplated his afterlife and God's right to punish him. His thoughts screamed for forgiveness and mercy, to a god he had long abandoned. Deep in his thoughts, the priest had shut out the world, until the mood was rudely interrupted by the sound of an engine starting in the far parking lot. Quickly the priest was shoved back to his unenviable and very unwelcomed present. Gathering himself, he fought the emotional roller coaster that whirled him from moods of fear, despair, anger, and remorse. It had been so long since the monsignor enjoyed life. The daily pain and fatigue caused by a relentless internal torture was winning and driving the man inside the monsignor very close to life's cliff. For the first time in his life, the priest came to understand the once-inconceivable thought of suicide.

The priest sat up straight, again peered upward, this time allowing the sun to dry his half-wiped eyes and cheeks. It was now almost 9:20 a.m., and the monsignor had to gather himself. Still, the chapel's courtyard was empty, although a quick view of the adjacent quad now disclosed a handful of students. They were quietly chatting and sipping on what appeared to be their morning coffees. The boys were dressed in slacks and collared shirts while the girls equally presented a clean, dressy image. The monsignor surmised that they were waiting for the funeral, perhaps unwilling to be the first to enter the chapel.

With the reality of the moment ending this morning's profound moments of reflection, the monsignor's demeanor of the past several weeks returned. Instantly, he felt his body present a language that seemed to shout for isolation. He felt his facial expression emit an air of avoidance, seemingly prepping a morning made to elude eye contact of any kind.

As he was about ready to stand and make his way to the chapel, his eyes gazed across to the far-side armrest of the wooden bench. There he noticed the words of the bench's donor. It read, "Our gift to Pious College—Dotty & Jim Castings—Class of 1968." The monsignor rose, took a few strides away from his seat, and with a Grinch-like disgust uttered the words, *"Fools."* His strides increased in both pace and length as he moved closer to the courtyard. The monsignor had returned to the moment.

It was nine thirty when he opened the chapel's front door and entered. Surprisingly, the room was empty, and a few feet from the altar rested a small waist-high table. On it sat a stand-up eight-by-eleven-inch picture frame containing AK's portrait, the same one used for the previous night's wake.

The monsignor strode to the left and sat in a pew situated on an angle to the altar. Behind him was a small frame holding a tray of several unlit candles. The tray lay atop a metal box with an ingrained cross. The front of the box displayed a manufactured slot, inviting bills and coin to be presented as donation for one's privilege to displace one of the thin wood sticks and light a candle. Typically, visitors performed this ritual in respect for a memory or deceased member of their family. Little did they realize that each custodian had received instructions to blow out all flames at day's end to preserve as much candle life as possible, thus affording the maximum donation for each dime-store circle of wax, just another perverted college procedure hidden under the soiled cloak of holiness.

Gary Lee, the athletic director, was the first to enter the chapel, holding a small bouquet of flowers. He was followed closely by Father Jon. Seeing the seated monsignor, Gary acknowledged his presence with a "Good morning, monsignor." Father Jon was a bit quicker with his greetings with a simple "Hello" as the monsignor reciprocated by nodding his head in their direction. The two men moved swiftly to the front table whereby the AD deposited the flowers next to AK's picture. Father Jon removed a folded piece of paper from his front priest shirt pocket and also placed it on the table.

"Would you like to welcome those who attend this morning, monsignor, or should I simply do so on your behalf?" said Father Jon.

"Yes, Father, that would be fine," stated the monsignor. "But once done, I will hand the proceedings to you with no need to revert back to me at the service's end."

"Okay, monsignor," Father Jon said, clearly ending any further conversation.

The two men then proceeded back to the chapel's entrance, each pushing one side of the double door until they clicked into the metal floor slots that held the doors open. The chapel, exposed to fresh rays of light from a brightening sun, seemed to signal that it was now open for business. Father Jon and Gary Lee stationed themselves on the outer side of the doorway, prepared to welcome the service's soon-to-arrive guests.

The next to arrive was Jenny Flopalis. Entering the chapel and noticing the monsignor, still seated in the far-left corner of the chapel, she let out a startled "ooew" as if his presence surprised her. A rather cold "Good morning" was all she could muster, still feeling the effects of the monsignor's previous night's car-ride beatdown. Weirdly, she jerked her head straight toward the chapel's altar, walked about halfway down the center aisle, and plopped in onto a pew on the right side of the walkway, opposite the monsignor. Appropriate for the occasion, Jenny was dressed in all black except for an out-of-place pair of brown open-toed sandals, clearly this morning's winner of the feeblest closet choice. Also, contrary to the warm (and getting warmer) morning, the assistant's black outfit included a rather tight-fitting turtleneck, covered by a tattered-looking black blazer and black slacks. As she gazed at the altar, the monsignor quickly decoded her intent to give off a somewhat cold and demure attitude in his direction. Overheating in an outfit better served for autumn or winter, however, her act was displaced with the need to deal with droplets of sweat gathering rapidly on her brow and under each mascara-laden eye. Thrust back in the familiar mode of being conscious that her master may be noticing another of her uncomfortable predicaments, Jenny eye-searched for something, anything, in the pew to provide a much-needed breeze. Stretching her hand into the little wooden pocket on the back of the pew in front of her, she pulled out a rather-thick, hard-covered songbook, unfortunately the only item available in the immediate area. Ridiculously, and as if the item represented a two-page paper pamphlet, she began to wave the heavy book back and forth in front of her face. Failing to create so much as a draft to cool her down, the book also became too much for her frail wrist to control. Pretending to act as if her action was succeeding, her grip gave way and the two hundred pages of songs with its dull reddish covers flew from her hand, over the top of the pew, and crashed on then off the neighboring pew. The flying songs made loud banging sounds as the book caromed off the pews until the heavy book mercifully laid rest on the edge of center aisle floor. Quickly glancing left, Jenny confirmed that the monsignor was curiously watching his assistant's latest talent show. Embarrassed, she swiftly stood, stepped out of the pew, stopped to consider picking up the book, but decided to end the show by ignoring it. Being in the way of her path out, she stepped over the displaced book like it was a puddle and walked exit north down the aisle and out of the chapel. Needless to say, there was no candle lighting by the monsignor, calling for an encore.

With the clock approaching ten, various staff members and even some students began entering the chapel. From the monsignor's perch, he sensed that all were entering rather cautiously, somewhat feeling trepidation in anticipation of the service. Not one outwardly acknowledged the monsignor; rather, each seemed to present an awkward but reverent silence as they timidly selected their seating positions. From the chapel's entryway, Father Jon glanced at his watch, peered out across the campus, and decided to give any latecomers a few more minutes before he began the memorial. This decision began to pay dividends as one by one, key Pious College personnel made their way up the pathway from the adjacent parking lot toward the chapel. Kevin McMatty was first to reach the doors. On his arm was an unfamiliar young and very pretty woman, a sweet thing that the fifty-something provost must have recently attached to, as it was not his way to keep his prizes in the background. Scurrying to two empty seats in the far back left was Patty Simon and her assistant, Britta. They had traveled together to the service, discussing their plans to move forward with the musical, each looking forward to the college returning to normal, an eventuality even bestowed on this world's most tragic events. Hidden and not to be addressed on this somber morning was their shared girl crush on Rae, Britta's partner. Rae, as with last night's wake, had stayed away. Britta had welcomed her gal pal's decision to temporarily remove herself from the Pious clan, although privately she was concerned that lately Rae's attitude seemed to reveal potential cracks in the proverbial wall of fidelity.

Following the theater staff into the chapel was Darlene Davidson, hand-pulling her stepdaughter Verona, intent on staying a few lengths ahead of the trailing Coach Sully. Coming off a night where she learned firsthand that sex can have the opposite effect to bringing two people closer, the CFO looked forward to ending this prolonged encounter. Looking to find a spot that fit only two, Ms. Davidson could feel all male eyes in her direction, knowing full well that most bypassed her to set on the voluptuous image of Verona, predictably scantily clad, her delicate cotton dress looking more for a day strolling the boardwalk than fit for a funeral mass. Unsuccessful in her quest to rid herself of the football coach, she settled for the end of a middle pew, with her stepdaughter being the shield between herself and last night's disappointment. Joining them came Shane Ferrigno, the coach's assistant and, as on most days, followed closely by his loyal companion Dolly Jackson.

Finally, upstaging all who had preceded her, Sister Dija made her grand entrance. With every step showing off her new look, the nun had doubled down on her role as the college's new rock star. If the now fully out-of-the-closet sister had been worried about any unwelcomed eye contact as she entered the chapel, those concerns were quickly quelled by her fresh sexy curves adorned in her tight-fitting low-cut short jet-black dress. As with last night, her redone light-and-soft headdress only seemed to add to her suggestive persona.

Content that most intended attendees had now arrived, Father Jon stepped into the chapel and nodded to Gary Lee to do the same, closing the doors behind him.

Father Jon strode down the center aisle. Prior to leaving his residence, the good priest had decided he would not even mention the previous night's wake disaster. Upon reaching the steps to the front altar he turned and reverently began to speak.

"Good morning, my friends. It is with sadness that we all meet on this morning to pray for our Lord's departed servant Adrian and ask for the Almighty's graces to accept his soul into the peace and love of heaven's eternal passage. As we begin our remembrance, Monsignor Clarke would like to say a few words." Looking in his direction, Father Jon simply said, "Monsignor," as he took a small stride backward, symbolically giving the floor to the college's president.

Rather than move to the front of the chapel, the ill-prepared monsignor rose slowly. About to speak, the priest was interrupted by the sound of the chapel doors being opened, exposing the dimly lit chamber to bright rays of the day's climbing sun. The monsignor and most others turned to the doors, a rather natural reaction to the disturbance. In walked two students, Katrice Brown and Dylan McMatty, the college's student council presidents. Oddly, Provost McMatty, Dylan's father, seemed to slump in his pew, a contrast to the usual "arm around his son's shoulder" great dad that the campus was used to enduring.

Dylan's sand-collared shirt and bright white dress shorts seemed formal compared to Ms. Brown's oversized turquoise beach top covering her one-piece black bathing suit, styling more for the boardwalk's nearby tiki bar than a funeral service. Rather than sit, the two students stopped and stood center aisle, eye-motioning to Father Jon at the front of the room as if to imply that they were on a mission, and once completed fully intended to do a *thanks but no thanks* on staying for the service. Getting the message, Father Jon pointed both students to the door, and as he walked toward them and glancing to his side, he looked at the monsignor and said, "My apologies, monsignor, please continue." With that, the young priest quickly exited the chapel to speak with the students, looking to understand the matter that was apparently deemed urgent. The monsignor began speaking, but tastelessly his words appeared more fit for morning intercom announcements than for a peer's funeral mass. He had no message about or relating to AK but rather he used his time to announce that the college would be closed for the remainder of the week, reopening on Monday morning. All activities, he said, could continue at the discretion of those in charge of such activities. As he continued, he found himself speaking over the rude and disrupting chatter of some students, who had attended the service, scattered throughout the chapel. One had to wonder whether the young students' disturbance was the result of their inquisitive reaction to their student council leaders' visit or perhaps an inappropriately timed response to monsignor's school-closing announcement. Perhaps it was neither, something less, a mere inbred reaction to act up when the teacher steps out of the room.

About to continue, the old priest was again interrupted, this time by Father Jon reentering the chapel. With a bit of pace to his stride, Father Jon made it back to the front of the altar, looked right, and said, "So sorry, monsignor would you like to continue?"

Done with his own poor acting and fed up with, well, with just about everything, the old priest responded, "No, Father Jon, I'm finished. You continue." Sadly, while such a feeble memorial-service discourse might have raised a few eyebrows elsewhere, at Pious College, nobody seemed to be at all fazed by just another of the college's dysfunctional exchanges.

The rest of the morning's service went as expected, with the exception of the communion ritual. Father Jon, as he had intended, stood stoically on the edge of the altar, preparing to lead the sacrament's distribution of hosts. He had called on Sister Dija to distribute the sips of wine. In Catholicism, partaking in the sacrament requires the recipient to be in good graces, typically having recently confessed one's sins and thus been discharged of evil's blackness and reborn into God's graces. Despite the religion's mandate, each attendee without exception, rose to receive communion. The fully participated procession line to receive communion inwardly disgusted the monsignor. He long felt that his school was full of atheists, almost all never confessing their sins and most never even attending mass unless it was an administratively required event. Receiving communion in the Catholic church had traditionally been based on the honor system, each sinner left to independently decide whether their souls were appropriately dissolved of sin and worthy of "receiving." Paradoxically, the black-souled monsignor felt little contradiction when, like the others, he rose and partook in receiving a host before returning to his seat.

Not surprising to anyone, Kevin McMatty had led the charge in being the first to advance to the altar, quickly pushing himself out of the pew, almost running over today's date, to be first on line. Almost grabbing the host from Father Jon, he appeared to swallow it whole, swiftly shuffling to the sexed-up sister where he changed pace from NASCAR to syrup. Slowly sipping her offered wine, he stood all too close, gazing lovingly at all things neckline and below. Finally realizing he was causing a logjam between host to wine, he begrudgingly returned the chalice back to the sister and returned to his pew, making sure to catch the eye of today's date as he bent his knee and made the sign of the cross. Even Father Jon was taken aback by everyone's sudden rush of faith, but his concern was more the possibility that he would run out of hosts, a clearly embarrassing but perhaps fitting end to this holy sacrament turned farce.

As the service ended, all slowly made their way to the exit, each nodding appreciatively past Father Jon as he stood just outside the doorway, content in completing his chore as the memorial service leader. The monsignor, wishing to remove any obligation to banter with his school's servants, stayed conspicuously in his seat, only rising when the chapel had fully cleared.

Making his way down the left aisle toward and out the doors, he was summoned by Father Jon, who was now alone outside the chapel.

"Monsignor, may I have a minute?" he said in a tone more like a command than a question. "I believe there is something you should be aware of."

"Yes Father What is it?"

Father Jon paused, a habit all at the school was used to, as the young priest often contemplated his words carefully before speaking. "The students, monsignor, Dylan and Katrice, they actually were looking for you."

"For me?" said the president, feeling the stomach pang, which now came all too normal during most of his interactions. "What's the matter, and why their apparent urgency to rudely disrupt the service?"

"They asked me to relay a message from two detectives who had stopped them as they walked past your residence a bit before 10:00 a.m. After identifying themselves, they instructed the students to find you and ask that you to call them today at the precinct. One of them indicated that you might know the whereabouts of Tony Sacco. Apparently, they had been trying to locate him. Dylan indicated their rather eagerness in finding him. That's all they communicated, monsignor. The detectives said they would be at the precinct for most of the day."

The monsignor said nothing. No response. Taking the pause as his cue that the conversation was over, the young priest politely wished the monsignor a good day, turned, and began walking up the path toward the main part of campus. With the message digested, being just the latest dagger into the psyche of the monsignor and with no direction that made any sense, the monsignor stood motionless contemplating which had ended worse, last night's wake or this morning's service.

Chapter Twenty-Two

Crossing the Line

Now ALMOST NOON, Sister Dija made the turn into the convent's parking lot, perching the nose of the car close to the gray steel guard-rail at the lot's far end. With school closed through the weekend, the nun sat still and thought about her day. The sister's old daily rituals, in step with her peer sisters and without much thought, no longer appealed to her. Her newborn freedom, while attractive and welcome, did also present a bit of a predicament. Frankly, she had nothing to do and no real friends. Before her recent self-revelation into womankind, her days didn't really require much thought. Most hours were taken up by holy masses, prayer, chores, school, and the many little obligations shared equally by the nuns inhabiting the convent. She had decided that the life of one rote mandate to the next must, at least for now, be put on hold. At some point, she thought, she would sit and explain her new way of thinking to her fellow nuns, owing them at least that. After all, her transformation did require an explanation.

Sister Dija was convinced that her new feelings held more depth than simply the extreme changes in her appearance and ward-robe. Until now, however, superficial changes—and extreme ones at that—were all the other sisters had seen. She recognized the need to, at some point, address the other nuns' very-raised eyebrows and

163

genuine concerns. Never had she discussed her long-closeted desires with any of her convent mates. She recalled that once, several months back, she was tempted to. She had entered one of the hallway bathrooms, not realizing that that it was occupied by Sister Ann. When her entrance went unnoticed by the showering nun, she quickly changed her immediate instinct to excuse herself and leave the room to delaying her exit, as she stood silently. She could hear Sister Ann groaning, first low, then louder. Realizing that the middle-aged nun was masturbating, Sister Dija stood still, hidden by the thick shower curtain separating her and her convent mate. Dija's embarrassment quickly turned to arousal, as she left the room and quickly returning to her quarters. Upon entering, she had locked the door behind her and sat quietly in the chair by the room's window. Determining that her bathroom intrusion was unknown to anyone but herself, she began to relax and her thoughts quickly returned to imagining Sister Ann touching herself. She recalled feeling that perhaps she was not alone in her struggle with a celibate lifestyle.

Her memory of that moment made her question her decision to keep silent. Perhaps, she thought, she should have confronted Sister Ann. If she had, maybe a meaningful discussion could have taken place, one in which the two nuns shared their feelings on the conflict between their vow to celibacy and urges as women. Her thoughts made the moment lonely, recognizing that her new way of thinking and acting bought full ownership on her and her alone.

Exiting the car, she walked around back, planning to sit for a while in her favorite room, adjacent to the kitchen. As she made her way to the door of the back porch, she saw a familiar scene in the distance by the rocky jetty cutting through the beach's sand and past the structure of the convent. It was Jesse, sitting passively in the spot where they had first met. He was staring aimlessly toward the water and the far edge of the jetty. His presence pleased her. She had been wondering what came of his conversation with the detectives. She had also wished to talk to him about his outburst toward the monsignor. Odd, she thought, that he was back again. Could it be her that again drew him to this isolated beach spot?

Feeling no choice, Sister began to walk toward him. The young man was dressed scantily. His frame was covered by a thin white T-shirt and cotton tan shorts that looked more like briefs. Flip-flops were sitting nearby their owner, serving little use as his feet were buried in the sand. As she got closer, he looked up toward her, and she could see he had been crying. Wiping his eyes with his sandy hands left his face dotted with sand grains on his cheeks and close to both eyes. Recognizing her presence, he said nothing so she brought herself to slowly sit next to him. The sun was hot, but the ocean breeze was strong, causing sprinkles of sand to be hurled at the seated duo. Perhaps from his mood or perhaps from the sand, both of Jesse's eyes were wet and tearing. He continued to wipe them, now with his forearms, although each was also sandy. Sister Dija recognized his plight and, now with a purpose, stood up, reached for his hand, and pulled upward, simply saying, "Come with me." Reluctantly, but without much fight, Jesses obliged and walked with the nun toward the back door. "Me clean you up," said the sister as she ushered Jesse through the back door and into the sitting room, her favorite room. As usual, during midday, the convent was empty as all of the sisters were off tending to nursing homes and care facilities in Cape May and Wildwood.

As Jesse sat still, the nun left the room and entered the kitchen where she wet a clean dish towel with warm water, bringing it back to Jesse, and sat next to him. He mustered a "Thank you" as he extended his hand to receive the damp towel, but she resisted and said, "Please sit back, Jesse, you full of sand. I help you." With that Jesse relaxed his body and sat back into the two-space love seat.

First, the sister took hold of his hands and messaged the sand off each. Next, she tenderly wiped down his forehead, eyes, cheeks, and lips bringing the freshness back to the good-looking young man's face. With her bare hand, she dusted some of the sand from his T-shirt and then moved the towel to his sandy legs, gently starting with his thighs. She couldn't help but notice that his shorts were skimpy, rising up almost to his lower groin area. Neither spoke as she softly cleaned the top and then the inner side of each thigh. As she moved the towel to his knees, her motions came to a halt, noticing a growing bulge in Jesse's shorts. Both had their heads down, until Sister Dija, without thinking, immediately placed her small soft hand into his shorts. Jesse began to groan softly as the nun, for the first time, felt passion for a man. She could feel the moisture between her legs begin to dampen her panties. Despite their unmistakable pleasure, neither seemed sure what the next move should be.

Knowing only old routines with his partner Steve, Jesse finally reached up and placed his hand behind the nun's neck and gently pulled her facedown toward his shorts. Sister began rubbing her face into his groin, wanting desperately to inhale the smell and taste of Jesse's private parts. Drunk with pleasure, the nun grabbed Jesse's hand and shoved it through the top of her dress until his warm fingers reached her swollen nipple. For the first time, Jesse felt the softness of a woman's breast. Sister groaned with pleasure, finally feeling what she had fantasized about so many times. Jesse pulled the nun's dress from her shoulders, exposing fully her breasts and dark, ripe nipples. He leaned forward, allowing his face to feel her breasts, now intoxicated with the newness of a woman's scent.

Abruptly, the scene broke stride, as Jesse could hold no longer, forcefully experiencing, for the first time, orgasm with a woman. Surprisingly, the nun did not jerk away. With a stronger sense of urgency, she pulled his hand to her groin whereupon feeling his awkward touch on and then in the lips of her vagina, her hips quivered as she came violently. Her breathing and gasps for air was new and welcome to the drained nun and her partner.

Savoring the aftermath, Sister began to kiss Jesse's lips, and for the first time protruded a man's mouth with her tongue. Both began to groan as Jesse's young penis again grew hard. Dija began to beg the man to enter her. As Jesse began to maneuver his hips toward her, the sex session was rudely and suddenly interrupted by the hard and loud clangs of the front door's knocker repeatedly contacting the convent's wooden door. Panicked, Sister Dija awkwardly tried to stand up, pushing her partner away. Sitting up, Jesse would have none of it, grabbing the small nun's hips and pulling them forcefully onto him. With Sister Dija now straddling her partner, without warning, he slid into her and began to thrust over and over until the petite nun could no longer avoid his action. As the door-knocking continued, Sister Dija turned back to Jesse, both now ignoring the intruder. She began to yelp with pleasure, wrapping Jesse's head into her breasts.

As fluids of wetness and blood dripped from her thighs and onto the love seat, Sister Dija now began to take the lead, thrusting herself up and down on Jesse. The knocking had stopped; neither noticed. With her eyes rolling back into her head, the small nun began grinding her bottom into Jesse until multiple orgasms rocked the small nun's body. Without thought, Dija screamed over and over with first-time pleasure. Gradually slowing her hips, the nun was done, but Jesse continued in his urge to experience his second orgasm. With the strength of a man, he lifted the sister off him and flung her around until she was facedown on the love seat. She was helpless as his strength lifted her hips toward him. Sister Dija screamed in pain as Jesse forcefully held her in place as he entered her rear. She began panting rapidly, partly to endure the pain but also because she was beginning to like the feeling of the man's domination over her body. Violently, Jesse erupted again with orgasm. Exhausted, he let her go, and she slid to the love seat and onto to the floor. Lying on her side, the young nun was motionless. Jesse rose and, seeing the bloodied love seat and the nun on the floor, quickly turned, pulled up his shorts, and ran to the back door.

Rising slowly to a sitting position, Dija's eyes focused on the soiled seat, not sure how to move or what to think. After a moment, she gathered herself and stood. Her thoughts were of Jesse as she limped through the kitchen toward a flung-open back door. Her hips and bottom were bruised and on fire from the roughness of Jesse's sex. Peering out, she saw Jesse, far in the distance, walking quickly down the beach, head down and away from the convent. Frozen, the nun neither called out or ran after him, settling for several deep, eyes-closed breaths before reentering the kitchen. Slowly and gingerly she staggered to its adjacent room. Surprisingly calm and not recognizing fully the scene for what it was, Sister Dija focused on cleaning up both herself and the room's rug and love seat.

Reentering the kitchen, she opened the cabinet under the sink and matter-of-factly removed a number of cleaning products and rags. She wet a clean rag and wiped herself down as best she could, realizing only a shower would fully remove the sweat and the cum and the blood from her body and crevices. She began to focus on the sitting room, and after some spraying and scrubbing, the seat and the rug were cleaned, save for now some light love seat stains, which she had managed to turn from red to a very light pink. She decided to deal with that later. She removed a throw blanket from an adjacent chair and placed it on the love seat to cover the remaining stain. After packing away the cleaners, she moved upstairs to the hallway bathroom, ran the shower hot, and stood under it, allowing the water to flow over all parts of her body until there was no trace of what her body had experienced downstairs. Without toweling dry, she moved naked to her room and sat in room's window chair.

Her thoughts returned to her violent sex with Jesse. Her thoughts quizzically ignored Jesse's forceful and final entry into her body. Her inexperience in sex caused little reaction to the end of her session and seemed not to bother her, thinking perhaps that such a man's action was normal, and not violating. She even had thoughts of satisfaction as having pleasured her partner into a second powerful orgasm. His quick departure troubled her, but in her thoughts, she committed herself to finding him and assuring him that she was good with all that had happened between them. She thought about maybe even kissing him again until he was calm and secure with her presence. Her thoughts overcame her, and she began to masturbate. Thinking of Jesse inside her and dominating her, the little nun came again, this time soaking her hand with her young juices.

Exhausted and after some time, she went downstairs, now remembering the knocking intruder and wondering if they had heard her screams through the door. She decided to go to the door and open it. There on the porch's sill was a FedEx package. She lifted it and went inside.

As she moved into the kitchen, her thoughts returned to her new way of life, her new way of thinking. The absence of dutiful rules, prohibitions, and obligations was exciting yet scary, passionate yet painful, and most of all thrilling, yet somehow very unsafe.

Back in the moment, Sister Dija glanced down at the package, the one that could not derail her first experience with intercourse. Spinning it on the table, she discovered that it was addressed to her, an odd occurrence at the convent, within what was so far a very odd day. She pulled the thin strip of cardboard at the top of the package, exposing an eight-by-eleven-inch white manila envelope, also addressed to her. At the top left of the envelope was the stamp of her Fraternal Order of Nuns. She could not remember when she had last received something from them. Opening the envelope, she began reading the letter, placed as page one of the package.

It read simply:

> Sister Mary Dija,
>
> It is with our commitment to God, and the Holy Father that we continue to serve the world's needs and those embellished in pain, poverty, and suffering. To this dutiful service, your presence is required in the Village of Loja, Ecuador, where you will, until further notice, serve the town's Catholic parish and its often poor and needy families. Your transportation has been arranged, and you are to depart immediately to begin this important mission. Enclosed you will find your travel passes and points of contact upon arrival.
>
> May God aid you and love you in providing the strength and graces to serve his people.
>
> God bless you, yours in faith,
> Sister Angelina Quapo, Hermanas
> Dominicanas de la Caridad.

Sister Dija reread the letter several times before placing it down on the table. Covering her petite, pretty face in her hands, the sister began weeping. Panicked and urgent, she made a hurried path to her room, spotted her cell phone on the night table, and quickly found

Sister Angelina's number and pressed it hard with two fingers. The call was answered after the first ring.

"Hello, Sister Enez speaking, how can I help you?"

"Si, sister, this Sister Dija in Wildwood, New Jersey. Me need to speak to Sister Angelina."

"Aye, sister, how are you? We miss you. Sister Angelina is not here. Can I help you with something?"

"Si, yes, si, sister. Me transferred to Loja. Sister, it very bad time here at school. Me want to stay longer. Can you speak Sister Angelina? Me need to stay longer at school."

"Oh yes, sister, I am aware of your new orders. Sister Angelina informed us at dinner several nights ago. But, sister, I don't understand. We were told that Monsignor Clark requested this. Something about your position at the school was changing, and he needed to hire someone with more experience in the new responsibilities. Sister Angelina was surprised, but the monsignor was rather insistent that he needed someone new and that your service was no longer needed at Pious. I'm sure he must have spoken to you, si?"

Sister Dija was momentarily lost for words. The monsignor had said nothing. *Why he doing this?* she thought. *Why was I not told of this? Maybe this because of Jesse's story to me.* Confused, Sister Dija continued the conversation. "Ay, sister, Me not know that. Me talk to monsignor. Me go now." With that, the nun ended the call, moved to the edge of her bed, and sat motionless. Teary-eyed, she gazed into an open closet at the far end of the room and became fixated on several long robes, neatly hanging on plastic white hangers. Sullen, her world, without notice, had been rocked by the powerful and hateful monsignor. Stripped of her newfound freedom, she sat silently, anguished by the news. With the palm of her hand, she wiped her eyes. Her body felt sore, the result of her first sexual encounter with a man. But it was her mind that was ravaged, forced to accept a life that she did not own or controlled.

Chapter Twenty-Three

The Chairman's Return

IT WAS HALF past two in the afternoon, and the campus was fairly quiet, with the exception of the school's theater. Patty Simon had decided to summon all actors in the spring musical to a mandatory meeting to discuss the schedule for the upcoming show. Given the option by the monsignor earlier in the day to continue activities, she and Britta had decided to at least get the troupe together to communicate the rehearsal schedule over the next two weeks. The show's opening was scheduled in a few weeks, with performances on Friday and Saturday night and then again ending with Sunday's matinee. With a rushed preparation and amid a campus dealing with AK's murder, the director and her assistant frankly had enough and privately wished to get the whole damn thing over with. The current mood on campus for the musical was less than enthusiastic, and that did not seem likely to change anytime soon. As the last actor hustled into the theater, the campus took on an eerie, almost somber, quiet. Beyond those in the play, most of the Pious students were readying themselves to return home on the news that school was closed through the weekend, while those who were not leaving were spending a sunny day at the nearby beach and boardwalk.

In step with the unnerving mood throughout campus, the president's residence felt soaked with apprehension and tension. The monsignor sat alone, deciding whether to oblige Father Jon's message and contact the local precinct. First, however, he had to think. While Tony Sacco's absence had worried him, the old priest could not think of a single connection for the detectives to link Tony to the murders. The monsignor's world, however, was filled with uncertainty by a lack of information that continued to haunt him. Not once since the day that the bodies had been discovered had he spoken to the chairman. Even now, he only assumed that Tony was involved in Summers's and AK's death, based solely on his meeting and request for help. Over and over he questioned his strategy to involve Tony or frankly his decision to trust him. But what choice did he have back then? Tony had been his only source with the means to remedy his dilemma, the only viable option that could make the whole disturbing mess go away. Still, too many questions remained unanswered. He continued to have no clue why AK was involved, and without access to Tony, there was no one to ask.

Today, however, he was certain of one thing. His approach and posture with the detectives must be convincing. He needed to muster a calm and confident appearance to simply communicate that he knew nothing of Tony's whereabouts…and if he could, to determine some reasoning for the cops' interest in finding him. He decided to take the most assertive of measures. He would visit the precinct in person. No phone calls. He figured nobody guilty of anything in this whole disorder would voluntarily go see the cops. He was convinced that this was his best move. He quickly went upstairs to freshen up, maybe change his shirt, and then head out to confidently answer a few questions.

It was a short drive to the Wildwood police precinct. As the monsignor pulled the car into a spot directly across the street from its front door, he determined that there was no turning back. Thinking about the possibility of street cameras, the old priest rallied a show of enthusiasm as he exited the car and strode quickly to the precinct door. He clutched the knob firmly, pulled the door open, and with a hop in his step that had been absent for a very long time, he bounced inside and up to the high desk in the middle of the room. With the exception of a uniformed cop behind the desk, name tag Carter, the room was empty. The cop looked down from the desk and, seeing the visitor's white collar, snapped to attention, uttering, "Oh, good afternoon, Father, can I help you with something?"

Drawing on his true self and the disdain he had for most people and things, he responded, "It's monsignor, actually, but yes you can help me. I'm Monsignor Clark, the president of Pious College. I apparently was visited by two of the town's detectives earlier today. They had asked a few of our students to get a message to me, essentially asking me to call them. I was in the neighborhood and figured I would stop by. My day is fairly booked, and I don't know if I will have the time later for any calls. I didn't catch their names, so I'm afraid that's all the information I have.

The desk cop rose, smiled down at the priest, and said, "Gotcha, monsignor, some of our boys are in the back. Wait here, and I'll see if I can find out." With that the cop walked the short runway from his chair to the three steps at the far end of the desk platform, navigated down the steps, and entered a door leading to the back of the precinct.

For the next few minutes, the old priest stood alone, waiting. His thoughts were focused on maintaining the confident, almost surly, demeanor that would convince the police that he had no role and certainly no knowledge in anything to do with the crime. Another minute went by, and then another. *What the hell is going on back there?* he thought to himself. For the monsignor, being in the dark was perhaps his quandary's most frustrating element—torture, really. All of his life, he was the one to drive the day; he was the powerful kingpin who decided who would know what and when. If he decided to shed light then that was his gift to you, a concession that warranted your undying gratitude. If his whim was to keep you in the dark, then well, so be it as that was the spoils to his commanding and victorious life. Lately, however, that power had been ripped from his arsenal. He was the one deprived of information. He was the one forced to endure sleepless nights wondering and worrying about facts unknown. Gone was the respect that demanded updates to him first, before anyone else was granted the leftover crumbs. His life had clearly changed, now relegated to feeling the frustrations of the common folk. In his day, if presented with undue waiting, he would simply leave and dispatch the penalty to those ignorant souls who kept him waiting. Today? Well, today was a different story. Today President Clark stood in the dark, a servant to his dilemma and merely a weak, frail impersonator of his former formidable self.

Finally, after another few minutes of awkward and uncomfortable waiting, Officer Carter emerged through the precinct's back door. Bypassing the steps to his desk's platform, the uniformed cop walked straight up to the monsignor.

"My apologies, Father, I mean monsignor. Didn't mean to keep you waiting. The boys were pretty busy. They don't come running to us uniform guys, you know. It's a pecking-order thing, Father, so I had to wait till I caught their eye. Anyways, you can go about your day. No need for you to wait. Turns out the boys in civvies found who they were looking for. In fact, they got him and his buddy in the back behind closed doors. Doesn't look too comfy, if you get my drift. I'm sorry you had to take the time to come down here. This morning, the boys thought you might know where to find the gold-club guy. Seems they knew he was affiliated with the school. Anyways, he's here now, so like I said, sorry for the inconvenience."

"Is Mr. Sacco in any sort of trouble, officer?" questioned the priest.

"Not sure, Father, *oh* jeez, I keep calling you Father, I mean monsignor. By the looks of it, the other guy is getting most of the attention. Shouldn't really talk about it though. Not right, otherwise yours truly will be the one in trouble. Anyways, thanks for coming down, Father."

With the conversation now over and with the monsignor not willing to push his luck or seem too interested, the cop turned, headed to the platform steps, and returned to his perch overlooking the front room of the precinct.

A bit wobbly with his confidence now shot to hell, the monsignor slowly turned, walked toward the front door, and quietly exited. He crossed the street, and with much less out of spring than when he got out of his car, he entered the vehicle and steadied his trembling hands by tightly gripping the steering wheel. *Need to go back to my*

174

house and regroup, he thought. About to pull out and drive back to campus, his eye caught the front door to the precinct opening. Out came Tony Sacco, by himself. He as always was dressed impeccably in a fine light summery gray suit and blue presidential tie. His jet-black shoes shone like mirrors, and his hands were trophy-like, endorsing gold bling rings that glistened in the bright early-afternoon sun. As he stood in front of the building, the chairman exercised his neck to adjust its fitting within the starched white shirt collar and pulled down on his suit jacket as if to reset its form over his tanned and well-bred frame. If he was just questioned as the suspect in a double murder, he certainly didn't show the effects of any such interrogation. After a quick glance at his Rolex, Tony Sacco looked both right and left like a guy without a ride looking for a way home. Monsignor Clark recognized as much, opened his window, and called out, "Tony!" Catching the chairman's attention, Tony Sacco gave a quick smile, waved an accepting hand gesture, looked both ways, and began crossing the street toward the monsignor's car. He walked around the back of the vehicle to the passenger front door, opened it, and got in.

"Thanks, monsignor," he said. "The guys inside tracked me down at the club and chauffeured me down here, so I could use the lift back. I hope that won't be too much trouble."

"No, Tony, it's fine. But don't you think we should start by talking about what's going on. Jesus…look where we are! What the hell is happening here? I haven't spoken to you in weeks. Fill me in, for Christ sakes."

"Easy, monsignor, easy. Foul language from a priest makes me nervous. And first of all, it was you who got me involved in this shit. Remember? And what's happening is fairly simple…we're generally getting fucked."

"What does that mean, Tony? Christ! Please give me details," said the emphatic priest.

"Okay, monsignor, let's drive and I'll explain it. Hey, does this piece of crap have air-conditioning. It's hot as hell in here."

"Jesus, fuck the air-conditioning, Tony. What was going on in there?"

"Well, they got Stain," said Tony.

"What?" said the monsignor. "What do you mean they got stained? What's stained? Stained from what?"

"Not stained! Stain. My guy, his name is Stain. They got him. He was inside with me. They are charging him with the murder of your two blackmailers."

"*Two?*" yelled the priest.

"Yeah, two," said Tony. "The other guy Kenny, Adrian Kenny. He was in on it with the fag. In fact, I don't know this for sure, but I think he started it. He wanted to bring you down in a big way. The other guy, Summers, he just wanted money for him and his boy toy. Kenny was the brains. Amazing how they spilled like girls as soon as we roughed them a little. Should have known better, though, than to give this job to Stain. The moron just wasn't careful."

"What did the Stain do?" questioned the monsignor.

"Not the Stain, just Stain. Oliver Stainwell is his full name. We all just call him Stain, an amateur mobster from way back. He's into me for a lot of creep."

"Creep?"

"Money, monsignor, cash!"

"What did he do? Why wasn't he careful? Give me some details," the priest bellowed.

"All was good until he dropped his pin at the beach where he dumped the bodies," Tony explained.

"Pin. What pin? asked the monsignor.

"Stain liked to wear his Club Eighteen lapel pin. Little gold pins that I gave my guys to promote the club. The moron had it on when he whacked your two guys. When he dumped the bodies at the beach, it must have fallen off near the two dead guys. Well, the cops found it, ran some DNA tests, and matched the DNA from the pin to some of the clothes on the bodies. While he is denying it at this point, the cops felt that they had enough for an indictment, so they charged him and held him."

"Oh my god," chirped the priest. "And you? What about you?"

"Well, they don't have anything on me. Not yet anyway, so they let me go. But these guys are no dummies, monsignor. They know the pecking order of it all. They can easily surmise that Stain is a guy who just takes orders. Low IQ, always in debt, loyal kind of guy. Stain would never initiate something like this."

"How loyal is your friend?" started the monsignor before being interrupted.

"Whoa, Stain is not my friend. He's a worker, staff guy so to speak."

"How loyal is your worker? Will he, I mean, could he bring you into it?"

Tony sat back and smiled, as the car moved down the Garden State Parkway toward Cape May and Club Eighteen. "You see, monsignor, it's all about deals now, a thing that guys like me know all too well. It's pretty standard stuff for cops. They want the guy who ordered the hit, not the animals who committed it."

The monsignor reacted quickly. "What kind of deals? Deals with Stain? You mean he would give you up? For what? To get off?"

"No, monsignor, that getting off ship has already sailed. Big difference, though, between ten years and twenty-five to life."

"You don't seem overly upset, Tony. What am I missing?"

"Listen, Padre, guys like me come to expect this kind of thing. It's the life we live and one we chose. Listen, I'm not happy about it. The guy's a fucken' moron. I never should have trusted him with this. If he were out here, I'd put a bullet in his brain. But he's not. Quite protected by now, I'm sure. But doing a little time is not the worst thing, beats getting whacked or even beats being poor."

As the afternoon sun sat high in the sky, the monsignor's car pulled into the lot of Club Eighteen. It was filled with high-end vehicles, guys' possessions that symbolized wealth and power. Tony took a deep breath, like a guy who was glad to be home.

The monsignor wasn't stupid. Always fairly good at leaping to implications, he pulled the car up to the impressive double doors of the clubhouse and restaurant/bar. "I can't believe how calm you are, Tony. I must apologize for getting you into this mess."

"I'm a big boy, monsignor. I could have said no."

"But deals, Tony. If Stain got you into it, would they offer you a deal if they suspected others were involved?"

"Of course, monsignor, that's how they play the game."

Pushed to get directly to the point before Tony could exit, the monsignor asked what was now on both of their minds. "Would you give me up, Tony? You know, if they offered you a deal."

Tony opened the car door and began laughing heavily. Through his laughter, he stepped out of the car and bent and peered back in. "You, monsignor? Nooo. I would never give you up," he said through a wide-mouthed grin.

"Thanks for the ride, Padre. Speak soon." Within seconds Tony disappeared through the doors and squarely back in his very comfortable element.

Chapter Twenty-Four

Say What?

THE NEXT MORNING's Wildwood Press headlines screamed yesterday's news.

ARREST MADE IN WILDWOOD BEACH'S DOUBLE MURDER.

The *Cape May Advance's* front page was glibber and a bit longer in its announcement.

A BAD DAY FOR EXCLUSIVE CLUB EIGHTEEN
Henchman Charged in Beach Hits; Sacco Questioned

Copies vanished quickly from newsstands all across both towns.

At half past seven in the morning, the monsignor was still unaware of the papers' morning banners. At the moment, he was more preoccupied with his own ultimate doom. Nervous, the monsignor sat quietly in his kitchen, sipping coffee from a fresh brew that sat hot on the gray-tiled counter. His meeting with Tony was a revelation on the mindset of a modern-day gangster and regrettably showed the old priest just how out of his league he was in dealing with "being fucked," as Tony had put it. Never one to not grasp the potential of a situation, the monsignor understood well: other than making a move that he virtually had no experience in, his fate was in the control of others. "Deals," as explained by the chairman, could throw him dead smack in the middle of this shit show, deprived of any recourse for a rational explanation and without any ability to control the media, and his almost assuredly shameful and most severe punishment.

Craving an update, the monsignor moved his tired body to the living room and turned on the morning's local news. Upon seeing the screen, "Oh Christ" were the only words that he could muster, with nobody but himself to hear them. There, for all locals to see, was the plain but energetic female reporter for WKRZ, Channel 10 on your dial, standing in front of the college's main office building. With her was a somber-looking Sister Mary Dija and awkward-standing Jenny Flopalis. In the bottom right corner of the tube was a small split-screen box showing a live shot of the entrance to Club Eighteen, with a male reporter waiting patiently to stick a microphone into the face of all who dared enter or leave the stunned clubhouse.

News crews were buzzing. Typically reduced to airing the rather passive report of events in the area, today reporters and camera crew alike were animated, as "real" news was in the air and the little TV station at the far end of town was looking to make the most of it. Put on hold was the story of the boardwalk's new taffy shop and the results of yesterday's local high school baseball doubleheader. Even the preparations for this weekend's sand-sculpturing contest would have to wait, merely filler to the morning's rare and sensational news-cast. In Cape May and Wildwood, the talk of the town was mur-der, and yesterday's revelations pinning the crime to those within the town's exclusive golf club was mind-blowing to the small-talk dinners and coffee shops throughout the southernmost points of New Jersey's shoreline. It was not every day that the town's less-than-wealthy majority got to scoff at the haves of the world, finally savoring their chance to bask and smirk in their check-to-check lifestyle.

The monsignor hit the up arrow on the TV clicker's volume button. The studio anchor had just passed the go-ahead to its sideline reporter.

"I'm here this morning with two of Pious College's employees, a place where for the past three years Tony Sacco has acted as chairman of the board. Let's start with Sister Mary Dija, the school's director of development. Good morning, sister. Can you tell us your thoughts on yesterday's shocking news?"

Back in her full nun attire, the litter sister responded, "Me very sad that I leaving. Me no want to go. Me love it here. I going to the monsignor today to complain. I tell him to keep me here and that I know how he hurt Jesse. And I know that he trying to hurt me!"

Showing an expression of confusion, the young reporter tried to make sense of the little nun's response. "I'm sorry, sister, but who is—"

Before she could get out her question, the monsignor's assistant jumped into the conversation.

Ignoring the reporter, Jenny scowled toward Sister Dija. "Wait, wait, wait, wait. No, sister, no, no, no, no! You have it all wrong. How dare you! The monsignor is a good man. He is the president now! That was a very long time ago, and you weren't even there!"

The baffled reporter took a slight step between the two. "Well—" Again she was interrupted. The sister would have none of Jenny's aggressive, however feeble, outbreak.

"I *not wrong*. You *wrong*," she blurted, then turned and quickly walked away, in the direction of the monsignor's residence.

Turning back to Jenny Flopalis, the reporter put the microphone up to her mouth, and before she could utter a word, Jenny darted from her spot and with long uncomfortable strides began chasing after the nun. The camera flashed in the direction of the departing pawns: Sister Dija in the distance and Jenny lagging behind, head down focusing on increasing her pace. As the two disappeared around the far campus bend, the camera panned back to a now-dazed reporter.

She in a "throw up her hands, I give up" fashion, looked straight into the camera, chuckled, and said, "Well, Dave, that may have been one for the ages. Let's turn it back to you."

In the newsroom, a different aura filled the space. While some sat dumbfounded, having just witnessed a most incoherent and dysfunctional interview, the station's manager abruptly snapped everybody back to business real quick-like.

"Okay, people, work to do! Looks like we have double stories here. Dave, you stay with our guy at the club. I want everyone entering and leaving that place to comment on Sacco and Stainwell. Tell our guy to f'n tackle anybody going or coming if he has to. We need reactions!" Turning to the small group on the other side of the room, he barked, "You guys, find out who this guy Jesse is *stat*! Let's follow up with the nun and see if we can get what the fuck she's talking about! And Sue, call the monsignor *now*. See if he will give a comment. Holy shit, people, when it rains it fucken' pours! Let's move!"

Within seconds, the monsignor's phone began ringing. Stunned, he had watched the live-interview fiasco literally occurring five walking minutes from his sofa. As Sister Dija departed abruptly toward his residence, the monsignor sprung up and quickly darted to the hallway closet, removing a black leather duffel bag. Smallish, the bag resembled an old doctor's bag during a time when house calls were made as a normal occurrence, both by neighborhood physicians and priests alike. Those days were long gone with the only heartfelt reminders residing in the older generation's nostalgic reminiscing during Sunday or holiday get-togethers. As he carried the bag to his bedroom and then to the adjourning bathroom, his fatigue with the whole mess caused brief inclinations of surrender but his will and, frankly, fear summoned the last bits of fight left in his shaking and stressed body. His thoughts quickly returned to escape, with an urgency to leave before he was confronted by an out-of-breath, but very angry, little nun. He consciously had ignored the phone's ringing and swiftly threw his cell phone, a few fresh clothes, a toothbrush, and his wallet into the bag. Heading for the door, he scooped his car keys off the front hallway table, exited, and walked briskly to his car. With Sister Dija and a now-disheveled and panting assistant within eyeshot but not earshot, he started the car and hit the gas, heading straight toward the Garden State Parkway north, destination unknown. His past once-private soiled secrets were gradually being exposed for all to see, including now those in the media with their salivating notebooks and stunted fixation to destroy.

The morning's sideshow instantly became the talk of the town. Over and over, the local TV station played the dysfunctional interview of Sister Dija and the assistant. Soon, larger networks picked up the story. Wildwood's antics had blown up into everybody's favorite "did you see" question around office water coolers and afternoon happy hours up and down the East Coast. Newspapers and their headline editors played Can You Top This? with one catchy, cute play on words, headline after another. Atlantic City's *Tribune* captured the moment rather frankly, simply headlining its story with *Wait? I'm Confused.* Not to be outdone, its rival, the *AC Daily Post*, coined the moment best with its two-word headline of *Say What?* Soon those two words caught traction, and newscasters from Philly to Boston played the clip over and over, now referring to it simply as the *Say What?* interview. What started as a story of murder, and the arrest of one of Tony Sacco's henchmen, had turned into comic relief bought to you by two of Pious College's finest. That was for all but those at WKRZ. This local station smelled blood, and they were hell-bent to find the monsignor and some guy named Jesse.

Back at the college, all was now quiet, emanating a peace that belied the school's tumultuous leaders and staff. Thrown into the limbo of a temporarily closed school, runaway leadership and headlines for all the wrong reasons, Father Jon walked into the theater to run a quick meeting he had called with the performing arts staff. As he made his way down the dimly lit center aisle toward the stage, he could see the back of three heads, seated in the front row. As he had requested, Patty Simon was there, along with Britta Holland. Seated next to Britta was her girl partner, Rae, there representing her role as volunteer for this year's production.

Approaching the three, he greeted them with a quick "Thank you for coming" and got right to the point. Standing in front of them, he said, "I believe we should cancel this year's play. Frankly, I was feeling quite opposite the other day, thinking that a bit of normalcy was just what this school needed. However, in light of the arrest and of course the recent press on Sister Dija, Jenny, and the monsignor, I think it's best to quietly finish an almost-finished academic semester and get to our spring, early-summer break. With summer classes not starting this year until mid-July, I am hopeful this publicity will have died down, and we can get back to normal. I think bringing people, you know staff, parents, local residents together at this time would be a mistake and only add to the chaos that we have found ourselves in. I am sorry, as I know you have worked hard on this, but I think for now it is the best thing."

Patty leaned forward, turning her head to observe the reaction of Britta. Secretly, Britta felt like doing cartwheels through the theater. Since the beginning, she had longed for the time when the play was concluded and a time when Rae and Patty had no venue to be together. With the cancellation of the play, if Rae intended to cheat with her boss, then they would have to do it on their own terms, not using the excuse that the play had brought them together. *Thank God,* Britta thought privately as she simply shrugged her shoulders in the direction of Patty as if to say, "What can we do, you heard the man…it's over." Rae, knowing her place within the threesome, kept silent with no visible reaction.

"Okay, Father, thank you," Patty responded. "While our kids will be disappointed, I do understand your decision. Perhaps we can use this production's preparation toward the same production next year. I will inform the cast of the school's decision, although honestly, I can't predict their reaction. If there is an overly negative or aggressive response by the kids or even their parents that, by the way, also may make the news, I will let you know."

"Thank you, ladies. Again, I apologize. Hopefully the spotlight will soon be off our school, and things can get back to normal…that is if you can leap to the assumption that anything we do around here is normal. Please stay in touch, as need be." With that said, the priest forced a cordial smile and began walking up the center aisle and out of the theater.

The three women momentarily sat in silence, until Patty felt the need to break the ice. She stood up, cueing to the other two to do the same. "Well, I guess that's it. I will call our cast leaders and ask that they spread the word. Perhaps I will send a group e-mail letting all the program's members know to expect a meeting sometime soon. I'm going to let the smoke clear a little bit, though. Sometime, say, midsummer. Do you agree?"

"Sure, Patty, that's fine," responded Britta. Rae simply smiled.

Patty again took the initiative. "Well, I'm outta here. You guys stay well. We'll talk soon." With that she moved into Britta and gave her a quick and somewhat forced hug. Turning to Rae, she stepped closer and placed her palms over Rae's ears and pulled her face toward her. As Britta watched in shock, Patty kissed Rae on the lips and, without notice, opened her lips and slipped her tongue into Rae's mouth and passionately swirled it for several seconds. Eyes closed, Rae responded by returning the action, forcing her tongue into Patty's open mouth. Rae placed her hands around Patty, squarely on to her bottom, pulling their vaginas closer. Finally, the kiss ended. Patty hugged Rae for a goodbye squeeze that was longer than normal. "Will miss you, girl," she said. Any reaction by Britta frankly was not noticeable, although neither Rae nor Patty bothered to look in her direction.

With that, Patty walked along the stage to the theater's front-side emergency door, shoving the horizontal bar, causing it to fling open. Off she went into the bright sunshine. Britta grabbed her knapsack from the first-row chair and, without so much as looking at Rae, huffed noticeably and quickly moved up the center aisle toward the exit.

Rae, stunned and quite provoked by Patty's hot kiss, ignored her partner's exodus and quick-stepped toward the emergency door. Using her body to the push the door open, she darted out, clearly urgent, hoping to catch up to the performing arts director.

Chapter Twenty-Five

Spilling the Beans

THE YOUNG GATE attendant's eyes went left and then right. Surveying the area for late arrivals, she raised the counter's silver microphone. Her announcement was heard throughout the Philadelphia International Airport's south-wing terminal. "Last boarding call for Quito, destination Mariscal Sucre International Airport, Quito, Ecuador."

Sister Dija slowly rose from the hard blue terminal chair, grabbed the handle of her rolling gray carry-on and moved toward the ticket post that stood guard to the flex mobile runway leading to the plane's entrance. Head down, she handed the ticket to the dark-skinned male collector, name tag Alde, and made her way onto the plane. With the bottom back of her long nun robes sweeping against the aisle's tan carpet, she stopped at row 22, seat A. An older gentleman, adjacent to the row popped from his chair and without asking, grabbed Sister's carry-on saying, "Let me help you with that, sister." Tucking the small suitcase in the overhead opposite Sister's Dija's seat, he nodded politely and sat back down. A fretfully low "Thank you" was all the little nun could whisper as she slumped into her aisle and shimmied her body over to the window seat, leaned against the plane's inner wall, and broodily gazed out the window. Her thoughts aligned well with her sullen body language. *Me going to miss USA. I no understand why monsignor do this. Me going to miss Jesse. Me miss*

186

Jesse now. As her eyes welled with tears, the captain's voice was heard over the loudspeaker. "Attendants, please be seated. We are ready for takeoff." Within minutes the LATAM Airlines' plane reached cruising altitude, and Sister Mary Dija was gone. Gone from Jesse, gone from the monsignor, gone from the free and cozy beach town of New Jersey, gone from Pious, gone from her comfortable convent sitting room and gone from her new way of thinking and a courage that gave her a joy never before revealed or experienced.

Back in Wildwood, Jesse Kane decided to keep himself busy by emptying the overly filled hallway closet in the off-road beach bungalow, the one that his deceased partner had described as their temporary little paradise. As Jesse removed one thing after another, each unrelated to the last, his thoughts were of Steve Summers. He forced himself to chuckle, thinking that his partner was a lot of things, but neat and tidy he was not. In the empty, unfurnished hallway, Jesse began laying each of the closet's articles on the floor next to him. Within minutes his feet were buried in beach mats, boardwalk trinkets, clothing, and numerous other possessions that now carried no meaning. As his pointless task was near end, under a strewn and tattered sweatshirt with the words *I Love New York* sitting atop a faded red apple, Jesse noticed a small tin box shimmied into the back right angle corner of the closet floor. Unfamiliar to Jesse, he lifted it and tried to open the lid, only to find it was locked. The cheap-looking silver keyhole on the front of the box reminded him of the one on his childhood keepsake chest, a curious memory and something that he had not thought of in years.

With finally finding the day's first purpose, he lifted it and carried it to the kitchen. Opening a long rectangle drawer, Jesse rummaged through another of the bungalow's venues for junk. From the back of the drawer, he grabbed a rusty old screwdriver, and intent on revealing the box's treasures, he shoved its tip into the keyhole and began twisting the tool determined to pop or at least break the locking device. Without much effort, his mission was accomplished as the box's lid cracked open, revealing a most unexpected but pleasant surprise. Jesse stuck his right hand into the box and grabbed a stack of cash and, opening his hand, let them fall on the countertop. Jesse had never seen so much cash in one place at one time. Lifting the box and turning it upside down over the counter, more cash spilled onto the counter, until the box was empty. Spreading the bills along the counter with the palm of his hand, the scattered view revealed bills of all denominations: tens, twenties, ones, even several fifties and hundreds.

Slowly and carefully, Jesse organized the loot into piles of the same value and counted it: 4,607 dollars…more money that he personally had ever owned. Confused why Steve had never told him about the box, Jesse switched his attention to the refrigerator, removed a half-empty carton of orange juice, and standing close to the appliance's opening to feel its chill, he gulped the juice carton until it was empty. Letting out a large and rather vile burp, he moved to the room's table and sat down in his favorite kitchen chair. Taking a deep breath of relief, his mind transitioned from boredom and despair to thoughts of his immediate future. He had wondered how he would survive without any money, what he would do or even where he would go. His thoughts of his sex with Sister Dija thrilled him, yet he felt awkward about how he had abruptly left. Since leaving, she had been a fixture in his mind. Earlier that day, he had masturbated thinking only of her, and later thinking it odd and somehow liberating that during the pleasuring, Steve had not even crossed his mind. Quick thoughts of visiting her were dashed in favor of catching a bus to Cape May. He had liked it there during the times that he and Steve had walked the town and visited the beach. He recalled riding into Cape May with Sister Dija to go to Steve's wake, even then feeling a fondness for the area. He decided to investigate renting a room in Cape May with his newfound wealth. Perhaps he would even look for some sort of a job. With the money, he at least now had the means to make a few decisions. He decided that on the bus, he would give it serious thought. Purposefully, he moved to the shower, stripped down, and stepped in. *Today will be a good day*, he thought, *a real good day*.

Closer to the boardwalk, Coach Sully, fresh from the shower, sat on his bed with a white hotel towel wrapped around his waist. A procedure followed for years, the coach at each football road game had always confiscated a towel from his hotel room to add to his apartment's collection. Frankly, that mentality was a fairly prevalent way of life for this head football guy. Taking advantage of life's access to free stuff prevented the unnecessary spending of his paltry salary on lots of supermarket and drugstore items, leaving a bit more for the essentials of betting and booze. His kitchen was evidence of this mastery, with each cabinet containing plastic utensils from fast-food joints, napkins from the island counter at Pete's Pizza, and disposable rinsed Dunkin' Donuts coffee cups set to last several weeks until their deterioration finally marked them for the garbage. His bathroom sink was lined with an array of hotel shampoos and conditioners, razors stolen from Club Eighteen's bathroom counter, and even little soap bars seized from the highway's gas station men's room. He had particularly scored big last summer at a local football camp when one of his tasks was to control the camp T-shirts for its paying campers. Till this day, he could vision several big dudes working out in under-sized tees as half the XLs and XXLs somehow found their way to the back floor of his beat-up truck. Not a proud man, the coach was also not shy nor embarrassed about his propensity to take advantage of securing necessities. In his mind, he was simply being practical.

Holding his phone on his lap, his attempts to contact Darlene Davidson had failed for several days, and this one was no exception. *How could that be,* he thought. *Fucked up that she would allow me to screw her twice in less than twenty-four hours and then not have the decency to return my calls.* Deciding he would follow up on this oddity and desperate to talk to someone about the arrest of Adrian's killer and the interview of Jenny and Sister Dija, he quickly got dressed, hopped into his truck, and made a beeline to the CFO's house. Like most guys, he ignored the obvious signals of rejection and envisioned the positive, thinking that maybe the bed romps had caused her to fall for him, and she was nervous with the feeling, not quite sure what to do or say.

Pulling up to her house and seeing her car in the driveway, he walked to the front door and rang the bell. In seconds, the wooden door opened, and sixteen-year-old Ash, Darlene's stepkid, spoke through the tattered screen door.

"Oh. Hi, coach. What's up?"

"Wondering if your mom is home. I've been trying to call her with no luck. Wanted to see if she was okay?"

"Sure coach," said the boy. "She's fine. She's around back. Quickest way is through the side gate," he said, pointing left to the side of the house.

"Thanks, kid," said Sully as he nodded and walked through the poorly maintained front-yard grass to the side gate, opened it, and headed around to the back. Intending to start with a rather demonstrative demand for an explanation on why his calls were being ignored, his strategy quickly blew up with a first glance into the yard. In the shade, under the yard's canvas awning, was Kevin McMatty, the school's less-than-dedicated provost. With his back to the approaching coach, he had both arms around Darlene courtesy of a pretentious attempt at instructing her on the proper movement in swinging a golf club. With McMatty's groin squarely stationed against her swaying rump and his soft instructions resembling more a rear-side whispering of sweet nothings in her ear, the coach could hear the pretty middle-aged CFO giggling like some innocent school-girl encountering some unexpected attention from the captain of the football team.

The coach interrupted the lesson with a few loud throat-clearing noises, causing the PGA provost to quickly release his grip on Darlene as they both turned to acknowledge the interruption.

"Hey, look who's here. What's up, coach?" said McMatty, in a very comfortable fashion. For the moment, Darlene's giggling and perhaps even her good mood was put on hold.

"You tell me, Kevin. Just stopped by to see why Darlene isn't answering her phone. I guess it was difficult to reach for it while she was in your bear hug." Talking past the provost, the coach looked at Darlene. "Playing all angles, huh, Darlene?" he said sarcastically.

"Easy, Sully, you're out of line." Smiling at McMatty, she continued, "Kevin was just showing me the perfect golf swing. And besides, who the hell are you? Last time I checked, the ink is real dry on my divorce papers. Free to do as I please, certainly without getting permission from you."

About to respond, the coach was thrown off by the entrance of Darlene's hot stepdaughter, Verona, casually striding into the yard with her now fully accepted lifeguard boy toy, Cory Penstar. Cory's arm was snugly wrapped around Verona, resting comfortable atop her curvy buttocks, held snug in her very tight blue jeans.

Letting out a forced one-syllable "*Ha,*" the coach blurted, "Like mother, like daughter," shaking his head in disgust.

"Fuck you, Sully" was Darlene's quick response. "Get the hell out of my yard."

Recognizing it was only downhill from here, Sully turned and headed toward the gate, only to turn and shoot one parting shot. "Oh, Kevin, say, how's that wife of yours doing?" he asked, referring to the known but never spoken about mentally institutionalized wife of Kevin McMatty.

"Low blow, dirtbag," responded the provost, ending the coach's unpleasant and very unsuccessful visit, just another dysfunctional episode involving Pious's cast of characters.

With the sister now traveling the friendly skies toward Third World territory, school temporarily closed, and the immoral monsignor hid away somewhere north of Pious College, Jenny Flopalis stood pointlessly outside the college's main administrative office. Wanting desperately to help the monsignor but without the brainpower to determine a course of action, the trusty assistant felt the pangs of uselessness that, more and more, had defined her being. As the good looks of a younger woman had long since abandoned her, she was left with only fading-fast skills; comically poor judgment; and of course, her never-disputed, but often-unproductive, good intentions. Her attempts to contact her master had all been instantly swept to voice mail. Even she had concluded that two incoherent messages blabbering her mission to help were more than enough. Confused with the remainder of her day, she decided to head home and try to figure it all out. Dressed in a spring-flowered dress that was old and overly tight that showed the ripple-after-ripple results from age's slow bodily metabolism, the assistant slowly and gingerly made her way back toward her modest residence, some ten minutes from the college. With the nuisance of almost always living these days with hurting, swollen feet, Jenny had turned the once-pleasant, short walk into quite the limping chore.

As she turned the corner, finally reaching her block, she saw that it was filled with people and a seeming endless stream of news trucks and vans. Never thinking such attention could have anything to do with her, she continued toward her house, ultimately realizing that the crowd seemed to be camped mostly in her driveway and in front of her house. Without any ability to move quickly or retreat, she was trapped as it became obvious that the reporters had spotted her and were now, complete with live mics, rushing toward her. Confused and unable to navigate through the herd of oncoming reporters and camera crews, Jenny stood still, oblivious that she was today's blood scent for the circling sharks masked as public-serving correspondents.

"Ms. Flopalis!" "Jenny!" "Ms. Flopalis!" chimed one reporter after another, hoping to be the one to throw the first dart.

The first to reach the baffled assistant was a young male scribe, complete with headset and audio-recording mic. "Where is the monsignor, Jenny? Has he been in contact with you? Who is Jesse? Where is Sister Dija? Does this have anything to do with the murders?"

Jenny, looking past the reporter as if searching for her rescuer, said nothing. Tears welled in her eyes and began rolling down her cheeks. Her vivid emotional state caused the reporter to back off, a silent interlude that allowed the full reporting mob to reach them, forming a horseshoe-shaped crowd around the shaky assistant. The young female reporter from WKRZ, the one who had conducted the *Say What?* interview, squirmed her way to a spot arm's length from Jenny.

Putting a microphone up to this morning's star, she calmly spoke, "Please don't be upset, Ms. Flopalis. If you can just tell us what Sister Dija meant when she said that the monsignor hurt Jesse? Who is Jesse? And what did the monsignor do to hurt him and Sister Dija?"

The reporter's civility momentarily calmed Ms. Flopalis and eased her toward a response. Jenny took an exaggerated deep pant as she alternated forearms to wipe dry each cheek. "Jesse is the little rectory boy, a long time ago," she said. "Monsignor didn't hurt anybody. He loved Jesse and took care of him. Of course, Jesse is grown up now. Sister is wrong. Monsignor is a good man."

Jenny's words reignited the frenzy, with various reporters barking new questions, until the young WKRZ reporter aggressively held up both hands, a motion that seemed to scream, "I got this!" Using the oft-used and well-known routine where reporters, looking to gain information, quickly ask multiple questions to get a wide-ranging response, the young scribe spoke again. "Why do you think the sister thinks that? Where is the monsignor and what did he do to Sister Dija?" Thinking for a second and not yet pushing the mic back to the assistant, the reporter took a calculated and, some would say, career-threatening risk: "Does Sister Dija think he abused Jesse when he was a little boy?" With each reporter's eyes opening a bit wider with the chancy question, one could see their arms stretch their recorders a bit closer to Jenny, awaiting her answer. With one word, the assistant to the monsignor cracked open a secret that had lain dormant for over twenty years.

"Maybe," said Jenny. With not a spark of understanding as to the ramifications of her answer, Jenny turned the situation from bad to worse by spilling whatever beans were left in the dreadful jar of what had become the old priest's nightmare. "But he didn't mean it. He loved Jesse. And besides, that's no reason to have your boyfriend commit blackmail. I know! I saw the letter." Without a clue as to the firestorm that she had just created, the reckless, dumb assistant had enough. As sternly as she could, she spoke, "No more, no more," and pushed her way to the outer edge of the hoard of reporters. Ignoring their attempts to follow up on her revelations, she walked across her neighbor's front lawn, reached her front door, managing to unlock it and enter the house.

Sitting on the first chair she came to, she took out her phone and again tried the monsignor. Disappointed that he did not answer, Jenny sat back, resigning herself to waiting. Filled with pride, she couldn't wait to tell her boss how she had helped him and how she had defended him. After all, she thought, *He could use some good news.*

Chapter Twenty-Six

Media Friday

IT WAS NOW Friday. This weekend would turn its page to June and the start of what typically was a peaceful and prosperous time in Wildwood. This year, however, was different. While Wildwood's streets, boardwalk, and beaches were humming with visiting summer dwellers and the town's locals, news stories had disrupted the peace usually attached to this time of year. Headlines had gone national, and news loops, from local to big-time network and cable stations, carried Wildwood's triangle story line. The words *murder, abuse, and blackmail* were repeated over and over, rousing the loins of even the mildest of the area's activists. News trucks and TV vans were parked throughout town and along the entrance to Pious College. Salivating scribes and reporters, some dressed in suits and dresses and others in logo-labeled golf shirts, could be seen sniffing for headlines and the reactions of town residents. Newspersons were stationed at key points on campus, at the courthouse and at Club Eighteen, looking to corner each story's main characters, hopeful of sucking out headlines for their nightly news shows or tomorrow's editions. Two-person crews, each with a camera guy and reporter in tow, could be seen spewed on boardwalks or outside supermarkets or restaurants intent on giving residents their minute of fame in exchange for comments: the stronger the opinion, the better. Yes, the sensationalism of murder and the potential of unveiling another pedophile priest were only superseded by the possibility that the stories were somehow connected, compelling various speculations by wannabe detectives and storytellers.

In Atlantic City, Exit 38 on the Garden State Parkway, in a remote motel almost a mile from the strip of now less-than-prosperous casinos sat Monsignor Clark, frozen, watching his life being ruined on the room's twenty-seven-inch TV. Once a player, and a powerful one at that, Shawn Clark had folded, drained from emotion, a sad personality with no hand to play. Ignoring three separate phone calls and requests for call back from the archdiocese of Cape May County, the morose shell of a man, once a powerful chess king, was trapped in the board's corner box, as the world screamed *check*!

Back on campus, on the sidewalk and street outside the monsignor's college residence, several college employees and students gathered in response to Josh Bromberg's e-mail. Josh was, as he liked to describe himself, a professor of mathematics at Pious College. Too often, he had a way of making others uncomfortable with his radical views of the world and his self-promotion as an atheist, usually during school events that demonstrated their Catholic affiliation. Many simply saw him as a nerdy-looking, glasses-wearing teacher, usually holding tight to his self-proclaimed intention to do good, but always on the lookout to quench his well-known thirst for self-promotion and activism.

Earlier in the day, he had crafted and sent a group e-mail to his peers at Pious appealing for the school community to get to the truth, the full truth, and nothing but the truth. His message enticed his fellow workers to participate in an almost-obligatory action to speak out through an organized protest. He implored them to demand clarity and detail regarding Jenny Flopalis's blurt that "maybe" the monsignor had abused Jesse when he was a boy. He raised the need for investigation into the assistant's claim that Jesse's boyfriend was blackmailing the priest. His message, like from any good math guy, had calculated that the boyfriend was Steve Summers, the man who had been murdered. He encouraged that his peers bring signs that pled for the truth and new leadership at the college.

In a particularly low move, on the list of the e-mail's recipients, he had included the school's two student council presidents, Dylan McMatty and Katrice Brown, privately hoping to stir students' inherent passion to save the planet from all evil. Josh's e-mail concluded with, what else, an equation. It read simply *Clark + Flopalis = Abuse + Cover-up*. Within minutes, the crowd included camera crews and reporters determined to use their presence to stir the pot of sensationalism. While the protesters took on the posture more of a sit-in than a vocal chanting mob, their signs were artfully crafted to do all the talking. *MONSIGNOR COME CLEAN* seemed to be the refrain of the day although posters targeting his assistant with signs that read *INVESTIGATE THE FLOPALIS COVER UP* and *DUMB & BLIND LOYALTY* were also in the running for the first-place ribbon. One sign's practicality drew noticeable attention of the growing number of cameras. It simply read, *FR. JON FOR PRESIDENT*. Chest out, Josh Bromberg walked through the crowd, nodding his head as if to congratulate his efforts to organize the pack. Making exaggerated eye contact with each reporter, his body language begged for attention until finally an equally goofy-looking scribe asked for a moment of his time. Acknowledging in the affirmative, he quickly hand-brushed his hair, separated himself from his eye specs, and began to tell the camera of his group's noble cause. "We gather for one reason and one reason only," he said. "And that reason is justice!"

Back at the assistant's house, Jenny Flopalis could be seen peeking through the drapes at the horde of reporters gathered in front of her house. Forgetting her past and uncomfortable encounters with the media, her ego flowed the juices born from attention, envisioning herself as the story's new star. She decided to rise to the occasion. Choosing to relish rather than avoid the attention, she seized the moment and began prepping for her grand appearance. Blindly envisioning her involvement as another chance to help her master, she waddled up the steps to the second floor. Quickly, she entered the bathroom and stripped down to her old-world undergarment. Deciding on her red-carpet wear, she slipped into her favorite evening dress, a black and rather low-cut frilly covering that she always thought did well to add a youthful look to her persona. Removing a blunt red lipstick from the medicine cabinet, she smeared it on both lips and puckered several times, making a series of puckering pop sounds more resembling a call for a mating partner than a pretty up. Stepping to the toilet, she unrolled a nice long strip of toilet paper, and making the sound that disgusts most in this world, she blew her nose hard into the paper. Turning to the sink, she placed the used and repulsive paper on the counter, looked into the mirror, puffed her hair with both hands, and headed downstairs to the front door.

As she approached the exit, she took one final gaze at the circular mirror, hung extra low on the hallway wall, some five feet from the door. "Showtime," she whispered to herself, and without so much as a hint of hesitation, she exited to greet her adoring fans.

Chapter Twenty-Seven

To Plea or Not to Plea

THE RING OF the phone in the four-bedroom penthouse suite caused the handsome young man to place down his gin on the rocks, raise his six-foot-four-inch bodybuilder frame, and walk across the stone-floored balcony and into the living room. Dressed impeccably in an expensive dark suit, mirror-clean shoes, and a silk white pullover shirt that played nicely to his broad chest and beach-tanned skin, he walked to the phone like a guy pretty damn sure of his role in things.

"Yeeaah," he said into the phone, demanding an explanation for his disturbance.

"Your cars, sir, one for five and one for your bags, has arrived. May I send someone up for your bags?"

Holding the phone away from his body, he looked across the room, past the three gorgeous playmates to his boss. "We ready?"

"Yeah, let's go" was the only response he needed to hear.

"Okay," said the man into the phone and hung up. Without hesitation, he walked into the bedroom where several black suitcases were neatly covering both beds. On a desk at the far corner of the room sat a carry-on-sized leather duffel bag, intentionally separated from the others. The man walked to the bag, unzipped the eighteen-inch opening, and pulled each side in opposite directions to expose the carrier's contents. Inside lay several, rather thick-wrapped, piles of cash, high denomination only. Placing his right hand into the bag, with a sweeping motion, he dug to the bottom of the case, revealing hard-covered banking books and four handguns, each nestled beside several loaded ten-piece magazines. As if a reminder, he moved his right hand to the bottom right side of his suit jacket to ensure that his short-nosed nine-millimeter was squarely in place. Satisfied, he zipped the bag closed, flung it over his shoulder, and walked out the room.

"We're good" was all he said to his four counterparts and led them out of the suite to the private elevator reserved just for the penthouse. Also seeming to know its place in this scene, the white gold-framed doors opened immediately on the push of the gold-plated call button. An oversized people mover, the opening allowed all five travelers to enter at once.

Perhaps new at this sort of thing, one of the three young ladies in the group, dressed smartly in a tight, low-cut white dress spoke. "So how long is this flight?" she asked.

Tony Sacco shot a quick glance at his bodyguard, prompting his instant glare toward the inquisitive beauty. Placing his index figure vertically across his lips, he uttered "Shhh" in her direction. Clearly, one got the feel that he didn't need to ask twice.

For the next twenty seconds or so, the elevator dropped to the underground parking floor where two full-size Escalades lay in wait. With all five exiting the people mover quietly, Mr. Sacco's plan was right on schedule.

Each of the women were young, sharing the attributes of tanned, model-like pretty faces, and showing wealth in the well-worn silver-and-gold ornaments that dangled from their ears and necks. Their frames' features were mesmerizing, each one possessing a sexy magnificence commanding some serious male charm, power, and wealth to be blessed with their presence. The private garage's dimmed lights revealed two wax-shined vehicles, and the group's procession into the front SUV reeked of some serious thought and planning that preceded this upscale getaway. As the driver, whose cockpit was separated from the fivesome with a tinted black remote-opening glass barrier, slammed his door shut creating a silent airtight transport, Tony Sacco finally spoke.

"Everybody relax, the flight is twenty-five hours, but my craft has comfortable bedrooms and as much entertainment and food as you want. Think of it as our own Air Force One. The chef is making steak and lobster for dinner. We'll have a good time."

The ladies smiled, each snuggling closer to their two Romeos and to each other.

"Carmine, make us some drinks and put some nice Italian music on. We got about an hour ride to the hangar." As the top-shelf liquor flowed and the vehicle sped up the Parkway to the remote and private aircraft hangar attached to the main Atlantic City Airport, the Cape May kingpin made one more domestic call, maybe his last for some time, maybe even forever.

"Ricco, its Tony. Listen, do me a favor. When the Stain scumbag gets out of the joint, go see him. Say my name and then put a bullet in his brain." Chuckling in reaction to something said on the other side of the call, he said, "Yeah I agree. You're a good man, Ricco. I won't forget." And just like that, he hit the end-call button.

By midafternoon, Tony's plane was above the clouds and headed for a private paradise island on the other side of the world.

Meanwhile, back in Wildwood in a small room under the courthouse, sat three of South Jersey's finest detectives. Patiently, they were awaiting the arraignment of Oliver Stainwell for the murder of Steve Summers and Adrian Kenny. In a short while, upstairs in the small courtroom, the defendant would be formally charged and asked how he pleaded, either guilty or not guilty. While never quite done until the plea left the mouth of the accused, this scene had already been decided. Stainwell had agreed to plead guilty under a plea deal that would limit his sentence to only ten years and out on good behavior in six. For this rather-generous concession, he had agreed to turn on Tony Sacco and provide collaborating testimony that Sacco had engineered the double murder, for reasons that were unknown to him. He would state that in his world you didn't ask questions. You just did as you were told. Law enforcement had been after Sacco for some time, and this was their best shot to bring him down. They were convinced that once he was indicted and charged, he too would squeal both about the reasons for the double murder and several other misgivings over the last five years. All knew that for the right deal, most criminals would give up their mother for a cushy prison cell and reduced time. There was no downside to this. Even if he took the high road and kept quiet, this charge would put him away for the vast majority of his remaining years. Stainwell, they knew, was the perfect pigeon to bring this arrogant sleazebag to his knees.

"Listen," said the detective in charge of the other two. "Once Stainwell utters the word *guilty* and we got him by the balls, you guys go find Sacco and bring him in. Make sure you read him his rights real slowly. I don't want any chance that this gets fucked up on a technicality. If you have to, involve our whole crew to find him. Start at the golf club. That's where he hangs. The word of Stainwell's plea is going to get out in a hurry. I don't want to give the boss man any time to think about fleeing. In fact, here's a better idea. You guys leave now and go sit by the club. I'll text you as soon as Stainwell pleads. Cuff that scumbag and bring him to me. I'll be waiting at the tombs in Cape May. We'll throw him in that tiny cell overnight…let him think about his fate for a while. I'll talk to the lieutenant and see how he wants to handle this. He may want the fun to talk plea with this jerkoff."

One of the listening detectives got out of his chair and motioned to the other. "Let's go," he said. "I'll look for your text, Sarge, and then we'll catch up at the tombs. He should be there, but I'll call you if we have to go looking. He can't be far."

With that, both men moved to the steps leading up to the courthouse's front door, followed by the man in charge. As they approached the exit, the sergeant called out. "Get a good look at his mug when he sees you. I want to hear how this surprise wipes that shit grin off his face."

As the two cops left the courthouse, somewhere now over the Atlantic, Tony Sacco dipped a big chunk of lobster into a dish of freshly melted butter and shoved it in his mouth. At the far end of the long white marble table his three playmates, already a bit tipsy from this afternoon's cocktails, were unintentionally giving Tony a show and perhaps a little coming attraction. As the petite dark-haired beauty tenderly stroked the hair of the taller blond, the third beauty was placing soft kisses on the necks and protruding cleavage of her two getaway partners.

Tony turned to his loyal buddy, grinned, and then looked back at the erotic trio.

"Turn up the music, Carmine, and pour some drinks. This party is about to get started."

Chapter Twenty-Eight

Over the Edge

WITH THE DAY'S events wrapped and in the books, Wildwood's police lieutenant, upon unending calls to his office, felt compelled to arrange a late-night press conference outside the small precinct house at the tip of town. The story had grown national legs, and frankly the brass within New Jersey's finest was not above soaking in some overdue attention and publicity. The news, however, was not all good, and for that the Lieutenant was, to say the least, quite pissed.

At 9:00 p.m., with the hastily called conference to begin in less than an hour, Lieutenant Burns sat sipping a lukewarm cup of bad coffee, as he dressed down his detective sergeant.

"Jesus Christ! How the fuck could you lose this guy?"

Knowing any answer wasn't going to be good enough, the sergeant had no choice but to respond. "Chief, someone must have leaked the plea on the street. No one was supposed to know the deal until the words came out of his mouth. I even sent our guys to wait outside the club before the scumbag's plead. Sacco must have gotten tipped."

Burns's face took on a deeper shade of an already-reddened nose and cheeks.

"*No!* That's shit work! No wonder you're still a fucken' sergeant! You should have been tailing the guy the minute we got Stainwell to agree to sing. Sacco got more chirpers on the street then we do, for Christ's sake. This should have been easy. Done by now. Jesus f'n Christ! The captain is gonna have my ass!"

The hour leading up to the press conference passed quickly. Just prior to stepping out the front door of the police station, the lieutenant paused and turned toward his mini entourage of detectives and uniformed honchos. In a low, firm tone he reminded them of his expectation. "Remember, no fucken' opinions. Keep it professional. Just the damn facts." Fortunately, for the lieutenant, over the years he had mastered the art of answering aroused beat reporters, manipulating his responses to always make his department look good. With the facade of competence and know-how front and center, he handled the press conference like a real pro, never letting on that both he and his men had royally blown it, and maybe, perhaps even probably, they would never see Tony Sacco again.

The next day's papers and newscasts all sang the same song, perhaps said best by Jersey's neighboring slime chronicle, the *NYC Town Post*. Above a less-than-flattering photo of Oliver Stainwell, standing downtrodden, hands cuffed and feet shackled in front of the day's courthouse judge, the bold ink headline summarized yesterday's news.

GUILTY PLEA! MANHUNT FOR MASTERMIND SACCO

As the hours passed from morning to afternoon, it became more and more apparent that Tony Sacco had outmaneuvered Wildwood's police force. The men with badges were looking for a win, anything to take the news away from the blunder of letting Wildwood's most-wanted mobster flee the coup. Speculation was that Sacco was not one to hide or bury himself in some hidden bunker. The man was gone, having the finances, influence, and power to now be anywhere, anywhere in the whole damn world. Humiliated, Lieutenant Burns was left with nothing but a really bad plea by a double murderer. A plea that, in the world of criminal justice, he must live up to. Stainwell would do his six years and walk. For that, the lieutenant had gained nothing: no Sacco, no complimentary headlines, no job well done from his superiors, just a whole lot of smelly egg dripping down each side of his face. He called for his sergeant, looking somehow to regroup.

"Sacco's gone, and the more we look, the more fucken' embarrassing it gets. Let's change gears. Go 'round up that assistant at the college, the bright light who gave up her boss, the old priest. Let's get her to turn. Make her agree to testify. Squeeze her with staying quiet on a felony, a sex-abuse felony. Then we talk to this Jesse kid. Maybe he'll sing on the priest too, and at least we can bring down a pedophile. It's not Sacco, but it will bring some headlines. And let's get to the bottom of this blackmail shit. Who knows, if we get lucky it might even lead us to our guy."

"Yes, sir, Lieutenant, we're on it," said the beleaguered but always-willing sergeant. Motioning to two plainclothes cops sitting patiently at their desks, he said, "Let's go, boys" as he led them out the door, up the steps, and out of the precinct, pumped with the opportunity to go for the justice and ruin a few more lives.

When they arrived at Jenny Flopalis's house, the sun had reached the day's peak, warming the air to a hot and breezeless eighty-seven degrees. Upon approaching the front door, the sarge felt it necessary to give instructions. "Listen, you guys stay quiet, let me do the talking. And take some damn notes," he said, prompting the trail cop to rather feverishly pat his lapels, determining—oops—that he had forgotten his pen and pad back at the station. Quick to the jump, the other plainclothes genius whipped out his pad and pen from his jacket pocket like some annoying grade-school kid who, far too enthusiastically, holds up his neatly written math calculations after the teacher instructs everyone to take out last night's homework.

The chime of the doorbell startled the dozing assistant as she slouched on the front room's couch. Thinking it was part of a disoriented dream, she didn't move. Today's newspaper, complete with its front-page story of yesterday's guilty plea, lay open and disheveled over her lap and legs, reminiscent of some poor-soul homeless guy trying to keep warm. With yesterday's makeup beginning to crust up on her aging eyes and cheeks, Jenny was, well, not having such a good day. Beginning to wonder if she would ever hear from the monsignor, she had spent the greater part of the day whispering gibberish to herself, eating far too many white-powdered stale Hostess Donettes, and staring at the phone.

Yesterday's encounter with her adoring fans from the media had turned sour by a bombardment of intimidating questions, most aimed at painting the confused secretary as the monsignor's cohort in covering up his degenerate pedophilia with an innocent little boy. Ms. Flopalis, realizing that stardom was not all it was cracked up to be, had once again abruptly ended the media's ruckus interview. As her confusion with their questions reached its peak, she had tightly closed her eyes, placed both hands over her ears, and repeated over and over, "Know nothing, know nothing, know nothing, know nothing," finally turning and stumbling up the front-door pathway and throwing herself into the entrance with the grace of an oversized fat guy, late for the airport, squeezing into a two-seat Corvette. Unbeknownst to the assistant whose lips were still covered in white sugary powder, her escape from another interview gone bad was setting records all day on YouTube. Perhaps the only three people in Wildwood not to have heard about or witnessed the trending video were the cops now broaching on her afternoon private time.

The second ring of the doorbell shook her stillness once again, this time making clear that it was not a dream. *Maybe it's the monsignor*, she thought, causing her to rise a bit too quickly. Dizzy and faint from the sudden doughnut sugar rush, she steadied herself by grabbing the top end of the couch. After a few deep breaths, she shuffled to the door and opened it to find three men, each standing in place, displaying police badges. One of the men, the sergeant in charge, spoke up. "Wildwood police, ma'am. May we have a few moments of your time?" Operating on a dysfunctional instinct, Jenny panicked at the sight of the three policemen and their very shiny silver badges. Attempting to escape, she turned and waddled briskly away in a straight line to the opposite end of the house, placing her square in the tiny enclosed laundry room where she slammed the door shut behind her. Making neither a left nor a right, Jenny's attempt at escape was comically in full view of all three cops, including her entrance into the closet of a room with only one way in and same way out. Delirious with fear, the assistant all but lost it, surrendering whatever sanity and lucidness was left in her loony-ridden state of mind. With nowhere to run, Jenny kneeled low in the room's corner, not quite fitting in the small space between the wall and the washing machine. She reached up and pulled down a fully loaded laundry basket of dirty clothes that sat on top of the washer. Crunching as low as she could get, she dumped the basket of dirty clothes over her head, somehow convincing herself she could hide from the menacing bad men.

Slowly turning the knob and opening the air-slat door, the sergeant peeked in, seeing the now-sniffling assistant balled up in the corner, strewn with dirty clothes, and acting as if she could not be seen despite hands, arms, legs, hair, even part of her face in clear view to the bewildered sergeant.

Turning to his men, the frustrated sergeant had already begun to think about how in the hell he was going to explain this one to his lieutenant. "Call backup," he barked. "Tell them we have a transport to the South River psych unit." And to no one in particular, he walked away from the door with a despondent "Good lord!"

Within minutes, one of the detectives was slowly guiding Jenny Flopalis's head into the back of a blue-and-white Wildwood police squad car. The instruction to the uniformed cop was made very clear. She should be driven directly to Wildwood's lone mental facility. There, she would receive much-needed and long-overdue care and evaluation.

Back on campus, Father Jon received word from the precinct of Ms. Flopalis's check-in to the town's mental-care unit. He was informed that the police were obligated to reach out to the patient's family. The young priest informed the detective that Jenny Flopalis had no record of any family. However, he would inform those at the school who needed to know, along with the powers that be within the archdiocese. Satisfied, the police ended the call by asking the good priest the whereabouts of the young man Jesse, the one referred to by Sister Mary Dija during her local news interview. Father Jon had politely ended the call with a direct and simple "I have no idea."

Without much discussion, and as if the news was simply another double bogey in today's Pious round of golf, the dedicated priest and his loyal coworker, Gary Lee, got back to work organizing final grades from the spring semester and the upcoming registration for July's summer classes.

In the accounting office, Darlene Davidson was sitting motionless, trying to decide if she had it in her to post then pay the school's past-due invoices. While she had been negligent and completely unsupervised in her job's responsibilities, at the moment she was consumed with attempts to just keep her emotions in check. Yesterday's news of Stainwell's guilty plea paled in comparison to her morning's shocking revelation, one that had rocked the pretty CFO and her already, somewhat, dysfunctional world. Queasy and nauseous now for several days, Darlene had given in to her fears by waking early and making a quick visit to the town's local drugstore. She then hurried home and locked herself in the downstairs bathroom. There she sat, anxious, on the down toilet seat, awaiting the results of her home pregnancy test. As the color shade confirmed the worst of her suspicions, she had begun to cry uncontrollably, not only because the test was positive but also because the timing matched up with her regrettable encounters with Coach Sully.

Holding a towel over her face in an attempt not to be heard by her sleeping stepkids, Ash and Verona, she hastily decided to leave the house and find recluse in her small but private office at the school. Frightening thoughts rushed through her, beyond the assuredly unborn's father. Most bothersome was the awful example such a mess would set for her kids during a time where both were budding teens and presenting more and more of a challenge to control. She anticipated Sully's reaction, guessing that he would use the situation to pressure her to be with him, a desire he had made very obvious. She had finally convinced him to stop calling and was actually getting on well with Kevin, her new boyfriend. Brief thoughts entered her head that maybe she could learn to feel differently about Sully; after all, it wasn't long ago that she had an attraction toward him. *My god*, she thought, *am I even considering such a thing?* She briefly considered deceit, waiting some time until she could present a viable conclusion to Kevin that the child was his.

Her thoughts moved away from the pain of the child's father to the potential that she wouldn't be able to handle the expenses and doctor's costs presented by a new child. Disgust quickly turned to fear. For several weeks now, she had been consumed with thoughts of the school closing down, and along with it the loss of her job. How would she even begin to pay for the essentials? While a believer in life, real thoughts of abortion crossed her mind, tearing at her, knowing deep down that she could never have the ability to get over such an act.

Cognizant that she was driving herself crazy, she decided to go home and say nothing to anyone. For now, this would remain private only to her. She chided herself to act normal, to calm the hell down and figure it out. Tonight she was supposed to meet Kevin McMatty for dinner. She would go, maybe even enjoy herself. There would be no rush to decisions. Nothing would be decided today.

Up on the boardwalk, in what had become his own sleazy replica of *Cheers*, the coach sat in the dark drinking, putting on a serious late-afternoon drunken buzz. Off-season for a football coach was a time that he once enjoyed, hanging out with friends, chasing ladies, and occasionally even getting lucky. These days, however, just weren't the same. His buddy AK was gone, and frankly he was lonely most of the time. His genuine and strong feelings for Darlene and her continued rejection served to pain him and magnify his loneliness. Like most at the school, he had little motivation to attend to his job. The many off-season football details that once consumed his every moment were now ignored, causing his program to deteriorate, in line with the rest of the school's activities. Mostly, though, he just felt old, or at least older than he needed to be. Low energy, bad habits, a lack of any real friends, and fading looks all represented elements that were beating down the once-scheming, but happy-go-lucky, coach. Never all that introspective nor ever being accused as a deep thinker, he was beginning to see himself as a loser, one of those guys that he and AK used to laugh about and mock. Coach Sully was desperate for a big win, anything that would transform his approach away from thinking that every one of life's glasses was half-empty.

"I think you had enough, coach," said the bartender after noticing that the very-drunk coach had begun to wobble in his stool. "How 'bout I order you some food?"

Too drunk to even respond, Sully pushed himself off his chair and stumbled along the bar till he reached the door of the men's room. Whipping it open, he moved toward the toilet, leaned over, and began vomiting into the bowl. Unable to support himself, he fell to his knees, keeping himself upright only by leaning his body against the soiled and most-disgusting toilet. Dizzy and incapacitated, the coach could do little more than incoherently mutter the word "Darlene" over and over again.

Chapter Twenty-Nine

An Opening

THE LOCAL PAPERS had milked all they could from Oliver Stainwell's plea and the disappearance of the Club Eighteen's CEO. Law enforcement, with mandates from the top to stay quiet while threatening anyone caught leaking, was mum on any details of the plea bargain gone wrong. They were just as tight-lipped on the investigation into the whereabouts of one Anthony Sacco. With Stainwell behind bars and Sacco nowhere to be found, local news chiefs were badgering their reporters for something fresh, something new, or something that served to keep the murder story alive. With the internet refreshing its byline litter every few hours, along with each cable station's endless looping of the same stories, the pressure on the media to keep churning digestible narratives, plots, and subplots was truly becoming problematic. Feeding the monster became the element that burnt most scribes into aggressively pursuing managerial roles, cushy anchor jobs, or if both had failed to eventually find a new line of work.

Finding new stories that could grow legs for more than one day was hard work. Public appetite for stories that offset their often mundane, shitty, and boring lives had led to a willingness within scribes and pundits to often stretch the truth, that is if it meant more internet hits or greater sales of their hardcopy dailies. Often in this whirlwind of grime, people got hurt, reputations got ruined, and retractions became rare—only something done when the reporter or station's ass was thrown on the line. "Integrity and honesty doesn't sell fucken' papers" was the way some local news chief had once put it to the paper's novice staff. Ethical news guys, those that refused to succumb to the pressure to fabricate or stretch the truth, were becoming a dying breed. For most in the business, bylines had become mylines, each sleazebag looking to grab some short-lived glory and maybe even get recruited by some rival station or periodical. For the sake of salary and a little exaltation, most reporters were willing to twist the truth, sensationalize stuff not very sensational, and ultimately cause more and more among us to view the news very much like we view professional wrestling. Problem was, half the audience in this world was dumb and getting dumber as many swallowed the hook, which dangled from the oily, fake-news fishing line. Editors and news owners relied on readership ignorance, finding no moral issue turning boring bedtime stories into X-rated cheap tricks.

Some local scribe, trying desperately to promote his daily but dying podcast, had posted the now well-known video of Jenny Flopalis, eyes squeezed shut, hands over her ears, muttering her repetitive *know nothings*. Using an internet crop tool, he had dressed the pathetic assistant in a hospital gown with the South River Psych Center's logo. Over her head was a dream bubble containing the face of Monsignor Clark, with the lyrics to Patsy Cline's song "Crazy" playing in the background.

"I'm crazy for trying and crazy for crying and I'm crazy for loving you."

Worse yet, the video caught some traction and was now being carried on many popular sites, mostly those that held few content boundaries or couldn't give a shit about being sued. When one of the local TV stations made reference to it, but in its reserved judgment decided not to show it, the internet hits soared, causing the school's soiled reputation to once again be front and center. Pious employees, initially intrigued at the attention for the school, were growing tired from following this never-ending story of the misgivings at their once-proud place of employment. Some even started to intentionally hide their association with Pious College, concerned that they too would be the dragged through the slime and the mud that had stained the school and its people. Even the righteous Father Jon surreptitiously cancelled his plan to go visit the ailing secretary upon finding, watching, and *(Oh my god!)* even privately singing along with the video.

Ironically, it was only Monsignor Clark who viewed the school's scorching, awful publicity as a good thing. Never one to fail in seizing an opening, the monsignor quickly put the latest chain of events together. With all thinking of Jenny as a mental case with little to no grip on reality, her previous blurt of "maybe" as to his despicable transgressions with Jesse could now easily be explained away as the blabber of a crazy person. He even envisioned himself posturing his denial with a modicum of sympathy and concern for his once-trusted assistant. Convinced also that his accomplice Tony Sacco wasn't surfacing anytime soon, he could now go on offense, taking an aggressive stance to deny these accusations as offensive and ridiculous. He decided that he would begin his winning touchdown drive with a return to his residence and a call to Bishop Duffy from the Cape May archdiocese. But first, he needed to devise a foolproof plan to silence Jesse Kane. While in the end he realized that, should the kid decide or be persuaded to come clean, it would be his word against Jesse's: not a good thought by any stretch but also not nearly the potential disaster he had been facing just a few short weeks ago. With Sacco's disappearance and the no-nothing Oliver Stainwell ignorant to his connection to Steve Summers, the probability that he could be linked to the murder was unlikely. And with Flopalis's entry into the town's loony bin with no friends or family to come to her aid, the threats against the monsignor were now limited to a single source—Jesse Kane.

The unforeseen streak of good luck had the adrenaline in monsignor's veins coming to life. While he knew he had to be cautious in his chess moves, this was at least a start for the once-powerful Shawn Clark to regain his dominance as conqueror. A plan to ensure that the whole mess would be buried for dead would take guile and focus. He decided that one more night at the motel to think, distraction-free, was his best move. Famished, his appetite was reborn. He decided to shower and drive to the local Crab Pot restaurant he had noticed back up the road a bit. Maybe he would even have some wine with dinner while he pondered how he would deal with Jesse. He decided to don a plain blue T-shirt that he had hastily thrown into the carry-on during his quick exit from his residence. Tonight there would be no collar and no black priest shirt. Just Shawn Clark, the man, who for the first time in quite a while felt some hope, an opportunity to carve a pathway to put this whole fucked-up fiasco in the rearview mirror. It had been some time since he felt unchained. He was finally rejuvenated to just sit and think straight. He was overcome to eagerly leap into his opening, one in which he could rid himself, and right himself, from the suffocating immensity that comes with thoughts of squad cars, of arrest, of handcuffs, of courtrooms, of incarceration, and of hell.

While the monsignor sat quietly in the almost-empty restaurant a little more than a mile from Atlantic City's casino strip, Darlene Davidson was on her way home from her get-together with Kevin McMatty. Since learning of her pregnancy, she had tried to convince herself that her relatively new relationship with the school's provost was still a good thing, but lurking doubts seemed to fill most spaces around her. Unfortunately, those trepidations surfaced more when she was with him than when she wasn't.

When apart, she tried to think of him as her handsome new boyfriend, someone she was attracted to and someone who seemed to return the feeling. But as relationships would have it, his initial gentlemanly approach in wining and dining his new girl, followed by walks on the beach and long thoughtful conversations, had rapidly advanced to expectations to expand the physical nature of their connection. She had for a few weeks now been good with that. It had only been a few days ago that she had given in and had sex with Kevin.

The provost was passionate in bed and a caring sort of guy who had shown a propensity to enjoy all their time together, including now the physical sex. He had been respectful when her kids were around, often displaying an appropriate judgment and decency. He had even confided his concern for his disabled wife and her institutionalized condition. He had described her as a woman whose condition had so deteriorated that he was now unrecognizable to her. Frankly, Kevin was turning out quite opposite to the selfish womanizer, a clear reputation that preceded him. Darlene had enjoyed all facets of their new relationship and was quite willing to be part of something that was moving to the next level. Until early yesterday, that is.

Her pregnancy had caused her to feel violated and dishonored. Nowhere was the joy that was so inherently meant for such a condition. She suddenly felt the need for complete privacy, building an armor around herself. Accepting physical advances from anyone now seemed impossible and repulsive. While in some reflective moments, her wanting to deal with this news better, the CFO could not help feeling angry, mostly with herself for allowing this to happen. Having to explain her new feelings to anyone, including Kevin, was equally offensive to her, clutching the right to be accountable to no one. After dinner, she had rejected Kevin's advances without explanation. Her mindset was, at least for the time being, to be alone and make herself available only to her two kids, Ash and Verona. Her condition served to urgently sober her and created an intense desire to be closer to her children. All others in her life seemed only like obstacles to that single, and now intense, priority. While today wasn't the day, she knew that soon she would have to tell Kevin of her desire to cool their relationship, although doing so in a way that wouldn't divulge either her real reasoning or her condition.

It was almost eight thirty in the evening, and the Wildwood sun was slowly dipping its toes into the west-side Wildwood Bay. Darlene gazed at the gorgeous sunset as she made her way back to her home. She had texted both her kids of her intention to arrive home early, offering them a nice dinner or even a trolley ride to Wildwood Crest to visit their favorite ice-cream parlor. Neither had responded. Amazing to her, the void that had overcome her since confirming her pregnancy could only be filled by them. In one way she felt blessed and in another ashamed that it took this event to smack her priorities straight. Still, she was determined to make it right and become what she had always wanted to be in their lives. The school, the beach, men, and her selfishness in all of these things had knocked her off course. The CFO was urgent to make amends.

A little after 9:00 p.m., Darlene Davidson made a left onto the street of her modest home in the heart of Wildwood Beach. As her car glided slowly toward her driveway, she couldn't help notice the stark difference that nightfall had revealed between the houses on her block. Her house was all dark, unlit, and barren. Neighbors' homes, up and down the street, seemed to be buzzing on this warm early summer evening, each lit with exterior lawn and porch lights. Interior lights signaled open and active households. The houses surrounding hers struck the CFO as warm and appealing. Her own house appeared cold and uninhabited. Anxiety filled her, as she vowed, beginning immediately to turn their house into a home. It panicked her when she realized that on most nights, this was what her kids saw as they typically arrived home before her. Too many times, she had come home to find them already sleeping with the remnants of fast food and junk soda cups strewn around the kitchen and living room coffee table. This was not what she had committed either to herself or the foster-child agency just a few short years ago when she convinced the organization to allow Ash and Verona to become her family. Coming to a full stop in her driveway, she pushed the car's console arm into *park* and turned the key to shut down its engine. She decided she would call Ash before exiting the car. As she reached into her bag to locate her phone, it rang. Since neither of her kids called her much, she considered the call a distraction. Quickly she grabbed the phone from her purse and looked at the screen, intending to send the call to voice mail. She didn't recognize the incoming number but noticed it displayed area code 609, Wildwood's area code. Relieved that it wasn't Kevin, and without thinking, her curious instincts made her answer, still intending to make short work of the caller.

Almost annoyed, she said "Hello" into the phone.

The caller was serious and to the point. "Hello, this is Sergeant Sanford from Wildwood's Police Precinct. Is this Darlene Davidson?"

Nervous, Darlene answered quickly. "Yes, it is. Is something wrong?

"Yes, ma'am, there is," the cop continued. "Miss Davidson, your son Ash has been arrested. Since he is a minor, it's police protocol, ma'am, to contact you and let you know."

"Oh my god," the CFO shrieked. "Is he all right? Is he hurt? What happened?"

"The boy is fine, ma'am. He's unhurt. He, along with another boy, was arrested late this afternoon. He is accused of assault. I should tell you, ma'am, that your son has admitted that he did participate in assaulting another male. That individual has been hospitalized with several injuries, including a severe concussion. The other minor who has been charged also confirmed his participation as well."

"Oh my god!" screamed Darlene. "Who did he beat up? Why? That doesn't sound like my son!"

"I'm sorry, ma'am. I'm really not allowed to provide details over the phone. If you would like to speak to the arresting officer, I believe he is still here. But you will need to come down to the precinct. I believe your daughter is still here as well. She has been questioned and released and has been sitting here ever since. She was offered a ride home but refused. We just now communicated to her that your son would not be released tonight. I will inform her that I spoke to you."

"I'll be right there, officer. I am on my way to get them." Quickly, before the frantic mom could hang up, the cop interrupted.

"I'm sorry, ma'am. Perhaps we can get you a moment or two with your son, but the boy must remain here for the night. The courts have long since closed. He will be arraigned in the morning, and bail will be set. After satisfying that requirement, you should be able to take him with you tomorrow. In the meantime, you can contact your lawyer and have him call the precinct. Should you not have a lawyer, the court will assign one of your son's behalf."

As if not hearing a word, Darlene blurted, "I will be right there, officer." And hung up the phone.

For now, the only unlit house on the block would remain dark. Taking a few very deep breaths to steady her shaking hands, she started the car and screeched backward out of the driveway, whirled the nose in the direction of the precinct, and forcefully stepped down on the gas pedal. The ride would take but a few minutes, and the CFO consciously forced herself to ease on the gas pedal, thinking, *Don't make bad worse by getting into an accident or getting pulled over.* As the red light in her path was met with an annoyed puffing sound from her lips, without thinking, she grabbed her phone and speed-dialed a number. As the light turned green, she sped forward as the outbound phone call produced nothing but the sound of an unanswered ringing. She hit the phone's speaker button and threw it on the passenger front seat, just as the call was going to voice mail. As the phone beeped its intent to start recording, Darlene Davidson started screaming in the direction of the phone.

"Pick up the fucken' phone, coach. Jesus Christ…where the hell are you when I need you! Ash is in trouble! Meet me at the police precinct the minute you get this!"

Focused on completing her ride, she let the phone record dead air until she grabbed it as she jumped out of the car and briskly ran to the front door of the precinct.

Flinging open the door, she hopped up the small flight of steps. Her eyes scanned across the room. As she headed to the room's raised desk manned by a uniformed cop, she spotted Verona sitting hunched in the left corner of the room, nestled on the corner seat of a hard wooden bench. Her head rested between her raised knees, supported by her sneakered feet sitting on the front end of the bench. Both her arms were crossed, hugging her legs. Withdrawn into a fetal position, the young beauty appeared worn and tired.

Reversing her course, the urgent mom headed straight for her daughter.

"Verona," she called but there was no response.

"*Verona!*" she said loudly, causing the teenager to raise her head and acknowledge the intrusion. Noticeably, she had been crying, her eyes red and teary.

"What happened? Are you all right?" Still, there was no answer from her shaken stepchild.

Darlene plopped in the middle seat of the bench, within arm's length of Verona. Changing her tone, she gently pulled her daughter's closest arm toward her. "Baby, please," she pleaded. "Tell me what happened. It's okay. Open up to me. Please, honey."

Verona removed her feet and legs off the bench, attempted to sit up straight, and finally spoke.

"Ash and Blo beat up Cory, Mama. They beat him real bad. They broke his teeth and slammed his head. At the end, a cop car came. They put me and Ash and Blo in the back of the car and brought us here. Another cop stayed with Cory. He was lying on the sidewalk. Mama, there was blood everywhere. He's really hurt bad, Mama. Then they put us in a room and talked to us. Ash told them I was his sister and that I didn't do anything, so they told me I could go. They wanted to take me home, but I wanted to wait for Ash. I was confused, Mama. I wanted to find Cory too. They won't tell me where he is or if he's okay. What are they going to do with Ash? Mama I'm sorry. I'm so sorry. Is Ash gonna go to jail?"

Tears began to roll down Verona's cheeks. Darlene pulled her close and hugged her. Verona, exhausted from the day's chaos, rested her head on her mom's shoulder.

"Tell me why, Verona. Why did Ash and Blo do this? I need to know. We need to speak to a lawyer. Ash needs our help."

As Darlene waited for an answer from her daughter, the duo was interrupted by a police officer that had entered their space.

"Good evening," said the cop. "I'm Officer Saro. You must be Ms. Davidson."

Gathering herself, Darlene stood and responded. "Yes, I am. Can we see my son now?"

"I can get you in the back for a few minutes. Your daughter should probably wait here," said the cop.

"*No*, please! I need to see Ash too. Please don't make me wait here," Verona said with urgency.

Officer Saro gazed at the room. It, except for the attending desk clerk, was empty. "Irregular and most likely breaking some rule, but it's late. Please follow me and only for a few minutes. Ms. Davidson, you should be aware that neither your boy, nor your daughter, has provided us with any reasoning for this. The boy who was assaulted is currently being questioned, but frankly, they won't push him tonight. He is being monitored for a serious concussion and any real discussion with him will not occur today. Your son will be arraigned about 10 a.m. tomorrow. Please see if you can get to the bottom of this. Your lawyer can brief the judge before the arraignment. If there is any helpful rationale in this type of charge, it can favorably impact the amount of bail set by the judge."

"Thank you, officer. I need to talk to my son," said Darlene as she and Verona followed the officer to the backroom holding cells where Ash was seen lying on a small cot in the corner of the cell. Seeing his mom and Verona shook the boy to jump off the cot and approach the cell door. Removing a set of keys from a hook on the side panel of an adjacent desk, the cop opened the cell door and let Verona and Darlene walk through, before locking it behind them and walking away.

"Ash, Verona, let's sit," said their mom as she motioned them to the cot, but a few feet from where they were standing. All three squeezed side by side, with Darlene intentionally positioning herself between them.

"I'm sorry, Mom. I know how mad you must be," said Ash, head down and grim.

"I'm not angry, Ash. In fact, I blame myself if you must know. But we can talk about that later. Are you hurt in any way?"

"No," said the boy.

The concerned mom reached and grabbed his hand in hers. "Then tell me what happened. Why would you and your friend do this? It took a while for all of us to accept Cory as Verona's friend. What happened between you and him that would make you do this? What did he do that could possibly justify violence? Tell me now so I can help us deal with this. This is serious, and you must cooperate with the cops, but mostly you must be honest with me."

Ash buried his head in his chest and shook it as if to say no.

His mom, frustrated and now angered, spoke forcefully. "Damn it, Ash! Do you even realize the trouble you are in? Kids get sent away for far less than this. Tell me why."

Ash refused to answer, looking past his mother at Verona. Tears welled in his eyes. All three sat silently, waiting for the other to speak. Finally, Verona broke the silence.

"He did it for me, Mama," Verona said, weeping. "He did it for me. I shouldn't have told him, but I did. I'm pregnant, Mama. Cory got me pregnant," confessed Verona as tears rolled from her eyes.

Ash too began crying. With no answers, their mom sat stunned, and she too began crying. Finally, the overcome mom put her arms around both of her stepchildren and squeezed them close to her.

Through tears, she took a deep breath. With the passion and forgiving love that is reserved for parents only, she whispered tenderly to both of them. "It's okay. I love both of you very much. We will get through this. I promise. Let's just stick together. We all make mistakes."

Holding hands, the family of three sat still and silent. Later, there would be much talk and needed action to address and hopefully do the things that would put all of this in the past. But for now, the mom and her kids leaned into each other, thrown into the irony of goodness and love that so often tragedy can foster.

Without notice, the ringing of Darlene's phone interrupted their special moment. Darlene Davidson put her arms around the shoulders of her children and squeezed tightly.

"Let it ring," she said. "It's probably that moron football coach from the school."

All three began laughing. All three finally became family.

Chapter Thirty

Raped

EARLY-MORNING WIND BLEW mightily throughout most of southern New Jersey. Forecasts were not good for the next few days. Today called for heavy rains and wind, for areas south of Long Beach Island, a small vacation spot just off the Jersey coastline, some sixty miles north of Wildwood. Today's weather, upfront on every network and cable station, was reported as just the prelude to tomorrow's dangerous storm, currently a category 2 hurricane named Andrew. Meteorologists were all labeling the storm's path as slowly moving through the Atlantic, in direct line to strike Virginia or North Carolina sometime late tomorrow evening. While, based on reports, New Jersey's coast would be spared the worst of the storm, Wildwood's businesses were already taking precautions. Storms were nothing new for those living on the coast, and while some hurricane seasons were worse than others, local residents were experienced in the various safety and preparation routines. Fortunately for the northeast, most storms hit landfall way to their south in Florida or halfway up the eastern seaboard. Andrew's expected path was no exception. Jersey was used to dealing with storm remnants, winds and rain just beyond the outer circle of a storm's path. As was customary in these weather events, businesses were shutting down early while warning patrons that in all likelihood they would be closed tomorrow. The grunts and groans of lost vacationer revenue could be heard up and down Wildwood's main street and boardwalk storefronts. Some business owners, taking no chances, had taken to boarding up their storefronts in case the storm altered its path northward, shifting the anticipated damage and havoc from the mid-East Coast states to those in the northeast. For now, though, Jersey was reported to be safe from the hurricane's most severe impact but could expect heavy rain and winds that threatened dangerous flooding, tree damage, and potential loss of power.

The monsignor was not bothered at all by the inclement weather as he had awoken early and readied his departure from the small motel room that had served as his hideout over the past few nights. As he saw it, rain and wind would ensure a path clear of staff, students, and even media, allowing hassle-free entrance to his residence. Without distraction, he would place the call to his superiors and aggressively communicate his innocence from any allegations directed toward him. After that, he had business to take care of, and planned to end his day by seeking out Father Jon and thanking him for filling in while he was away. He planned on unequivocally informing him that he was back and that all things should return to normal.

Without an umbrella, the monsignor scurried through the rain, dropped his key in the box directly outside the motel's main office, and headed across the parking lot to his car. With the body language of someone who knew exactly where he was going, he started the car and navigated the rainy roads toward the entrance to the Garden State Parkway south.

On his ride home, the scheming priest rehearsed his pending discussion with the archdiocese. He concluded that it was actually pretty simple and, more importantly, quite feasible. Flopalis would be labeled as a harmless, confused, and dementia-riddled assistant that he had cared for and compassionately carried at the school. She had earned this temporary kindheartedness given her tenure and unwavering loyalty to the church. She had been his assistant and nothing more. Rumors of any inappropriate relationship between them were absurd and unfair to both of them. Steve Summers would be characterized as a conman and a liar simply attempting to extort the school and its leader for quick cash. AK was to be painted as a disgruntled employee and a drunk, probably amassed in large debt from gambling and who knows what else. He had recruited the help of Steve Summers in extorting the school to conceal his involvement in the scheme. In fact, their murder, as had been suggested by unnamed law enforcement, was probably the result of unpaid gambling debt with the wrong people. And finally, Jesse would be portrayed as a victim, not of pedophilia, but rather a pawn used by AK and Summers, given his sick relationship with Summers and his short employment many years ago in the rectory. His connection to the church and the monsignor was needed to make the ridiculous accusation seem feasible and prompt him and the school to comply with their blackmail. The monsignor would say that he initially had viewed the whole thing as absurd, refusing to let it interfere with his daily and always-busy duties. He would convince his superiors that he considered it, at the time, nothing more than an idle threat and one that could be ignored since at the time he had no idea of AK's involvement. He would explain that like so many things in this decaying culture, once the media got hold of the story, the truth became irrelevant for the sake of greed and sensationalism. He would suggest that things needed to get back to normal, and that meant communicating to the Pious family—all staff, students, and parents—the need to ignore the rumors and fabricated news streams. He would insist that Pious College, beginning Monday, should move on undaunted by false allegations against either its staff or administration. He would conclude that, like any story based in untruths, it would blow over quickly. The strength and integrity of the school and its leaders, vehemently refusing to give merit to false allegations and corrupted individuals, could even be used in marketing and recruitment efforts.

As the monsignor pulled into his private parking spot in front of his residence, he summoned all the grit and guile left in his tank, muttering the words "Let's do this," as he exited the car and headed for the front door.

Prepared and confident that no stone was unturned and that surprises in this roller coaster of a mess were a thing of the past, the monsignor saw no reason for delay. Kicking off his wet shoes, he sat in the chair intentionally situated for phone calls. He removed his little directory book from the top drawer of the small table supporting the phone. Locating the number, the monsignor dialed the offices of Cape May's archdiocese and boldly spoke up to the answering secretary.

"Please connect me with Archbishop Duffy. This is Monsignor Clark from Pious College." With no success in contacting the monsignor for the past several days, the archbishop quickly answered the incoming call.

For the better part of the next hour, the conversation went remarkably according to plan. With the monsignor's convincing and impeccably delivered explanation to each and every comment and question from his superior, what started as a skeptical and inquisitive tone from the archbishop rapidly turned to an accepting and almost apologetic attitude from the archdiocese's leading on-site member. The archbishop had agreed to instruct the church's public relations division to craft the positive message to the Pious community and additionally monitor the need to timely respond to any resulting negative press. With a back-to-business-like final comment, the monsignor received instructions to "Get back to work in making Pious College the area's premier educational and service-minded institution, so important to the church's mission to accommodate the many young and talented students of faith."

Monsignor Shawn Clark thanked the archbishop, hung up the phone, and joyfully slapped his bent knee, rejoicing at his status of now being back in the game. It was onto phase two of the day's critical business. Stepping into his shoes, the monsignor exited his campus residence, walked purposefully through a now-steady rain, and bent into the shelter of his car. Leaving Wildwood for the short drive to Cape May, Shawn Clark felt rejuvenated, feeling once again that he had pulled the proverbial wool over the inferior world's eyes. There was little time to contemplate whether his performance with the archdiocese was that good or if the archbishop was just that gullibly stupid.

While the wicked priest was by all measures having quite a start to his day, on the other side of town a sick and hungover Coach Sully was struggling to lift his head and reach for the half-empty bottle of water that had been sitting on his nightstand for days. Dehydrated from a night of bad bets and too much booze, the embattled coach had failed miserably on yesterday's afternoon's intent to clean up his act, stay sober, and stop by Darlene's house with a pizza-box peace offering and a bottle of dry wine. After purchasing a nine-dollar bottle of red, his afternoon decision to have one quick drink at the liquor-store bar had made swift shambles of the day's attempt at romance. One drink turned to three and when the bartender shift changed, sometime around 4:00 p.m., the hot twentysomething cutie now serving drinks took up all of his attention to well after eleven. Getting stone-cold ossified, the drunken coach had stayed on guzzling cheap scotch with beer chasers, delusional that he somehow had a shot with the pretty young bartender. Not quite remembering leaving the bar or even how he had gotten home, the coach stood over the bathroom sink contemplating self-induced vomit as this morning's prelude to his breakfast of stale bread and coffee. Like any authentic drunk, his thought pattern quickly shifted back to booze as his mood deflated, realizing that he had left the bar without the wine bottle. Not quite fully sober, any real adult thoughts were temporarily replaced with actually considering a quick return to the bar to claim the crushed dry grapes that filled the cheap bottle way before its time.

The coach sat on the edge of his bed to steady the queasy feeling of a drunk's next morning. Convinced that lying back down could only make his aging frame feel worse, the coach stood and with a rush of unintentional thought suddenly panicked, thinking that his phone may likely have gone the way of the wine bottle. As he staggered from the bedroom to the parlor, his first glance, however, was a lucky one, spotting his phone resting comfortably on the musty couch pillow across the room. With his day having no purpose or reason, he went to the device, simultaneously grabbing it as he plopped into the couch apparently fatigued from his long walk from the bedroom. There on the tattered screen of his outdated version iPhone was a missed call, a missed call from Darlene.

With a rush of adrenaline, Sully hit the number-one circle six times, a code signaling a guy who couldn't be bothered with phone security and then quickly hit the green phone cube to access his calls. *Damn*, he thought, seeing that the call was made early last night. Encouraged to see that Darlene had left a voice message, he hit the voice mail button, then the message and hoped for the best. Hearing last night's panicked call for help, the coach instantly knew that he blew it. Gone was his opportunity to be Darlene's knight in shining armor. Like the dad who couldn't avoid the urge to stop at the bar rather than go home to his ailing family, a shame overtook the meaning-well of a man who just couldn't seem to get out of his own way. Not sure of his pending excuse, the frantic shell of an adult dialed Darlene's number only to hear several rings and then her voice mail message. A man of few suitable words on a good day, the coach decided not to make matters worse and just hit the end-call button and slumped back, challenging the couch for the room's most tattered and pathetic element. The moment, their moment, had passed and with it quite possibly his best opportunity to be with Darlene.

Unbeknownst to the coach, Darlene's morning left little time for superfluous phone calls. She had just arrived at the courthouse with Verona for a pre-arraignment meeting with the public defender who had been assigned to Ash's case. Shortly after arriving, she was summoned to a back room past the high desk and through the far-end dark wooden door. Today, Verona was given no choice but to wait on the bench that had been yesterday's only friend. She watched as a short and rather plump uniformed cop led her mom through the door and out of sight. In familiar territory the pretty, and now-pregnant, teenager assumed yesterday's pose, knees raised and head resting comfortably between them, eyes staring down at her summer-white sneakers.

The cop escorted Darlene to a door halfway down the left hallway, opposite a small kitchenette. Another uniformed cop, back turned, was brewing up a fresh pot of the precinct's morning coffee. Hearing their footsteps, he turned his head and acknowledged Darlene's presence with a smile and slight head nod. Darlene smiled back and paused as her escort opened the door and allowed her to enter the room. Facing her entrance, seated on metal folding chairs tucked neatly under a plain-white folding table, was Ash and a young man in a gray suit. To most women the lawyer was a heartthrob, a ten with movie-star good looks, clean and polished. Forgetting the moment, Darlene momentarily stared at his handsome looks, unable to turn away. Her quick glance at Ash brought the mom back to the day's purpose. Obvious to her, Ash had been crying. She headed straight for her son, leaned down, and hugged him, assuring him things would work out. The man stood and addressed the mom.

"Ms. Davidson, my name is Jack O'Brian. I am with the Public Defendant's Division of Wildwood, and I have been assigned to your son's case. Please sit down."

Darlene quickly took a seat opposite Ash and the lawyer.

"Mr. O'Brian, please explain the proceedings, as I am in unchartered waters here. Is everything all right? You both seem very concerned."

Ash's lawyer looked squarely into Darlene's eyes and confirmed the worst.

"I'm afraid I have some very bad news, so I will get right to it. Mr. Penstar, the young man who was beaten yesterday, has tragically passed away overnight. Apparently, the trauma to his head caused a severe brain hemorrhage. The hospital's urgent attempt to rush him to surgery to stop the bleeding was too late. While we will eventually receive a report, I am told the hemorrhage came on swiftly, and there was not anything anyone could do to prevent this. I am also told that every precaution had been taken in caring for this man, including every protocol in dealing with a severe concussion."

Darlene, mouth open and tears welling in her eyes, reached out and grabbed Ash's hand, squeezing it tightly. "Dear god," was all she could mutter.

A few seconds of silence filled up the room, threatening to suffocate the shocked and confused mom. Seeing the panic on Ash's face, she gathered herself and matter-of-factly moved the conversation forward with the only thing she could think of to defend and protect her son.

In desperate screams, she shot back at the lawyer.

"HE RAPED MY DAUGHTER! HE RAPED MY DAUGHTER! We have proof. My daughter is pregnant! Ash was just protecting her. Oh my god! Oh my god! What will happen now?"

Darlene's passionate response caused Ash to lose control. He began crying and violently started to bang his fist into the table, causing a ruckus that forced the lawyer into action. He grabbed Ash's wrist aggressively, and with a tone that demanded rather than asked, he spoke, "Please, Ash! Please, Ms. Davidson! Calm down. If they are forced to enter the room, the police will take Ash with them, and there will be no meeting. Ash gets arraigned in less than an hour. We must talk this out. Your anger and emotions are not helping matters. Please! Both of you must calm down."

The lawyer's words were received loud and clear. Both mom and son took deep breaths, controlling their urge for outburst. Darlene was eager to proceed.

"So how does this change things? Will we be able to explain how this happened? Can Ash still come home today?"

The calm lawyer slightly raised his hand, palm out, as if to indicate his intent to talk and explain things. His words were carefully stated and brutally honest. He was a man who clearly had gone through this before.

"At his arraignment, Ash's charge will be changed to murder."

"*Murder*," shrieked Darlene, as Ash buried his face in his hands.

"Please, Ms. Davidson, please let me finish. We will of course plead not guilty. In cases such as these, it is typically not too difficult to convince the prosecutor of the absence of intent. I should be able to, fairly quickly, get the charge reduced to manslaughter."

Darlene interrupted, "What does that mean?"

"It means that Ash had no intention for this outcome. Murder charges require a level of premeditation. That is not the case here. The prosecution understands that during this initial proceeding, many things will ultimately change, including perhaps the offering of a plea deal. I also should be able to get Ash's statement from yesterday thrown out given he provided nothing in writing, and at the time, he had not yet been provided a lawyer."

Ash interrupted the discussion. "Will I be able to go home today? I want to go home." Darlene accentuated her head nod in the direction of the lawyer and peered at him awaiting his response.

"Ash is a minor. I will fight to have the courts continue to consider him as such. In rare cases, the prosecution has the flexibility to treat minors as adults. I don't believe that will be attempted here. After we make our plea of not guilty, the judge will give us a date to return. During that time, I will speak to the prosecutor and have much more information for us to consider. In any case, I will ask that bail be minimal, and that Ash be released as a minor, in your custody. The prosecution may argue otherwise. It will be strictly up to the judge to grant bail and then, if granted, set the bail amount. I will make clear that Ash has no prior record, which should help. Once bail is set, it will be up to you to provide the bail amount, and then Ash may return home. In my experience, rarely is bail denied for a minor, especially one with no record of previous aggression or crime."

"Thank you, sir," said Darlene. "What will we do after that? How will we defend ourselves?"

"Ms. Davidson, may I suggest that we get through the day. There will be plenty of time to carve out our strategy. I must have a chance to talk to the prosecution, and based on your previous and very serious accusation against Mr. Penstar, we must talk and determine many facts related to that claim. I don't believe this is the right time. Frankly, your claim is different than how Ash described your daughter's relationship with Mr. Penstar. We must be careful what we say moving forward. We must align all stories before we communicate them. That said, your daughter is also a minor, and willing or unwilling, we may have a clear statutory rape claim here, if we can clearly show, through testing, that the pregnancy matches Mr. Penstar. *But*, and I emphasize *but*...we are getting way ahead of ourselves here. Let's get through the arraignment, and then we can set some times to meet and discuss our plan for defense. This is a serious matter, and Ash clearly was involved here. That much cannot be denied, particularly with a codefendant involved."

"Blo. Oh my god, Blo. Where is he? Is he all right? Oh my god!"

"Your son's friend," started Mr. O'Brian, "has been assigned his own public defendant. I am told he is fine. It *is not* the time to talk to him, nor would the prosecution or the police allow it at this time. Let's just concern ourselves with Ash today." Beginning to stand, the lawyer ended the meeting. "We must go, Ms. Davidson. The cops will take care of Ash. We will see him in the courtroom. Ash, please don't discuss anything with anybody. We will see you shortly upstairs."

Upon leaving the room, two cops entered and quickly began escorting Ash back to the building's holding cell. The lawyer leaned into Darlene and whispered that he would meet her upstairs. Without waiting for a response, he began walking toward the back private steps up to the courtroom. Darlene, a bit mesmerized by the handsome young lawyer, watched him walk away and then headed back to reunite with Verona. Opening the door, from across the room Darlene could see Verona staring up at her like a loyal dog waiting for her master. She gave her mom a hopeful smile, appearing desperate for good news. Darlene felt sick with anguish. She had to hurry and get upstairs for Ash's arraignment. First, however, she needed to spend a moment with Verona, somehow telling her that Cory, the father of her expected child, was dead.

Striding toward her daughter, Darlene knew that language contained no words to communicate these painful circumstances. Over the last few days, the worn-out mom's strength had been tested like never before. The shock of her own pregnancy could at least be personal, a sullen regret born of her own poor decisions. But it was on her and her alone. Upon the reality that she had no choice but to accept her condition, she realized that she had the power to own it and mask it to her children in a way that was positive, with little effect on their lives and their futures. She had gathered a committed determination to use her condition as a catapult for change, to be home more, to create an environment of a loving home and to make up for the self-centeredness that instigated and caused her predicament. Before news of Ash's arrest, she had been moving toward an inner peace and a frame of mind that made her pregnancy a constructive event in her family's lives. Unsure how she would deal with the coach, she considered that secondary, something for down the line and only after it was all good with Ash and Verona.

But this was different. Ash and Verona's situations were way beyond what she could control. Their hurt and the impact on their futures were almost too much to take. She was overwhelmed, inexperienced, weakened, and frankly out of her league. Worse, she was without the support of anyone close in her life. She was in solitary agony. She blamed herself for their mess, as it was her selfishness that allowed her kids to veer off course. She had condoned Verona's relationship with Cory partly because she didn't commit the time to communicate and guide her away from such a potentially destructive relationship. She also gave in, accepting a quick fix of happiness for Verona, rather than imparting a discipline born through hard love and one that was knowingly in Verona's best interest. The possibility or the apparent probability of her teenager's unsafe and premature intercourse was staring at her and she did nothing, a passive and derelict acceptance that would serve to haunt her forever. She had failed her children, and now they were paying a price owned by her, not them. The magnitude of these events was overwhelming her, and the lack of any real answers to make it better left her fragile and helpless.

Darlene approached her daughter slowly while she searched for words that were not to be found. Crippled with emotion, she sat and hugged Verona, uttering, "I'm sorry, I'm so sorry for letting you down. I love you, baby. Mom is so sorry." Feeling her mother's pain, Verona began crying in her arms.

Darlene, holding her daughter tightly, began to whisper into her ear.

"Baby, mom needs to tell you some bad news before we go upstairs to be with Ash."

Verona pulled back, freeing herself from her mother's grip. "Ash, Mama. Is Ash going to go to jail?"

Darlene was about to answer, but the two were interrupted by the room's front door swinging open. Rushing in, head on a swivel turning right and left, was Coach Sully. Spotting Darlene, he quickly approached, transforming the ladies' quiet and somber conversation to an aggressive and frenzied urgency. Ignoring Verona, the coach addressed the mom, whose was clearly upset over his intruding presence. Typical of the crude coach, his body language and demeanor was contrary to the needs of the moment.

Before Darlene could rein in his oncoming interruption, he divulged the traumatic overnight news. "Darlene! What's going on? It's all over town. Cory's dead! They're saying it was Ash. Jesus, Darlene! Is it true?"

The coach's words threw Verona into shock. Staring at her mom, the young girl's breathing became erratic. Struggling to react, Verona let out her one-word reaction, as she cocooned her body into a ball on the bench. "*Nooo!*" The word hurled Darlene off the bench. With the ferocity of a mom whose child was being threatened, she slapped the coach's face with all her might. Grabbing Verona's hand, she pulled her off the bench and rushed out of the precinct, down the cobblestone sidewalk, and up the stairs to the public entrance of the adjacent courtroom. At the top of the stairs, she hugged the limp body of her daughter.

"Baby, please. I'm so sorry. Be strong for me, honey. Be strong. We must help Ash now. We will talk later. Please, honey. We will get through this. Please, baby."

Without allowing a response, Darlene flung open the courtroom door and pulled her daughter through. Together they entered the room that would ultimately hold the fate of Ash's freedom. Darlene scanned the room. The handcuffed boy could be seen being led into the courtroom through a doorway and up the far-right aisle where he was summoned to a seat next to an already-sitting Jack O'Brian. Darlene continued to pull a crying Verona to the bench directly behind Ash. Verona, sniffling and weak, leaned into her mom, who wrapped both arms around her. There they sat, quiet and motionless, Verona's head buried into her mother's body and Darlene's eyes staring at the back of her troubled son. All present, including now the brash Coach Sully who had followed and taken a seat in the room's last bench, they sat silent waiting for the judge to enter.

Finally, from the court's comfortable chambers and through the back door came the judge. To Darlene's pleasant surprise, the judge was an African American woman. The court officer issued the opening mandate. "All rise. This court is in session. The honorable Kay Anton presiding. Your Honor, the case before the court is the County of Wildwood Beach vs. minor Ash Davidson. The charge, Your Honor, is murder in the first degree."

Showing no emotion, the mid-aged judge peered from her high-top desk as the stenographer, sitting below and just under the witness stand, stood ready.

Addressing the prosecution, the judge asked, "Has the prosecution been fully briefed?"

"Yes, Your Honor" was the answer from the tall, plain-looking, gray-suited man sitting at the table opposite Ash and his lawyer.

The judge, looking now at Jack O'Brian, continued, "Has the defendant's office and its lawyer been fully briefed?" Similarly, Mr. O'Brian responded, "Yes, Your Honor."

"And how does the defendant plead?"

Mr. O'Brian, without hesitation, matter-of-factly answered, "Not guilty, Your Honor."

The judge took a moment to silently read some papers that had been placed on the desk prior to her entrance and then stared down Ash. It was as if she was letting her experience compare the feasibility of the charge to the look of the young boy before her. Placing the papers back down on the desk, she spoke. "Hearing is set for two weeks from this day, in this courtroom. I expect that, between now and then, the counsels from both sides communicate with each other and then prior to the hearing state their intent to me. The defendant is a minor and therefore shall be detained by the Security Division for Minors until he reenters the court for this hearing. Are there any questions?"

Jack O'Brian quickly responded. "Yes, Your Honor. The defendant is sixteen and resides in a caring home. The boy's mother recognizes the severity of both this event and this charge. The boy has no previous arrests nor has he, at any time in the past, been in any trouble of any kind. We respectfully request that a reasonable bail be set and the boy be authorized to stay at home until the hearing, under the supervision and custody of his mother."

"Counselor, I have considered those facts long before I entered this courtroom. This, however, is a charge that does not warrant any further consideration. Request denied." Rising from her chair, the judge barked one final statement. "This court is adjourned." And with that the no-nonsense judge turned and exited through the back door and into her chambers.

Darlene reached out to touch Ash. The boy turned to his mom, tears welling in his eyes. With the hardness of a routine that contained no room for compassion, two court officers quickly led Ash out of the courtroom. Darlene turned to Verona, who stood frozen with both hands over her face. Darlene reached out and hugged her daughter closely. The arraignment, along with any hope for a positive day's outcome, had ended. Both the distraught mom and her distressed daughter would leave the building with only worries and a host of unanswered questions.

Chapter Thirty-One

I Quit

FRANKLY, SISTER DIJA could have done worse. While generally a poor area, Loja, Ecuador, had over the last ten years developed itself both economically and culturally. With 98 percent of its people considered *mestizo,* that of combined European decent, the town had developed into a region of both music and culture. Lives were simple in Loja, and living standards were rising above many of the poor and struggling areas of Ecuador. In Loja, while development was slow, it was steady, with most of its inhabitants following daily unpretentious and modest routines integrated within long-standing religious values.

Ten years ago, the little Spanish servant of God would have accepted her place and her work in this little province capital, nestled nicely in the southern part of the country bordering its neighbors of Peru. But that was then, not now. Dija had changed. Gone was the satisfaction born from selflessness, overcome by new feelings of self-identity and personal desires. Even for nuns, Wildwood Beach had a way of magnetizing people in front of their mirrors, assessing what they had and more prevalently what they were due. In Wildwood, most pushed for accelerated self-fulfillment. People led lives filled with superficial sequences that reached for a selfish destiny, one that ignored the values of virtue and generosity. Too many people of decency and faith had hightailed it out of Wildwood, making room for egotism and a general air of dishonesty.

Sister Dija, having now tasted the spoils of pleasure, didn't fit anymore in a place like Loja, and today she was determined to take the plunge into a world unknown. Sitting at her small desk in the cramped room provided by her order as home, she began to write.

> Dear Sister Angelina, Hermanas Dominicanas de la Caridad
>
> Today I tell you that I leaving the order and no more can be Sister Dija. Now I need be just Mary Dija. Me sorry to tell you this but my heart tell me what to do and my job to follow my heart. I go back to Unites States to live and make my life. Me sorry. Me go see Monsignor Clark and talk about job. Thank you for all Hermanas Dominicanas do for me. I hope you be well and understand.
>
> Mary Dija.

Finished with her resignation letter, Mary Dija gently placed the letter on the bed next to the neatly folded robes and habit head-dresses, all that was left of her once-meaningful way of life. She was leaving in a short cotton skirt covering her only clean pair of skimpy white panties. Tattered flat sandals covered the bottom of her feet, and her top was scantily covered with a clean and soft little white T-shirt. With her bras tucked tightly in her small travel bag, her breasts' dark nipples bulged into her top, bound to arouse any lucky traveler who happened to cross her path.

Before leaving, she stared down at her garments that laid claim to the vocation she once loved. Gently, she kneeled on one knee by her bed and lowed her head.

"Me sorry, Lord. Please forgive me," she whispered. And with that, after only a few days into her new assignment, it was over. Mary Dija was on her way to the airport, headed back to Wildwood Beach.

What little money she had saved as a nun wouldn't last long. She would quickly go see the monsignor and pretend not to be mad at him. She would beg for her job back, but this time as a layperson that wanted desperately to make a sustainable life for herself. She would also go see Jesse. Not experienced nor versed in the world of relationships, she viewed her single encounter with the young man as an awkward commitment between the two.

It was her plan to talk to Jesse and tell him that she wanted to be his partner, clearly exposing herself as a naive beginner in relations with a man. She was a newcomer in both love and sex, whose inexperience in such matters was teenage like. Her gullibility and lack of any long-formed opinions made her vulnerable but also attractive beyond her outward beauty, a cute obliviousness from a drop-dead gorgeous and petite young woman.

In her favor, Jesse too was a novice in these matters. Sheltered and without the guile of a normal mid-twenties male, he had for years been treated as half-lover, half-child by Steve Summers. His growth had been stunted and his attributes misused by his selfish and conniving partner. Like Mary Dija, he had little savvy regarding relationship normalcies and lacked any real understanding of what was appropriate versus what was not.

Conceivably it was possible that, for Mary Dija and Jesse Kane, their stars were well aligned in this universe or perhaps that the world's fate stood by chuckling as it had comically threw two like creatures together to form one unusual but stimulating duo.

As her plane took off, headed for the States, Mary Dija sat in the back row of the aircraft and stared out the window. Although nervous, she was determined not to spend the whole flight questioning her decision and her future. After landing, she decided that she would head straight to monsignor's residence and beg for her job back. She felt confident that he wouldn't refuse her. She would then stay in the town's motel until she could find Jesse, assuring herself that he would welcome her. Together, they would take care of each other.

Back in Wildwood, the town was patiently readying itself to clean up the fallen branches and debris left behind by the outer rims of Hurricane Andrew. Like most storms on the East Coast, the worst of the hurricane had hit landfall far south of the Jersey coastline, flooding the shores of South Carolina and causing havoc on beach towns and small communities. Declared a natural disaster, crews from far north and south of the storm were providing all they could to restore power to the thousands affected. South Carolina's tourist towns like Hilton Head Island and Myrtle Beach were frantically attempting to address the mess left behind by Andrew. Square in the midst of their prime revenue seasons, personnel from local businesses and resorts were all in, doing what they could to clean up and open their doors for business. The storm had hit Carolina's coast hard, then boomeranged like a horseshoe back out into the Atlantic and was making its way north some 150 miles off its coast. For New Jersey, that meant continued heavy rains, weather that was impacting the town's efforts to get on with its summer fun.

For Jesse Kane, the weather represented a distant second to the day's threats for disruption. He had started his day by answering the knock on his newly rented room's front door in the small community of Cape May. The Wildwood police had tracked him down and asked that he come with them back to Wildwood to answer a few questions. His response that he had already done that the night of AK's wake didn't seem to impress either of the uniformed officers, so without choice, he had taken the short ride north in the whistling squad car and was now sitting in the precinct's small room reserved for such a proceeding. Remarkably, his nerves were steady, and he reminded himself to keep his answers brief. From all appearances, the good-looking young man seemed surprisingly calm and collected. For Lieutenant Burns who was conducting the questioning, Jesse's demeanor was frankly just a bit too well prepared.

The lieutenant, still seething from letting Tony Sacco disappear, stood in the corner of the room peering out the window, as Jesse sat at the table patiently awaiting the first question. As he sat still, the young man eyed the stripes and ribbons up and down the cop's arms and chest. He remembered Steve telling him that cops, like firemen, were really only guys that were going nowhere in life so they became servants of the people, instantly transforming themselves from losers to men who commanded respect. For Steve Summers, Jesse recalled, he didn't buy any of it. He had told Jesse to remember his words if he was ever confronted by a cop. Such thoughts he had said will allow you to be relaxed and incapable of being intimidated.

On this day, Burns had decided to take the casual approach to his inquisition rather than any attempt at frightening the youngster with the darkroom-and-spotlight approach. With the grace of a dog in heat, he turned toward Jesse and got right to the point. "Is there any truth to a blackmail attempt by Mr. Summers, or even by you, against the priest at Pious College?"

Jesse immediately responded. "Officer, not that I know about. Steve never told me anything like that."

The detective approached Jesse and sat across from him. With a tone that attempted to put Jesse at ease, he calmly spoke. "Listen, Jess, there is no reason to be nervous here. It is not you we are interested in. You are not in any trouble. We are more interested in the priest. You know, the president of the college."

"I'm not nervous. I just don't know how I could possibly help."

Lieutenant Burns followed up. "You know, Jesse, some at the college have seemed to imply that perhaps the priest had done some bad things to you a long time ago. And that somehow those things are connected to your friend's death. Is that true?"

Jesse's answer was quick. "No."

Taken aback by Jesse's blunt response, the lieutenant leaned back in his chair, displaying an exaggerated look of disbelief. "Why then would the nun and even the priest's assistant seem to say that he had hurt you in some way? Surely you must be aware of the protest that was attended by many of the faculty. Why would they gather like that? Could they *all* be wrong?"

Jesse paused to think, and then spoke in a tone of candor. "I can't say what they were doing. I wasn't there. The priest, actually he's a monsignor, was always nice to me back then. Frankly, I was a kid. I don't remember much other than I didn't work there very long. It was a long time ago."

Frustrated and going down yet another fruitless road, the lieutenant became more blunt. "Are you denying that the priest, the monsignor, abused you in any way? In any way, Jesse! Are you absolutely sure?"

"Abused? What does that mean? No, I don't remember feeling abused."

Burns, now a bit desperate to hear something, anything, to act on, came very close to pushing his questions toward the desired answer. "Jesse, please try to remember. You were just a kid. Did the priest ever say things to you that made you feel uncomfortable? Did he touch you at all, maybe even where he shouldn't have? Did he ever ask you to do anything that an adult shouldn't ask to a kid?"

Jesse Kane, showing an uncharacteristic firmness, simply looked straight at the lieutenant and stopped the exasperated cop cold. "No, sir. None of that ever happened."

"Then, Jesse, this conversation is over. Frankly, I'm surprised at your answers."

Jesse said nothing, shrugging his shoulders as if to say, "Sorry, Officer, but I can't help you."

Walking out of the room, Lieutenant Burns turned with all the words he had left for today's very unsuccessful encounter. "Okay, Jess, if you think of anything, give us a call. I'll have one of the boys take you back to Cape May." With that, he was gone, whispering to a newbie cop standing in the hallway, "Get this lying bastard back to the Cape," and within minutes, Jesse sat silent in the cop car's back seat, content that he had done good. As he gazed out the window, watching the rain continue to fall heavy on the streets of Wildwood Beach, he had, as he intended to do, passed today's exam.

Chapter Thirty-Two

The End That Wasn't

THE PLANE FROM Loja, carrying the former nun, would land at Philadelphia's International Airport at 7:00 p.m.

Mary Dija had booked a 7:40 p.m. Amtrak train that would get her into Wildwood Beach before 10 p.m. She planned on catching a cab to campus, and if all went well, she would be at monsignor's residence by 10:30 p.m. She figured that arriving late would be to her benefit as the monsignor would surely be home. The campus would be dark and quiet, a setting she thought might help to secure the answer she desperately needed from the college president.

What the ex-nun had not considered was the torrential rain forecasted to flood the South Jersey coastline well into the night and through most of tomorrow's morning. The plane from Loja had departed on time, and only as it got close to its destination did the aircraft's captain inform the passengers that the rather bumpy ride was the result of some nasty rain and wind that was here for the night. Seatbelt signs, he noted, would stay lit for the remainder of the flight. With such details out of her control, the petite woman of determination stayed the course, resolved to willing her way to achieve the night's mission.

Considering the weather, Mary Dija's flight did well to make time into Philadelphia, landing at seven ten and giving the anxious little traveler more than enough time to walk the short path through the terminal, down the escalator, and onto the train-track platform where she would stand, patiently awaiting her connection to Wildwood. She barely noticed the other scattered passengers, mostly male, who had gathered on the platform, eyeing her skimpy outfit on an unusually chilly night that clearly called for a light jacket or cover-up. The chill in the air only exasperated her now goose-bumped nipples, which seemed to be begging for their freedom from her nearly see-through T-shirt. As she stood there glancing down the track's tunnel waiting for the train's headlights to break through the darkness, she was unaware that her breasts and petite exposed legs were the centerpiece of each man's fantasy stare down. The platform was silent, mostly the result of each man's refusal to waste such moments with chatter and of course the natural physiological fact that penises grew into erections, typically without making a sound.

Mary Dija was caught up in her thoughts, surprisingly past her upcoming encounter with the monsignor, to Jesse Kane. She was engulfed in her own vision of love for the young heartthrob, never considering that such feelings were merely infatuation with a man who she really did not know. Consumed by her memory of her first and their single sexual episode, her brain sent waves to her senses, as she could smell the scent of his seed dripping down her cheeks and into her mouth and nose. Without warning, her thoughts were rudely interrupted with the sound of a rumbling train and its bright lights barreling down the tracks and into the station. Her focus quickly shifted to the present, attempting to read the moving destination signs posted on the side scroll of the train. Her face squinted in confusion, like she was expecting a clearer sign, maybe one that read *Monsignor Clark's Residence*. Worried, she confirmed with the closest, and luckiest, passenger that the train did stop in Wildwood. Told that it did, she boarded and took a seat snugged in the mostly out-of-sight back corner of the train, generally to the chagrin of her new fans from the platform. She decided to spend the ride now thinking about her pitch to the evil priest of power.

The rain back in Wildwood was heavy, at times horizontally pelting the modest line of mourners waiting to get in to the funeral home to show their respects for the young lifeguard who had passed way before his time. Umbrellas, of the cheap kind were generally useless in this windy downpour. Still, those who were enduring this soaking seemed intent on paying their respects to Cory Penstar, a well-known native of Wildwood Beach, a liked young man who was many things, but mostly one of their own. Those who had showed up on this stormy night had been closely following the story of his murder in the papers and were well aware of who had committed this heinous crime. Few, however, actually knew Ash Davidson, and none understood the reason for his uncharacteristic act of violence. Since Cory's death, Ash's stepmom had become the town outcast, with many spouting the rumor that Darlene was just another case of a white lady taking in a black kid for the foster care money, with little intent to provide proper parenting. Most saw Ash and Blo as two of the many new undesirables in town. These savages had killed their Cory, and they should be punished severely, never again allowed to walk the streets of their hallowed beach village.

Up the road, caged in a small dirty cell in Ocean City's north-side penitentiary, sat Ash. Like lunch, he had not bothered to touch the mush that had been provided for his dinner through the plate hole in the locked iron door of his cell. Late the previous night, he had been transported to his new quarters from the holding cell of Wildwood's precinct. He would stay confined in Ocean City, await-ing his pending case to start, still weeks away from this very gloomy evening. His mom, who had paid the single allowable daily visit ear-lier in the day, was now sitting at home with Verona. Not up to the task on this night, Darlene, at some point in the near future, did plan on telling her daughter about her own pregnancy. Her delay in telling Verona stemmed mostly from the anxiousness caused by Ash's plight but also to ensure that she captured the right words, in the right time. There was still work to do in convincing herself that her news would serve to bring the two mothers-to-be closer, maybe even rendering a bond used by both to somehow get through this ordeal.

Darlene had decided not to solicit another attorney, as Ash's assigned public defender had impressed her. She assured herself that her decision to stick with Jack O'Brian had little to do with his charm

244

and good looks, although privately, she knew that a male's strength and companionship would go a long way in offsetting her daily feelings of fear and loneliness, not to mention her oft moods of being downright horny. Despite those feelings, Darlene was staunchly unwilling to reach out to Coach Sully, having now considered it a mistake calling him the night of Ash's arrest. Her belly was still flat, and she had decided not to even consider discussing her pregnancy with him until she began to show. Even then, her message would be one that demanded financial support and little else.

Sully, having failed miserably to support his heartthrob during her time of need and with no knowledge of his pending fatherhood, was back to generally what he did best, or worst as one might think of it. Each day was filled with recovery time from the previous night's boozing, followed by forcing himself out of his disgusting apartment to some local gin joint where he would repeat the rerun of placing a bet that was not very well thought out, and drink himself silly while waiting for the results. He lived spending all that he made, promising himself that he would sometime soon stop the routine of slowly killing himself and get back to coaching his team. He justified everything in his decaying life to needing a break from football and this was, after all, the off-season.

Back at school, most of the faculty members and staff were nowhere to be found, except for those whose responsibilities caused them to be occasionally at the school during the summer. Minimal effort by all was clearly the popular approach, as fall opening was still weeks away. That is with the exception of Gary Lee and Father Jon.

The young priest and his informal assistant kept busy with the multiple tasks that helped the school get through its summer sessions and ready itself for the coming year's fall semester. Privately, Father Jon had begun the task of researching other job opportunities, knowing full well that with the monsignor back, nothing of substance would change for the positive. Until such an opportunity presented itself, the good priest did what he always did—what was right and what was best that day for the school.

Gary Lee, well, he was ridiculously wealthy and generally enjoyed his role as AD. He had convinced one of Jersey's top track recruits to register for the fall semester, somehow selling his family that he would be a big fish in a small pond, and that would allow his star to shine brighter. With recruiting, he was well aware that most parents had an inflated opinion of their child's ability and promising consistent headlines for their little superstar often did the trick. Without Pious, Gary figured he would have to be closer to the source of his wealth, his father. Deep down, the Pious AD was proud of his dad's success but was always uncomfortable watching the way his family flaunted their money within a general air of arrogance. The farther he was from his father, the better. Mostly, though, Gary had a practical way of looking at things. While generally a good soul, he saw the series of headline events at the school as a good thing, maybe not good publicity but in the end positive opportunities for change. While not blind to the fact that Pious College seemed to be marred in a chain of less-than-flattering headlines, he continued to think that Pious was a good place, a worthwhile institution of higher learning. For as long as he could remember, he viewed Dean Kenny as a drunk who didn't deserve his noble position at Pious. Never wishing him dead, Gary simply viewed the facts as the facts, and with AK's passing, he saw an opportunity for the school to materially upgrade this important post. With Sister Dija, he viewed her transformation as one from an underqualified director of development to a wannabe Hooters girl, nothing more. For some time, he felt that the head of Pious's Development Division should be experienced in marketing and fundraising, neither relying on a religious vocation nor Sister Dija's undeniable sweet and petite curves. With her departure, he would push for a knowledgeable fundraiser who was apt at branding the school in a professional and worthwhile light to both alumni and philanthropists. Lastly, with Jenny Flopalis, he saw her recent exit as mere addition by subtraction. For years, he had little patience for the nimble-minded assistant. Often, he had felt she was a detriment as one of the "faces" of the school.

Yes, Jenny, like AK and the little nun, were now gone. Ms. Flopalis was now a full-time resident at the town's lone center for the mentally disabled. Sad, really, that her days and nights were filled with the same abstract behavior so often the case with her disease.

Minds inflicted with dementia typically latch onto a single theme and repeat that theme endlessly, unaware of their continual reiteration of the same words or story line. Just after her arrival at the center, Jenny had found a Raggedy Ann doll in the small pile of toys and books, a collection of mostly children's items that were used to entertain the ward's population of dementia patients. The aids had long since realized that those with this serious mental diagnosis seemed to be interested in, and even comforted by, the various assortment of kids' toys and articles. Instantly, Jenny had picked up the tattered red-haired doll and held it close, eating, sleeping, and comforting the little doll, convinced that it was her own child. Tens and tens of times each day, Jenny would approach one of the ward's workers and ask, "Has the monsignor come today to see me? He must know that I have found our baby. We never really wanted to give her away, you know. But he said we had to so we did. But now I've found her. I must tell him. Has he come today to see me?"

Over and over, to anyone who would listen, often even to visiting guests of patients, Jenny would ask about the monsignor and tell her little story. It had gotten so dominating to her daily routine that the nurses and other aids, never considering any validity to her rants, had often played along. They would compassionately or even between themselves comically continue the conversation by telling her such things as the monsignor was busy today, or he had called and that he would come soon to see her and their baby. While some might have viewed these responses as somewhat cruel, the staff was only applying a sense of calm to Jenny, doing what was required to get her through each day. Playing along seemed to ease Jenny's mind, keeping it free of the agitation and mood swings that often accompanied dementia. The nurses played a critical role in these wards, often while the physicians struggled through the trial and error to find the right medication and dosage levels for each patient. A nurse stationed in a dementia ward was one of the true servants of God, people of patience and compassion, the world's most loving souls. If kindheartedness and an unwavering ability to sustain it weren't inherently part of your internal fabric, then frankly, you wouldn't last long in such a position. For Jenny, still measured by the center's physicians as only in the early stages of her dementia-like condition, the nurses were her daily lifeboat in the babbling assistant's very turbulent sea.

It was 9:55 p.m., and the Amtrak slowly came to a squeaky stop in the outdoor Wildwood station. Except for a few overhangs, the stone and concrete platform yielded little cover from the continuing downpour that would drop over two inches of rain on the soaked little beach town. Holding nothing but a carry-on sized bag that now claimed her life's possessions, Mary Dija braved the weather and struggled to the small cab station some fifty yards from the platform. Within seconds she was drenched, her soaked shirt stuck tight to her breasts and body, the white tee now taking the shade of her young and smooth Spanish skin. Sopping wet and now shivering from the night's chill, the X-rated looking little dynamo moved quickly across the small parking lot and opened the door to the small taxi hut. Entering, she found only a single female dispatcher sitting behind a small desk cluttered with communication equipment, strewn papers, and the leftovers from tonight's McDonald's meal.

"Oh my god, girl," said the nose-ringed twentysomething-year-old. "You must be freezing."

"Yes, me very silly," said Mary Dija, noticing that the wide-eyed young woman was now intently staring at her swollen dark-brown nipples stuck firmly to her soaked shirt.

"Silly? What does that mean?"

"No, silly, silly like cold," said the ex-nun.

"Oh chilly, haha, you funny girl. Come with me, quick before you catch pneumonia." She grabbed Mary's hand and pulled her to the back room where she pulled off her Jimmy's Taxi Service gray hoodie, exposing her arms and Save the Planet T-shirt, each arm displaying full sleeves of tattoos, wrist to shoulders.

"Here, sweetie, gimme that shirt and put this on. It's not much but at least it's dry." Mary Dija, taken aback and leery of her request, stood still and said nothing.

"Jesus, girl, I don't bite. Gimme that shirt. I'll throw it in a bag, and then we'll get you a car. Return the sweatshirt the next time you're around." Placing the hoodie over the top of an open locker, the woman reached for the bottom of the dripping ex-nun's top, grabbed each side, and lifted firmly, pulling the soaked shirt over Mary's head, exposing her young ripe breasts. "Jesus, girl, you sure do got it going on. You have a killer body. You into girls? 'Cause I can go both ways."

Mary Dija, unusually calm considering she was now topless, uttered slowly, "Me need to go. I have important meeting in college."

"Yeah, no problem, sweetie. Can't fault me for trying. You kind of leave a girl no choice with those things staring me in the face. Here, put the sweatshirt on, and I'll get you on your way." With that, Mary Dija grabbed the hoodie and swiftly navigated the top hole over her head, finally engulfed in a dry cover-up. "Me need to get to the college," she repeated.

Getting the message, the dispatcher made her way back to her desk and picked up the little walkie-talkie, turned the sound knob up, and spoke loudly into the front screen. "Jimmy, wake the fuck up. I got a ride here going to the college. Hurry up, she's gotta go."

Within two minutes, the taxi's headlights shone brightly in front of the hut, and Mary Dija was quick to leave, first turning to the girl worker, saying, "Thank you, me bring back your jacket." The dispatcher, disappointed at letting a very rare opportunity at Jimmy's get away, just nodded and winked at her departing visitor. As Mary stepped through the pouring rain and into the back seat of the car, the dispatcher leaned out the door and yelled, "Hey, Jimmy, no charge, this one's on me."

It was a short ride to the college entrance or to anywhere else in Wildwood for that matter. East to west or bay to beach, as some liked to refer to it, was only four short blocks while one could get north to south by car and fully across Wildwood Beach's one and a half miles in a matter of minutes. Mary sat in the back seat, again soaked, this time simply from her six-step exit from the hut to the car. Her light cotton skirt was soaked through to her panties and presented little cover to her wet, exposed legs and feet. The Jimmy's Taxi hoodie served as an around-the-shoulders towel, allowing the tips of Mary's wet hair to rest comfortably while catching the drips from her ears and neck. The sweatshirt's dampness had unleashed a scent of stale cigarettes, no doubt the result of the dispatcher's pack of Newports, which Mary had noticed sitting amid the debris on the hut's lone desk. Despite her discomfort, however, and with her confrontation with the monsignor almost at hand, the former Sister Dija stayed determined to the night's mission. She would be relentless in her effort to convince the monsignor to return to her a life that was now her best chance at normalcy and one that would support her independence. Sister Dija was a novice in most things. Only now did it strike her that her heedless exit from her vocation meant loss of salary, residence, and benefits previously provided from her order as a nun.

As the taxi approached the entrance to Pious College, Mary Dija was confronted with yet another hurdle, this one also unforeseen. The vehicle gate to the campus was closed and locked. Unusual but not unprecedented late in the evening, access was restricted to a walking passage gate, directly to the left of the main vehicle gates. The three-foot-wide swinging iron entry was open and represented Mary Dija's only path to the college's walkways and ultimately to the monsignor's residence. Unfortunately for the soggy visitor, the weather continued to be in no mood to accommodate a pleasant stroll through campus. The wind and rain remained relentless, intent on soaking to the bone anyone caught outdoors on this chilly summer evening. The monsignor's house was one quarter of a mile into the heart of campus. With a single-minded persistence, the young lass had little choice but to brave the downpour with short-legged quick steps through the puddles, up the path past buildings and grassy lawns, finally logging up the residence's path and arriving at the priest's front door. During her approach, she had been encouraged by the sight of the monsignor's car in his private parking spot and further warmed by the various dimmed lights throughout the first floor of the residence.

Standing on the home's half-moon platform, Mary Dija could feel her strength fading as she approached her finish line. Her hoodie was soaked and now heavy on her back. Her hair, face, and neck were draining streams of water down onto the platform, and her skirt, legs, and sandals were drenched. On her toes and fully stretched, the sexy little ex-nun could see into the home from the lowest glass panel some five-and-a-half feet up the door. Recognizing how ridiculous her late-night visit would appear to the monsignor, but captive to no other choice, the ex-nun rang the doorbell, then again and then again. There was no response to the bell's chimes, rings that she could slightly hear from outside the door. For a brief moment, the worn traveler gave into her fatigue, and the night's mission left her. Still being battered by rain, she was exhausted, hungry, a bit confused, and now almost desperate to get out of the deluge. She briefly considered walking away, maybe to a dorm hallway or to the student center to find shelter and warmth, but these buildings were across campus, and frankly her vigor and determination were on empty.

With a long, deep breath, she willed herself to regroup from her disoriented state. From desperation, she began banging the door with her fist and then yelling, "MONSIGNOR! MONSIGNOR! PLEASE OPEN THE DOOR! MONSIGNOR, PLEASE!" Thinking that he was sleeping, she pressed on in hopes of waking him. Exhausting herself, she went back to pressing the doorbell over and over and over. Finally, and about out of all hope, she grabbed the doorknob and twisted. To her astonishment, the door was unlocked. Instinctively, she pushed the solid wood barrier open a few inches and paused. Tattered and distressed from her journey, she quickly decided that entering was a matter more of survival than intrusion. She stepped in cautiously, leaving the door cracked open behind her. Standing still, drips of water began collecting on the linoleum floor beneath her feet. With the back of her wrist, she wiped the soaked sleeve of the hoodie across her forehead and eyebrows to keep the water, dripping from her scalp, from entering her eyes. Over the last half hour, she had been unmercifully pelted with rain and wind, and only now—standing in the warm, dry entrance to the president's home—did her ability to focus begin to return to her.

Silent and still, she could faintly hear the sound of a shower at the far end of the first floor. Again, attempting to dry her eyes, she peered across the foyer's entrance through the dimly lit living room. To its left was the kitchen entrance, also barely lit like the room's dimmers had been turned down low. To the right of the living room was a narrow hallway, heading back away from her, with two doors at its far end. It was from one of these doors that the faint sound of a running shower could be heard. *The monsignor is in the shower*, she thought. *Now what?*

Caught in a place where movement in any direction seemed terrifying, Mary Dija's demeanor reeked of fear. Her body was filled with trepidation, and her spirit no longer possessed the courage to initiate confrontation. The life force of this morning's decision to abandon her vocation, the willpower that pushed her through her travels, and the fortitude that carried her walk through the campus's monsoon was spilling out of her. Her eyes welled with tears. For the first time in this day, she was out of answers, divested of the needed drive to continue. With only instincts carrying her movements, she slowly crept into the living room and took a seat, almost hiding, in the room's corner wicker chair next to a small table holding up a single black phone. Unknowing to her, she was sitting in the exact spot that the evil monsignor had called her superior to get her kicked to Loja, the root cause of today's stressful and traumatic journey. There she sat, still, in the shadowed corner of the room resolved to having her confrontation with the monsignor begin while feeling frail and weak. Her earlier intent to be demanding had all but vanished. She felt herself on the edge of passing out and struggled to physically stay in the moment. Ironically, it was the absence of sound that kicked the last dribbles of adrenaline into her bloodstream. The shower noise stopped. The intruding ex-nun braced herself for her clash with the priest who ruled all things at Pious.

Within seconds, the door on the left side of the hallway opened. The monsignor, wrapped only in a white towel around his waist, entered the hallway and began slowly strolling toward the kitchen, never looking her way. Forty feet turned to thirty, and then twenty, and soon the topless priest, unaware of her presence, began to cross the path through the living room to the kitchen. Still the dark corner and her frozen silence kept the terrified young woman out of his view. She wanted to call out, but petrified, she remained silent. About to enter his kitchen, the priest caught a glimpse of his front door, noticing it was not fully closed. Alarmed, he turned to face the living room. His eyes scanned all corners until he saw Mary Dija sitting in his corner chair. Shocked, his eyes squinted as if to verify the presence of another. His posture turned aggressive and, about to call out and confront the unwelcome stranger, the scene drastically changed. Without warning a second man, naked, exited the bathroom and, with some pace, walked into the living room. The monsignor, stunned by his presence, called out, "No, Jesse! Go back." But Jesse ignored the panicked monsignor. Unlike the priest, he quickly spotted Mary Dija in the corner of the room. Her presence froze him cold in his tracks. Exposed fully to her, he made no attempt to cover himself, only interrupting his stare toward her to take a quick glance at the speechless monsignor, who was using his right hand to grab the corner of the wall in an attempt to steady himself against the tremors overtaking his body.

The dumbfounded threesome stayed wordless: the monsignor surrendering to the moment, Jesse dripping and moist from his clergy cleansing, and Mary Dija clinging desperately to a fate largely unknown.

Words, all words, seemed unsuitable. Useless. Like the storm, this night was passing, having—as was usual for this small beach town on the coast of southern New Jersey—missed its mark.

For this was the Wildwood Beach, a town never perfect, never loyal to prediction, a place of characters mostly dysfunctional but rarely dull. This was Wildwood Beach, where its final outcome lay as close as its next chapter, tantalizing and teasing an ending that would never come.

For this was Wildwood Beach, a story determined and destined to continue.

About the Author

RICHARD POST'S WIFE is fond of saying, "Everything my husband touches turns to gold," but she follows that line quickly with "and for some reason that seems to really piss people off." Controversial, mostly old-school, and honest to a flaw, Richard discusses issues from a lens of common sense, a mindset often spurring criticism and attacks from today's woke "tweeters and "gramsters." Spending the greater part of his career as a Wall Street executive and a coach of almost forty years, the author has had a positive influence on the lives of many. Typically leaving political correctness at life's doorstep, Richard's writings land on the side of a realist, a dying breed of silenced voices that have given way to our nation's agenda-filled barking. His experience and background contain the success and rewards that are often derived from talent and hard work, but like so many others both before and after him, he has also been mudslinged and the subject of those hell-bent on sensationalism. When speaking of our society's trendy war on reputation, he simply states, "It merely was my turn, not more complicated than that."

Mr. Post's first book, a nonfiction titled *Beyond Real: Surviving 9/11 and How It Changed the Way I Think* was a compelling story of his thirty-year Wall Street ride. It is a purposely unruly-written memoir and a simple tale of truth about a cutthroat business within a diverse and divided nation. It is about a "beyond real" day that contained a man's worst and luckiest hour. The book is an American male's transformation of views, from believing that he lived in the best of all worlds to thoughts of stark realism...perhaps too real for his own good or for the good of those around him. Frankly, it is a serious opposite to the entertaining story of *Tuition*, demonstrating a talented diversification in writing style reserved only for the most versatile of authors.

CPSIA information can be obtained
at www.ICGtesting.com
Printed in the USA
BVHW030213070621
608928BV00005B/133

9 781662 418693